Blood Lands

She moved her sights over to the parson, then to Evans, then to Muller. They fit the description Reese had given her before he died. These were the ones; if by some fluke they weren't her attackers, her father's killers, too bad, she thought. If that was the case, they had simply picked the wrong day to come calling.

Her sights homed onto Muller, the one farthest away, the one most likely to get atop his horse and make a run for it. She rested the sights there and waited, breathing slowly, calmly.

Strange, she thought, how not long ago she had looked for the slightest reason not to kill these men, these men who had violated her, who had taken her father's life, and in that sense destroyed hers. But that had changed. Now, if they fit the description, or matched the names, or came close to doing either, she wanted them dead.

The killing had begun. The quicker they were dead, the sooner she could live in a home of her own—something she'd never had. And more than that, she could hold her head up and live there in peace, like regular, everyday folks—something she'd never known. A tear glistened in her eye, but there was no time to wipe it away. She wouldn't let it affect her aim.

BLOOD LANDS

Ralph Cotton

A SIGNET BOOK

SIGNET
Published by New American Library, a division of
Penguin Group (USA) Inc., 375 Hudson Street,
New York, New York 10014, USA
Penguin Group (Canada), 90 Eglinton Avenue East, Suite 700, Toronto,
Ontario M4P 2Y3, Canada (a division of Pearson Penguin Canada Inc.)
Penguin Books Ltd., 80 Strand, London WC2R 0RL, England
Penguin Ireland, 25 St. Stephen's Green, Dublin 2,
Ireland (a division of Penguin Books Ltd.)
Penguin Group (Australia), 250 Camberwell Road, Camberwell, Victoria 3124,
Australia (a division of Pearson Australia Group Pty. Ltd.)
Penguin Books India Pvt. Ltd., 11 Community Centre, Panchsheel Park,
New Delhi - 110 017, India
Penguin Group (NZ), cnr Airborne and Rosedale Roads, Albany,
Auckland 1310, New Zealand (a division of Pearson New Zealand Ltd.)
Penguin Books (South Africa) (Pty.) Ltd., 24 Sturdee Avenue,
Rosebank, Johannesburg 2196, South Africa

Penguin Books Ltd., Registered Offices:
80 Strand, London WC2R 0RL, England

First published by Signet, an imprint of New American Library,
a division of Penguin Group (USA) Inc.

First Printing, June 2006
10 9 8 7 6 5 4 3 2 1

Copyright © Ralph Cotton, 2006
All rights reserved

Ⓡ REGISTERED TRADEMARK—MARCA REGISTRADA

For Mary Lynn . . . *of course.*

And in fond memory of Evan Hunter (Ed McBain), whose work inspires me and keeps me reaching. Long live the boys of the ole 87th.

PART 1

Chapter 1

At daybreak, in a cold drizzle, Julie Wilder, her father, Colonel Bertrim Wilder, and the colonel's former orderly Shepherd Watson rode up into sight above the low-rise north of Umberton. Upon seeing the three riders and behind them the string of finely attended horses each was leading, Davis Beldon, the livery owner, stepped out of the corral beside his barn and stood in the middle of the muddy street, waving them in with his calloused hand.

"Here comes the colonel, bringing his horses in, just like he said he would, soon as the weather broke," Beldon said over his shoulder to his helper, Virgil Tolan, who stood at the barn door, a pitchfork full of clean straw in his hands.

"Yep, he's doing it," Tolan replied, staring out through the grainy morning light, "but it's not going to sit well with Ruddell Plantz and his militia riders."

Behind the livery barn a rooster crowed into the

gray stillness of the morning. "I expect *Captain Plantz* and his *so-called* Kansas Border Militia will be making themselves scarce now that this confounded war is ending," said Beldon. "Good riddance to them too." A slight smile of satisfaction came to his face as he spit and watched the three riders bring the horses forward along the north trail. "I have no doubt Colonel Wilder would have dealt soundly with those scoundrels, had they tried to stop him from bringing those horses to town."

"All this time he's never once paid Plantz and his militia any protection money like the rest of the 'steaders did," said Tolan. He pitched the clean straw and stepped out beside Beldon, both hands resting atop the long pitchfork handle. "I expect even Plantz and the rest of them knew who to mess with and who not. Some men have guts; others don't, I reckon." He gave his employer a guarded look.

"Well, thank God the extortion is ending." Beldon's smile faded as he squinted for a better view of the three riders, realizing that like most businessmen in the area during the war, he too had paid the Kansas Border Militia more than just a few times to keep his property and himself safe. Beldon decided it best to change the subject. "I recognize old Shep," he said, "but who's the wrangler on Wilder's right?"

"I have no idea," said Tolan, also squinting a bit as he stared out with his employer. "I reckon it's some cowpoke drifter the colonel let winter with him for beans and a roof. There's plenty of them these days."

"Yeah," said Beldon, "and it's going to get worse before it gets any better, war or no war."

No one in Umberton had ever seen or even heard of the colonel's daughter, and for good reason. Julie had not been born to the colonel and his late wife, Laura Nell Wilder. The girl's real mother had been a camp follower known only as Sudie, who'd given birth to the colonel's child during his tenure as a young captain along the wilderness frontier. Sudie had revealed Colonel Wilder's name to her daughter shortly before her death ten years earlier. Over the next decade Julie had written to her father many times, but only recently had she traveled down from the north country to meet him face-to-face.

"I sure hope Colonel Wilder knows what he's doing, taking in every saddle-tramp that blows in off the prairie," said Tolan.

"I expect the colonel doesn't need you or me telling him how to conduct himself," Beldon said a bit sharply. His eyes stayed on the three riders and their strings of horses, most particularly on Julie Wilder, whose identity and gender lay hidden beneath a broad-brimmed Montana crown Stetson and a faded gray riding duster.

Once atop the rise, Colonel Wilder slowed his mount long enough for Julie and Shep to sidle their horses up to him; riding abreast, the three led their strings at an easy pace all the way to the livery corral where Tolan unlatched the gate and swung it wide open.

When the riders and their horses had all passed into the corral, Beldon stepped across the mud-rutted ground toward the colonel, grinning, with his hands shoved down into his back pockets. Tolan closed the gate and walked forward quickly until he'd passed Beldon and stood close enough to take the three lead ropes from the riders. He pulled the horses to the side and began looking them over as they milled around him.

"Morning, Colonel," said Beldon, deliberately showing little interest in the well-cared-for horses. "I expect you realize the price of horses can drop most any day with the war nearly over."

Without stepping down from his saddle, the colonel touched his hat brim courteously toward the two livery men and crossed his wrists on his saddle horn. "One thing for certain about war," said the colonel, "is that it takes *horses* to carry men and equipment there, and it takes *horses* to carry them home again."

Beldon scratched his jaw and said, "Well, I can't argue that. But the thing is, I don't ordinarily keep this many horses on hand. I have to consider my cost in feed and upkeep until the army purchaser comes through Umberton again." He shrugged. "It could be a week; it could be a month."

Julie and Shep backed their mounts a few feet to the side and sat quietly.

"Or you could take them on over to Rulo," said the colonel, leveling a fixed stare at the livery owner, "the way *I would have done* had you not asked me to first bring them to you for an offer." The colonel paused a second, then said, "If need be, I still know the way to Rulo."

"Now hold on, Colonel," Beldon said with a nervous smile, squirming a bit in place. "I'm not about to let you take these animals all the way to Rulo! I'm just looking for the best price. You can't fault a fellow for that."

"No, I suppose not." Colonel Wilder allowed himself a thin smile beneath his wide white mustache. Water dripped from the brim of his hat. "If you need to dicker a bit before you meet my price, let's do it over a cup of coffee, out of the rain."

"Where are my manners!" Beldon said, chastising himself with a mock slap on the side of his wet head. "Of course, let's get inside and get some hot coffee, while I try getting you to listen to reason."

Before swinging down from his saddle, Colonel Wilder raised an arm toward Shep and Julie. "Speaking of manners . . . you both know Shepherd Watson."

"Howdy, Shep." The two livery men acknowledged the old cowhand, who touched his frayed hat brim and returned the courtesy.

"Now for a surprise," said the colonel. "I'd like both of you to meet my daughter, Julie Wilder."

"Your *daughter?*" said Beldon. Both he and Tolan looked doubly stunned, first by hearing that the person beneath the sweat-stained Montana crown was a woman; second, that Bertrim and the late Laura Nell Wilder had a *child* neither of them had ever mentioned. "My goodness . . . ," Beldon added in a hushed tone.

Colonel Wilder gestured his daughter forward with a gloved hand. "Julie, come on over here beside me," he said cordially. "Let me introduce you to some of your new neighbors." As Julie stepped her horse forward, the colonel added, "Even though we *will* be leaving this part of the country before long."

Recovering from their surprise, Beldon slicked his wet hair to one side. Tolan took off his wet flop hat and held it against his chest.

"Ma'am, it is our pleasure to make your acquaintance," Beldon said, speaking for both himself and his helper. "If there is anything we can do to make your stay here in Umberton more comfortable, please allow us to do so."

"Obliged," Julie said, keeping her reply short and her tone of voice lowered as if its natural huskiness made her feel awkward. She pushed her hat brim up out of courtesy, at the same time revealing her face.

Looking her over without being too obvious, Beldon asked, "You've been back east, I take it, in boarding school, no doubt?" Yet, even as he asked, Beldon silently answered his own question. The young woman sitting atop the big buckskin bay had not been back east, not in any boarding school anyway.

Julie Wilder sat atop the buckskin loosely and comfortably, yet in a confident command, like a vaquero, Beldon told himself, not like some boarding school equestrian. He gave a cutaway glance at old Shep, then back to Julie as she said, still quietly in the same husky yet warm rich voice, "No, sir, I have never been back east. I've been—"

"Not until now, that is," the colonel cut in. "This will be our first daughter and father trip back east. We're both looking forward to it." He swung down from his saddle and held his reins out to Tolan, who stepped forward and took them obediently. "Daughter, why don't you and Shep go over to Molly Lanahan's and order us all three a nice hot breakfast? I'll be right along as soon as Mr. Beldon and I thrash out a price we can both live with."

Beldon looked back at Julie Wilder, expecting her to complete the response she had started, but she didn't. Instead she smiled modestly, saying, "Yes, Colonel," and backed her horse a step as if in dismissal. As she did so, Beldon noted a short jagged scar on her left cheek as she turned her dark eyes away from him.

The young woman had a rawboned toughness to her that presented itself clearly at first glance. Her eyes bore the same haunted look the livery man had seen on countless young drifters, eyes that were sharp and alert, but in sore need of rest, or perhaps reprieve.

Beldon and Tolan turned sidelong and gave Julie and Shep a nod as the two stepped their horses past them, out the gate and up the narrow mud street.

Turning back to Colonel Wilder, Beldon started to speak, but as if anticipating further questions about his daughter, the colonel said tactfully, "I hope you'll both understand that Julie and I have missed many years together. You might say that we're only now getting to know one another. Julie isn't comfortable talking about her past . . . not that it's anything to be ashamed of." He finished speaking with a firm, level gaze.

"Of course not," said Beldon. "Whatever caused you two to be apart all those years is you and your daughter's business. Let's all just be happy that you're together now." The colonel's gaze softened.

He smiled. "Obliged, gentlemen. Now, let's go do some dickering."

Watching from the upstairs window of a weathered clapboard rooming house across the street, a young gunman named Nez Peerly saw Julie Wilder take off her hat and shake out her long dark hair. "Whooiee!" he said over his shoulder to his trail pardner, Clarence Conlon. "Charlie, come take a look-see! This ain't no *ordinary* wrangler the old colonel has riding with him!"

Clarence, chewing on a cold fried chicken leg left over from last night's dinner, stepped slowly over to the window, running the back of his hand across his glistening lips and black mustache. Looking down into the street, he caught only a glimpse of Julie's long hair as she placed the hat back atop her head. "What's the deal?" he grunted, still chewing. "I don't see nothing."

Looking disgusted, Peerly said, "Well, maybe you would have if you'd gotten here when I told you."

He looked the big man up and down, eying the chicken leg in his hand and the grease shining in Clarence's full black beard. "That's a woman down there, Clarence." He pointed.

"Down where?" Clarence asked thickly, craning his big head forward a bit.

"Down *there*, gawddamn it!" Peerly said angrily. "The one on the right, riding that black-legged buckskin! She just stuck that big hat down over her head, else you'd seen what I mean!"

"So what?" Conlon shrugged, exposing a slash of dirty white lining in one of the ripped shoulder seams of his ill-fitting uniform. "Long hair don't always mean *woman* where I come from." He sucked grease from a large dirty thumb. "I could stand a little barbering myself."

Peerly stared harshly at him. "Didn't you see the house rules downstairs, 'No food allowed in rooms'?"

"That's not *my* house rules," Conlon said flatly. He switched the chicken leg to his other hand and wiped his fingers on his already badly soiled tunic.

"Do you know *why* that's a house rule?" Peerly asked, getting more and more put out with him.

"I couldn't care less," said the big burly Conlon, turning his gaze back down to the street as Julie and Shep rode slowly on toward the restaurant.

"Because it draws rats up here," Peerly informed him.

"Rats don't bother me none."

"I can see why," said Peerly, "but as long as we have to share a bed, I don't want rats crawling over me just to lick your whiskers."

"Then sleep on the gawddamned floor," Conlon said gruffly, staring down at the two riders. He watched Julie swing down from her saddle out front of the restaurant. "A woman, huh?" he asked, noting something different about the figure in the wet riding duster. "I don't even remember how long it's been since I laid my hands on a woman's warm furry belly."

Hearing Conlon's voice take on a slight tremble, Peerly stared at him bemusedly and said, "*Quite* a damn while from the sound of it." He stepped closer to Conlon, who stood staring down at the street as if mesmerized. Shaking his head in disgust, Peerly plucked the gnawed chicken bone from between Conlon's large thumb and fingers and pitched it away. "Pull your tongue in and let's get going," he said.

"*Going?* We just *got here* yesterday!" said the big bearded man.

"We're spying here, remember?" said Peerly. "Don't you think Ruddell Plantz is going to want his due *payment* when he hears the colonel slipped all them horses into town? Hell, he might even want to confiscate these horses for our own men."

"So, chances are we'll be coming right back?" Conlon asked, staring down toward the restaurant as if in contemplation.

"Once we tell Plantz about all these big good-looking horses?" Peerly grinned. "Oh yes, I'm pretty sure you can count on us coming back here."

"Then let's go," said Conlon, sucking a piece of chicken from between his teeth. He looked out through the window. "The rain's stopped anyway."

"Yeah," Peerly said with sarcasm, shaking his head, "I wouldn't want you to ride in the rain." He paused for a moment and looked the big man up and down. "Let me ask you something, Conlon. Would you be riding with us, Plantz, me and the others, if this war wasn't going on?"

Conlon shrugged his broad shoulders inside his too-tight uniform jacket. "Hell, I reckon. Why not? A man's got to do something."

"You don't mind all the killing, robbing, burning, purging?" Peerly asked as if pursuing a point.

"Naw, not me," said Conlon. He offered a wide crooked grin. "Every day, somebody has to die. If it ain't us that kills them, something will."

"Now, there is what I call a real deeply considered opinion," Peerly said, returning the grin.

"Why'd you ask?" Conlon cocked his head a bit in curiosity.

"Just making conversation, Charlie," said Peerly, turning and walking away.

Chapter 2

Ruddell Plantz sat at the kitchen table with his tall muddy cavalry boots propped up on the edge, right beside a cold plate of half-eaten beans and hoecake. On the floor near his chair lay the body of Harvey Shawler. In front of the smoldering hearth lay his wife, Mattie Shawler. On Plantz's lap lay a big Colt horse pistol and the feed sack with eyelets that had covered his face as he rode in. He'd taken his Union saber and scabbard from around his waist and laid it alongside his forearm on the tabletop.

At the open door to the Shawler farmhouse, Carl Muller stood holding two young boys by their shirt collars. The youngsters squirmed and kicked, but to no avail. "What about these Shawler tadpoles?" Muller asked.

Plantz hardly gave the boys a glance. "I didn't know they were still alive," he said. He picked up the cup of coffee one of his men had poured him from the steaming pot hanging above the hearth coals, swirled it, then said before taking a long sip,

"Kill them both, Carl. Missouri tadpoles today become full-grown Missouri frogs tomorrow."

Muller shot a dark grin to Rance Sawyer standing beside him on the short wooden porch. "See? Ain't that what I told you he'd say?"

"It never hurts to check first," Sawyer said sullenly. He jerked one of the farm boys from Muller's hand and helped drag the two away, down off the porch and farther away from the house. "If you ask me, the war will be over before these two ever make Johnnie Reb's roster."

"But see, the thing is," said Muller, giving a nasty grin, "nobody did *ask* you." He paused, then said as he raised a boot and kicked Davey Shawler forward, "If you want some good advice"—his big Remington pistol came up from its holster and fired a round into Davey Shawler's back—"you'd do well to keep your opinions to yourself, especially when it comes to showing mercy for this Missouri border trash."

"Davey!" young Martin Shawler screamed. He lunged forward against Sawyer's grip, trying to go to his fallen brother.

"Let him go," Muller said quietly. When Sawyer turned the boy loose, Muller let him get to his dead brother, then raised his Remington again and fired.

Sawyer winced at the sight of the two brothers lying dead in their own side yard.

"You see," Muller continued as if nothing had happened while gray smoke curled from his pistol barrel, "the shorter this war gets, the more folks will start to wondering what kind of trouble they might get into over stuff just like this." He gestured his pistol toward the two dead Shawler brothers. "Not everybody realizes that our cause is just."

Hearing the two gunshots from inside the farmhouse, Plantz turned a tired look toward a small bedroom separated from the kitchen by a wool blanket hung over a length of twine. "Parson, are you going to sleep all damned day?" he called out.

After a grunt followed by a short silence, a voice replied from behind the blanket, "How in God's name can a man sleep . . . all this shooting and screaming going on all night."

Plantz gave a dark chuckle. "Now, it wasn't all that bad. Only a couple of young women and these two last night. Muller just shot a couple of boys out in the yard. Come on out and have some coffee with me. Tell me some things."

"Damn it, Ruddell," the voice grunted. In a second a large hand wearing fingerless leather gloves drew the wool blanket to the side. "As long as we've been riding together, you'd think I've already told you all you'd ever want to know."

"Naw, I can never get enough learning," said Plantz. He turned and watched Preston Oates, "the parson," step into the room, shoving his gray-black hair back out of his eyes. "I followed your advice too. The blind man is still alive. Hurley and Kenny Bright have him tied to a post out in the barn."

"Thank you," said the parson, "I appreciate it." He cleared his throat and spit into the smoldering coals on his way around the table. Picking up a half cup of cold coffee, he slung the contents out onto the dirt floor and filled the cup from the steaming pot. "I felt very strongly about that."

Plantz offered a thin smile. "I could tell you did.

You come near throwing down on Kiley when he started to cut the man's throat."

"Killing a *blind* man on a moonless night?" said the parson, shaking his head as if in fear. "That's the kind of bad luck we neither one want to bring down on us . . . not when things are going so well."

"Especially a *one-legged* blind man," Plantz added with a feigned sense of caution. "Ain't that what you told all of us last night? Or was that whiskey talking?"

"That was no whiskey talk," said the parson. "That was just me reading all the signs and looking out for all of us." Easing down into a chair across the table from Plantz, he gave the man a look and said, "I know you don't put as much stock in these things as I do. But it's widely known in *my* inner circle that Napoleon had a blind man put to death the night before his battle at Waterloo." He paused for effect, then added flatly, "It was a moonless night." His beady dark eyes stared gravely at Plantz.

"But was he one-legged?" Plantz asked, showing a trace of a teasing smile.

"Whether he was or not, it's not a matter to treat so lightly," said the parson.

Plantz shrugged a bit, sipped his coffee and said quietly, "Sorry, Parson, I'm just not superstitious the way you are."

"This has nothing to do with superstition, Ruddell," said Oates. "This is a matter of carefully accumulated scientific fact." As he spoke he made the sign of the cross, only instead of making it on his chest, he made a smaller version on his forearm.

Noting the gesture, Plantz said, "Well, fact or

not. It's daylight now. I expect we can go ahead and kill this Reb sonsabitch and get on about our business."

"Did we do ourselves any good here last night?" the parson asked. Then, to keep from appearing greedy he added quickly, "Enough to support our *just cause,* that is?"

"Naw, hell, these people have been picked to death the last few years," said Plantz. "We're doing them a favor, killing them." He sipped his coffee. "We're leaving here with a little grain for our horses, a sow hog and some skinny chickens."

"Chicken thieves, then, is what we've become," said the parson, looking down stoically into his coffee cup.

Plantz stared at him in silence for a moment. "You know, I've been giving it some serious thought. Soon as this war simmers on down, I'm thinking about making my own *private* little war. Think you can go along with that?"

"You mean . . . ?" The parson gave a sly grin and let his words trail.

"Yep," said Plantz, knowing he didn't really need to explain himself any further, but doing so anyway. "I mean doing for ourselves what we've been doing for the cause all this time. Instead of throwing the proceeds to the Free Kansas Militia, we keep it all for ourselves."

The parson raised his partially gloved hands as if in dismay. "But there's nothing left now. This is what we should have started doing a couple of years back when there was still something worth stealing around here."

"As soon as this war stops, it'll just be a matter

of time before there's more money circulating than we've ever dreamed of. It'll be real *Union* dollars too. Not these worthless gray dollars." He gestured a hand toward the Confederate bills strewn on the dirt floor, some of them stained with blood.

The parson sat in silence for a moment as if having to give it some thought. Finally he said, "Hell yes, I'm with you. Only, why wait for the war to end? We could head out tonight, rob and kill all the way to San Francisco, far as I'm concerned."

"We've got a total of eleven men . . . nine of them right out there, Parson," said Plantz, jerking a short nod toward the barn and the surrounding yard. "How many do you think we could count on to ride with us if we broke away from the Free Kansas Militia right now?"

"I'd like to say all of them," the parson replied after pondering it for a moment. "But to be honest and practical, I'm going to say six or seven."

"Yeah, that's about the same number I came up with," said Plantz. Raising another finger each time he mentioned a name he said, "I figure, Carl Muller, Kid Kiley, Goff Aimes, Clement Macky and Buell Evans." He held up five fingers, then added, "Clarence Conlon, and Nez Peerly too, once they catch up with us."

"What about Delbert Reese, or Rance Sawyer, the ones who won't go along with your idea?" the parson asked, lowering his voice lest anyone outside hear him.

Lowering his voice as well, Plantz said, "Well, if there's one thing we've all learned from this war, it's that 'He who is not with us is surely against us.' "

"In other words . . ." Staring intently at Plantz, the parson raised a finger and ran it symbolically across his throat.

Plantz gave him a thin guarded smile. "If it comes to that," he said, "but maybe we tell them we're disbanding, and shake loose of them without having to . . ." He made the same sign across his throat.

"Right, of course," said the parson, catching himself before he appeared too bloodthirsty. "I meant only as a last resort. God forbid it come to that."

"Yeah, I agree," said Plantz, without much commitment in his voice. "God forbid it come to that." He hesitated for a second, then said, "I've got Peerly doing some checking around, seeing who we can count on when the time comes."

"You say *when,* not *if,*" said the parson.

"Yeah," said Plantz with a level gaze, "I suppose I did."

The two fell silent and turned toward the sound of a young gunman named Kid Kiley whose high-welled cavalry boots pounded up onto the wooden porch. "Ruddell! I mean, Captain Plantz, sir!" he said in an excited tone, sticking his head inside the open door. "We're bringing this blind basta— That is, we're bringing *the prisoner* from the barn, sir!" He gave a quick, awkward salute.

"At ease, Kiley," Plantz chuckled, rising from his chair. "Get out of the doorway and go calm yourself down. You're panting like a hound on a deer trail." Turning to the parson, he said as Kiley ducked away and pounded back off the porch, "Come on, Parson, let's see how these boys handle this. We'll see who fits in our plans and who doesn't." The two stood with their coffee cups in hand and stepped onto the porch.

Propped up between Kenny Bright and Joe Hurley, Avrial Shawler hobbled toward the house. He turned his blind eyes back and forth aimlessly, searching his endless darkness for any sign of his kin. "Davey?" he called out. His ears piqued for a response. When no response came he called out, "Martin . . . Marty boy, can you hear me? Jed? Speak up, one of you! Where's Sister Loretta? Sister Rose?"

"You don't want to see Sister Rose and Loretta," Muller chuckled. "They're a mess."

"Jed . . . ?" Bright said curiously, almost to himself. He looked all around the yard.

Kid Kiley, who had hurried to join Hurley and Bright in accompanying the blind man across the yard, snickered and answered in a mocking, teasing voice, "Here I am, big brother. I'm down over here with a bloody hole in my back, deader than hell!"

Avrial Shawler stopped abruptly and stiffened in place, causing his two guards to stop also. "What have you devils done to my kid brothers?" he cried out. "Where's my ma and pa?" He swung his head back and forth wildly, shouting, "Pa! Ma! Where are you? Somebody answer me, for God sakes!"

"I did answer you, you stupid bastard!" Kiley called out in the same cruel taunting voice. "We're all dead! Every gawddamned rebel-loving one of us! Except you!" He ran in close in a short circle, spit in Avrial's hapless face and kept circling, preparing to do the same again.

Some of the men hooted and laughed; other men only looked on in shame. "All right, Kiley, that's enough!" said Bright, jerking the blind man to the side, away from the circling Kiley.

"See?" the parson said quietly to Plantz, the two observing from the porch. "Kenny Bright is a good man, but his heart just isn't in it, not the way Kiley's is. Wouldn't you agree?"

"Yep, I see what you mean," said Plantz, staring straight ahead. He sipped his coffee, his big Colt in his right hand, hanging down at his side. "All right, both of yas, stand down!" he called out to Bright and Kiley, seeing their tempers begin to flare.

"He started it," Kiley replied. "I'm only doing my job! My job is to *hairy-ass* the enemy any chance I get!"

"This man is no longer the enemy," Bright said. "He's been sent home, out of the war! He's harmless!"

"As long as he's alive, he's still my enemy!" Kiley shouted.

"You've got a knack for harassing the blind and the infirm, Kiley," Bright said flatly. "I can't wait to see you someday have to face up to—" His words stopped short beneath the roar of Plantz's big pistol. Kiley ducked away as if he'd been shot.

"Damn it," said Plantz. "Didn't you two woodenheads hear me tell you to stand down?" He stepped off the porch and sauntered forward, eying both men sharply. Hurley turned loose of Avrial Shawler's arm and stepped away.

"Sorry, Captain," said Bright, one hand on the blind man's thin upper arm, helping to steady him. "I see no need in all this killing . . . and certainly no need in torturing a man this way."

"Torture?" said Plantz, turning his harsh stare to Bright alone. He gave Kiley a gesture with his pistol barrel, sending him away. "This isn't torture. You haven't *seen* torture." He reached out with a muddy boot and kicked Avrial Shawler's wobbly leg out from under him, dropping the blind man to the wet ground. Bright could only turn loose of the downed man's arm.

"If you want to know about killing and torture, ask me about Lawrence, Kansas, the night Cantrell and his men rode through!" He kicked the helpless blind man in the side, causing him to roll into a ball, gasping. "Ask me about Centralia . . . about Whitfield, or Logansport."

"Captain, I—" Bright tried to reply, but his words cut short again as Plantz took him by his forearm and pulled him away from the man on the ground.

Hearing the big pistol cock in Plantz's hand, the blind man said with tears streaming down his face, "Go on, kill me then, you murdering sonsabitch! I ain't going to beg! I ain't going to crawl!"

"Is this daylight enough for you?" Plantz called out to the parson. "Does this fit your *accumulated scientific* tastes?"

The parson only nodded, watching with a firm grin of satisfaction.

On the ground, Avrial Shawler had heard enough to know that his life would end any second. "Ma! Pa! Little Brothers! I'm gone. Can you hear me? I love all of you!" He sobbed and shook his bowed head, his blind eyes seeming to search the wet ground beneath him. "Ma!" he said. "*Please* say something. Let me hear your voice!"

"She can't talk," said Plantz, reaching his pistol out at arm's length. He gave a trace of a cruel grin. "We cut her tongue out." He paused for only a second to let it sink in; then he added, "So she can't tell what we're all going to do to her."

"Noooo!" Avrial Shawler shrieked and swung his hands wildly back and forth, trying in his desperation to grab on to his tormentor.

Plantz squeezed the trigger on his big saddle Colt and watched the impact nail the screaming man's head to the ground in a spray of mud, blood and brain matter.

In the sudden silent wake of the explosion, Plantz turned to Bright and said, "You heard him mention another brother, didn't you?"

Bright stared at Plantz for a moment before finally saying, "I heard him call out the name, *'Jed.'* I don't know what he meant by it."

"If you were to guess though," said Plantz, "would you think there might be another brother around here somewhere, maybe somebody who saw everything that just happened? Maybe somebody who will spill everything he saw to the regulars, first chance he gets?"

"I suppose that could be," said Bright.

"Yeah, I suppose that could happen too," said Plantz, staring Bright harshly in the eye. "Why didn't you say something right then, when you heard him mention it?"

"Hell, I don't know," said Bright. "Everybody else heard it; why didn't they mention it?"

Plantz didn't answer. Instead he gave the parson a knowing look. Then he turned to the men gathered in the yard and called out, "Goff Aimes! Get mounted and get up here!"

A tall man with a black powder burn tattoo on his right cheek stepped quickly into his saddle and gigged his horse forward, sliding to a halt in front of Plantz. "Yes, Captain?"

Plantz grinned and said to Bright, "See, that's the attitude a man needs to have around here." To Aimes he said, "Circle this yard a good ways out. If you come upon any fresh tracks, hoof or foot, follow them till you know who made them."

"Then kill them," Aimes stated, as if issuing himself an order. Without having to hear another word from Plantz, Aimes turned his big roan and kicked it up into a trot out across the yard toward the hill line.

"See? Gawddamn it, Bright," said Plantz as Aimes cut his horse back and forth, his head lowered, searching for prints in the dirt. "That's what I need more of."

"I follow orders, Captain," Bright said in protest. "If you are unhappy with how I—"

"Kenny," said Plantz, cutting him off, "I think you'd do well to join another band of riders. This war is nothing *but* killing and torture."

Chapter 3

———

Jed Shawler did not hear his brother Avrial call out his name before Plantz's bullet resounded out across the woods and hollows. But even if he had heard Avrial, he would have been powerless to help him. Earlier, when the militia riders swooped down onto the Shawler farm, their gunfire shattering the predawn stillness, Jed had been tucked away in the cover of a downed cedar, keeping vigil on a large squirrel's nest high up in the bare branches of a sycamore tree.

Upon hearing the gunfire, he had run back to the edge of the woods and looked down into the clearing where the Shawler farmhouse sat beneath its rise of morning wood smoke. Seeing the riders circle the house, some of them splitting off to the barn and dragging his brothers out into the dirt, his first instinct had been to raise his squirrel rifle to his shoulder and draw a bead on the leader of the hooded riders.

"Damn you, Plantz, I'll kill you!" he'd said aloud to himself, recognizing Ruddell Plantz's big dun horse and the man himself, in spite of the grainy light and the white flour-sack mask over his face. The shot would be difficult at this distance, but he'd made harder shots in the course of his short years, bringing down both deer and elk for the Shawlers' dinner table.

As he took aim, he instructed himself to calm down, breathe deep and make the shot count. He knew how many shots he carried in the leather shooting pouch draped over his shoulder. He'd brought seven loads, enough to bring home seven squirrels for the noon meal. But would seven shots be enough to draw the militia away from his family? Enough to save his family from Plantz and his killers?

He didn't know, Jed told himself, centering his rifle sights on Plantz's chest as the man came to a halt out front of the farmhouse. He only hoped that seeing their leader fall might scatter the rest of the men, or draw them hurrying up toward him, giving his family a chance to arm themselves. He felt his right index finger begin its slow, steady squeeze on the hammer. *Now,* he said to himself, knowing from experience at what point the hammer would fall and the stream of fire would belch forth from the barrel.

Yet, before that thin deadly second arrived, his hands began to shake violently; his steady breathing suddenly became tight jerking gasps. He watched Plantz wobble back and forth in his sights until he finally lowered the rifle barrel an inch, batted his eyes and tried to settle himself. *It's a whole different thing killing a man,* he recalled Avrial saying when he'd returned from the war. The image of his brother and his blank lifeless eyes came to his mind. He clenched his teeth with determination and raised the rifle back into position.

"Please, God," he said aloud. But his shaking hands and his trembling knees would not allow him to make the shot. *You've got to do it!* he demanded of himself, trying desperately to calm his shaking hands. Yet, even as he'd struggled for self-control, he watched Plantz swing down from his saddle and step out of sight into the farmhouse.

Jed swung the rifle to a new target, but he realized the moment had slipped away. His hands shook uncontrollably. His breathing remained shallow and tight. The world had begun to swirl around him. He heard his mother scream; then he heard her scream cut short by gunshots from inside the farmhouse. *"Noooo!"* he shrieked in a muted, almost dreamlike voice, feeling what little was left of his nerve and his self-control slip completely away from him. In his hysterical condition, he suddenly hurled the squirrel rifle away, turned and ran wildly, mindlessly deeper and deeper into the woods. . . .

In the front yard of the farmhouse, Delbert Reese heard a sound on the trail and turned quickly, his pistol already raised and cocked. "Captain," he shouted to Plantz, "we've got riders coming!"

Plantz and the others turned their attention toward the sight of two horses coming across an open stretch of land between the Shawler farm and the Umberton Trail. "At ease, everybody," said Plantz. "Hold your fire. It's just Peerly and Conlon."

"Yeah. I wonder what the hell brings them

here?" asked the parson, staring intently at the two approaching riders as they galloped into the yard.

"Looks like we missed all the fun!" Peerly called out, looking all around at the bodies, the pillaged barn and house.

"You didn't miss a thing," Plantz said in a grim tone, stepping over closer to the horses as the two stopped. "I thought I told you two to stay put, keep an eye on Umberton for us?"

"Oh, you did. But you're going to be damn glad to see us today, Plantz!" said Peerly.

"I doubt it," Plantz said sharply. "And it's *Captain* Plantz to you." As he spoke he grabbed Peerly's horse by its bridle and held it firmly. "Do you understand me, Peerly? Or am I going to have to give you something to hold on to as a reminder from now on?"

"No, sir, Captain Plantz." Peerly's attitude changed instantly; his demeanor turned serious. "My apologies, Captain." He nodded at Clarence Conlon. "We saw the colonel bring three strings of horses into Umberton. We knew you'd want to know about it right away. So we came running!"

"What about Tolan?" Plantz asked. "When was I going to hear from that hay-pitching son of a bitch?"

"We saw him." Peerly shrugged. "I reckon he would've told you about it first chance he got." Peerly smiled proudly. "But I knew you'd want to know right off. So I wasted no time. Was I right to do that?"

Plantz nodded his approval, turning loose of Peerly's saddle. "Yeah, you two did right bringing that information to me."

"It was all my idea," Peerly quickly pointed out, not wanting to share any recognition with Conlon.

But Plantz, having gone into rapt contemplation, appeared not to hear him. The parson spoke to Peerly and Conlon, saying, "You two go water your horses."

"Wait," said Plantz, seeming to snap out of his deep thoughts. A sly smile came to his face. "That old colonel is just testing me, that son of a bitch." He turned his eyes back to Peerly and Conlon. "Who did the colonel have riding with him?"

Conlon sat slumped and uninterested in his saddle. Peerly responded quickly, "Two wranglers! One was—"

"Shepherd Watson," the parson said flatly, cutting in and finishing his words for him.

Looking taken aback, Peerly gave the parson a curious look. "How did you—?"

"Because old Shep is always with the colonel," said Plantz, sounding unsurprised. "Who else?"

"You ain't believing this, Rudde— I mean *Captain Plantz!*" he said, correcting himself. "He had a young woman riding with him!" He blurted it out quickly about the woman on the outside chance that once again the parson would finish his reply. When the parson said nothing, Peerly gave him a passing glance, then said, "She was dressed like a man and sat her horse like a man. But she was a woman, no mistaking that. Was there, Conlon?" he said, turning to the big hulk of a man for support.

"She was the prettiest thing I ever saw," Conlon grunted, rising to the question.

"I wouldn't go so far as to say that," Peerly said,

taking over. "Fact is, she was a might on the plain and manly side, for my taste."

"A woman wrangling for the colonel," said Plantz. He turned his amazed expression to the parson. "What do you make of it?"

The parson looked flatly at Peerly and asked as if he already knew the answer, "How old do you say, early to mid-twenties? Dark eyes, dark hair?"

"Yes, that's her," said Peerly, impressed and unable to conceal it. "How'd you know that?"

"It's the colonel's daughter," he said confidently to Plantz, ignoring Peerly.

"Begging your pardon, Parson," said Peerly, thinking he had caught the parson in a mistake, "but it's a known fact that the parson's wife was barren of child."

"Peerly's got you there," Plantz said to the parson, as if standing neutral between the two in some kind of mental sporting contest. "It *is* widely known about the colonel's wife."

"The colonel's wife had nothing to do with it," the parson retorted, his confidence unwavering. "This daughter of his came from a whore named Sudie . . . one of the camp followers from back during the Indian campaigns. She took up exclusive with the colonel for a whole winter and got her belly blown up. By the time the baby was born, the colonel was gone on back to Texas. Instead of hat-pinning herself, or knocking the baby in the head when it was born, Sudie decided to keep the girl child." He grinned. "You never know what's in a whore's heart."

The men stared in silent fascination at the parson.

The parson grinned, liking the attention. "She named the child Julie, but being from Wildwood, Virginia, Sudie liked to call the girl her *Wildwood Flower*."

"Damn, Parson," said Plantz. He shook his head slightly in wonderment. "I just don't see how you come up with so much."

"It's a gift," said the parson, shrugging it off. "Sudie's little Wildwood Flower has been the colonel's deep and best-kept secret."

"Except for you knowing about it," said Plantz.

"Of course," said the parson, a bit smugly, "except for me knowing about it." Pausing as if to reward himself, he pulled a twist of tobacco from inside his uniform coat, bit off a plug and rolled it over into place inside his left jaw.

"*A gift?* Jesus!" said Plantz, with total and unquestioning belief. "I don't know what to think of you sometimes."

"Nor do I, sometimes," said the parson. He grinned, spit and ran the back of his hand across his mouth. Looking back and forth at the other men as if they had become his audience, he went on. "Sudie died young of consumption as many of her occupation do, still working the flesh circuit—railroad camps mostly. But early on she'd told her little bastard daughter all about the colonel. Of course he'd only been a captain when she knew him." He looked off as if in deep contemplation for a moment, then said, "She built him up to be a hero. Must've wanted her child to grow up and try to better herself, I suppose, knowin' she'd come from such good stock."

Looking at the men and seeing their undivided

attention to the parson's words, Plantz suddenly grew restless and said, "All right, Parson, before you go passing a collection plate. Let's get everything gathered up here and get going."

The parson gave him a look. "Don't you want to hear more about our Wildwood Flower? What she's done all her life? What's she apt to do?"

"Later maybe," said Plantz, seeming to have snapped out of the parson's spell. "Right now, it's time to go."

"But it's always best to hear these things while the information is fresh and pouring through me," said the parson. "There are things about this woman," he cautioned, raising a half-gloved finger.

"I said, *put it away for now,* Parson," Plantz said, a bit sharply. "It'll make for good entertainment around the campfire. Right now I've got other things to do."

Put it away . . . ? The parson stared flatly at him, not allowing Plantz to see how offended he'd become. "As you say, Captain," the parson replied submissively.

"Captain?" asked Conlon. "Are we riding back into Umberton? Make the colonel pay tribute?" He'd straightened upright in his saddle at the prospect of riding right back to town and finding the young woman.

"Hush up, fool," Peerly growled at him in a lowered voice. "It ain't your place to ask such a thing."

Ignoring Peerly, Plantz said to Conlon, "I think not. We'll let the colonel complete his horse sale." He grinned. "We know the way to his house . . . He's not getting away with anything."

Chapter 4

On the trail back from Umberton, Julie, her father and Shep nooned in a stand of white oak trees near the base of a stretch of low hills bordering the rolling plains. The colonel watched proudly while Julie stooped down onto one knee and watered her big buckskin bay by pouring water into her tall-crowned hat and holding it to the horse's muzzle. To old Shep, who sat nearby, trimming himself a slice of jerked elk, he said quietly, "Tell me, Shepherd, how does a child—especially a girl-child—who grew up without me, remind me so much of myself?"

Old Shep didn't venture a reply. Instead he watched Julie water her horse and said, "She's a top hand with horses."

"Yes, isn't she though." The colonel smiled, watching his daughter rub the buckskin's muzzle with her gloved hand.

Standing up beside the buckskin, Julie slapped her hat against her leg and held it at her side as she looked off along the base of low hills where a short stream of dust drifted upward and away on a warm breeze. "Colonel," she said, keeping her eyes on the dust as she spoke, "there's something coming our way."

"Oh? Man or beast?" The colonel smiled and gave Watson a look, proud of his daughter's trail ability.

"Could be *man* . . . somebody on foot," Julie replied in her husky but pleasant voice.

Not seeming too concerned, the colonel looked off in the same direction, judging the distance of the small billow of dust. "Well, whoever it is better hurry if they expect to catch up to us."

Julie said, "I just figured, you carrying money and all."

"That was sensible thinking on your part, but this money is as safe as it is in a bank," the colonel replied. "Safer," he added. "There's three of us here, *well armed*. No bank has that kind of protection."

"I expect you're right, Colonel." Julie nodded. She glanced again toward the short rise of dust, then appeared to dismiss the matter. She walked the buckskin over to where the other two horses stood hitched to a small white oak sapling.

As she hitched the buckskin, the colonel said, "Julie, come on over here and rest yourself beside me. I've got something I want to give to you."

She walked over to where the colonel and old Shep sat in the shade of a towering oak tree and eased down onto one knee, the same position she'd taken while watering her horse. "All right, Colonel," she said, facing the two from four feet away. "What do you want to show me?"

The colonel noted the space between them, but smiled to himself as he reached down into his shirt pocket. "Just a little something I thought fitting for a lovely young lady."

Julie felt herself blush, and she lowered her eyes. She was not used to such talk, or to such kindness. She was not used to the warmth and trust of kin. She had to remind herself that this man was her father in order to coax herself forward.

"There now," said the colonel, "you needn't be bashful with me, young lady." He liked the self-protective caution in Julie's character, but he wondered at what cost she had developed such a trait. They had grown closer since her arrival, yet that growth had been slow in coming.

Where have you been, my daughter? He asked himself, capturing her dark eyes for a moment. *Where has this life taken you?*

At times the colonel reminded himself of a man befriending a young wolf cub. He saw a deep aching need in his daughter; in spite of Julie's strong self-reliance and independence, the colonel saw that his wild, beautiful wolf cub yearned to *belong,* to something, to someone. She had been drawn across the wilds to him as if following the scent of the kindred blood coursing through their veins.

"I want you to have this," the colonel said. He raised his closed hand from his pocket and, opening it, allowed a silver necklace to spill from his calloused hand and dangle from his fingertips. On the chain a silver medallion the size of a quarter swung back and forth gently; in its center a single engraved silver rose glistened in the flickering sunlight through the leaves of the white oak.

"For me?" Julie whispered in a hushed tone.

"Colonel, I can't have something like this." Her words faltered for a second. I— It's— It's too fine a thing for the likes of me."

"Too fine a thing for *my daughter?*" the colonel said with mock reproach. "Nothing is too fine for my daughter." As he spoke, he reached out with the necklace, as if insisting she take it. She did so, reluctantly.

The colonel's voice softened. "Julie, by all rights this necklace has belonged to you your entire life."

Without a word, Shepherd Watson stood up and moved quietly away, giving the two the privacy he felt they needed.

Julie removed her stained trail glove and allowed the colonel to lower the medallion into her hand. She lifted her gaze from the silver rose and searched the colonel's eyes for his meaning.

"It belonged to your mother," the colonel said softly, "or, that is, it would have." After an awkward second's pause he said, "I bought it for her from a Mexican silversmith and had her name engraved on the back."

"It's beautiful," Julie whispered, turning it and seeing the name *Sudie* engraved in fancy letters.

"I meant to give it to her the day I left the territory and went to Washington. It was—" The colonel stopped, unsure of how to phrase his words.

"A going-away present," Julie said quietly, looking back down at the silver rose, then raising her face back to the colonel with a bittersweet smile.

"Well, yes . . . exactly," said the colonel, knowing she could have called it something else. "Thank you for understanding," he added. "I want you to know, I would've come and brought you home with me, back when you first wrote to me. Why did you turn me down?"

"It wasn't meant to be right then, Colonel," Julie said. "It wasn't meant to be until now." She clutched the silver rose in her hand and remained quiet for a moment, her eyes closed, as if collecting her emotions. Then she opened her eyes and said in the same quiet voice, "Colonel, I realize how things stood between you and my mother. I know how she lived."

"Julie," said the colonel, "you know how Sudie lived, but I don't think you know that it wasn't that way between the two of us. There was something between us. I wasn't just another face behind the curtain."

"You needn't try to clean up my or my ma's life, Colonel," Julie said. "I didn't come looking for that. All my life I have wanted to find you, to see you. I can't even explain why. I suppose just to hear you say something to me, something that anybody's pa might say to them, except, hearing you say it, I would tell myself, that's *my pa* talking to *me*."

"And it is your pa talking, Julie," said the colonel, deeply touched by her simple words. He moved forward and brushed a strand of hair from her face with his fingertips. He felt his own eyes well up. "I did something while you and Shep waited for me at the restaurant. I hope you find it agreeable." He paused for only a second, then continued. "I hired Fortney, the attorney, to do whatever he has to do to *legally* make you a Wilder."

Julie looked delighted, yet stunned. "Oh, Colonel, you needn't do that for me," she said, although the very idea of having a last name made her heart soar. "I know who I am, and that you are my pa. Nobody can take that away from me, not ever."

"I feel the same, Daughter," said the colonel, "but since you are a Wilder, let's make it formal. "From now on, you are Julie Wilder, daughter of Sudie and Colonel Bertrim Wilder." He beamed.

"But, Colonel," Julie remarked, "hearing it said like that makes it sound as if you and my ma were married."

"Then so be it," said the colonel. "Let folks make of it what they will. You *are* mine and Sudie's daughter. Under different circumstances, perhaps your mother and I might have been—"

"Please, Colonel." Julie stopped him. "I told you, you don't have to say things like that for my sake. I'm a big girl." She offered a wan smile.

The colonel gazed deep into her dark eyes, and saw so clearly those traits of his own, so much so that he knew it would be futile to try to convince her. "All right then," he said with a slight sigh. "I won't mention how things were with your mother and me, ever again. But remember this: There *was* more between her and me. That's why the silver rose."

Julie nodded and gazed lovingly at the necklace and medallion in her hand.

"Welcome to the family," the colonel added softly. "The Wilders of Virginia—what few of us are left—are fortunate to have you."

"I don't know what to say," Julie whispered, a

bit overcome, still studying the silver rose. "There were never any fine, pretty things in my ma's life. I wish she'd seen this."

"Perhaps this day she has," the colonel offered softly, seeing the features and reflections in Julie of both himself and the young woman who'd mothered his only child. "I thank God she had *you* in her life," he whispered. "You were all of those fine and pretty things."

He closed her hand gently yet firmly around Julie's hand, closing it over the medallion and necklace. The two sat in silence for a moment until the colonel said in a lighter tone, "Now then, Daughter Julie Wilder, the next words out of your mouth better not be, 'Yes, Colonel.' " He smiled and said, "It better be, 'Yes, Pa.' Is that going to be all right with you?" Opening her hand, he took the necklace between his weathered fingers. He opened the clasp, reached out, strung the necklace around her throat and fastened the clasp behind her neck.

Julie felt a tear run warm down her cheek. "Yes, Pa," she whispered, touching the silver rose ever so lightly. She raised the medallion from the front of her dusty shirt and let it slip down out of sight into her bosom.

From over by the horses, old Shep said, "Colonel, there's a single rider up in the hills, coming down. The dust we saw a while ago on the flatlands is back up too. What do you make of it?"

Before standing and ending the conversation with his daughter, the colonel looked to her for approval. "Are we all right, Julie?" he asked.

She smiled and nodded. "We're getting there, Pa."

The two stood and walked over beside Shep. "I don't know what to make of it," the colonel said, gazing out to where the thin spiral of dust drifted sidelong on the early spring breeze. He spotted the distant figure on horseback farther up on the hillside move in and out of the shelter of trees and rock.

"This is rough country to be afoot in," Julie offered.

"It is indeed," said the colonel. "I'm thinking we need to ride back and see who this is on foot. It could be somebody in sore circumstance, needing help."

Before the colonel had finished talking, Shep had begun reaching out to unhitch the horses. "We'll ride wide of the worn trail, *Comanche style*," the colonel said to Julie, "just in case there's trouble brewing." He gave her a thin smile. "We never let the other party see us as well as we see them."

"Right, *Pa*," Julie said, liking the feel of calling him her father, liking the feel of having a last name like everybody else. Taking the reins to the buckskin from Shep she started to step up into the saddle.

"I don't suppose it would do any good for me to ask you to stay here and wait for us, would it, Daughter?" the colonel asked.

Julie gave him a firm smile. "Not a bit, Pa," she said.

"That's what I thought," the colonel chuckled, taking his reins from Shep and stepping up into his saddle.

* * *

Jed Shawler did not realize one of the militiamen was on his trail until he found himself rolling and tumbling the last few yards down the hillside to the wide plains. There he pulled himself to his feet and clung to the trunk of a cottonwood tree where he stood panting and looking back up along the hill trail. When he spotted the lone rider coming down the trail, a rifle propped up from his lap, the boy knew that the horror of this day had not yet ended for him.

In a broken, sobbing voice, Jed said under his panting breath, "Forgive me, Ma . . . I'm so sorry. Forgive me, Pa. Forgive me Avrial, Marty, Davey. I shoulda stayed with you!"

It had come to him in a jolt as he'd fled the scene of the carnage, that it would have better had he stayed and died along with his brothers and his parents. Yet, what had he done? He'd thrown down his rifle, turned and run, *like only a coward would do,* he chastised himself.

Staring up along the hill trail where the rider had disappeared for a moment into the trees and rocks, Jed ran his shirtsleeve across his cold face. *Only a craven coward . . . ,* said a voice inside him. But before that voice could finish denouncing him, Jed saw the rider move back into sight, and a new voice cried out, *Run! Hurry*

Jed had pushed himself away from the tree trunk and now ran with all of his waning strength, with no direction in mind, no plan for staying alive beyond his next stumbling steps onto a dry dusty trail cutting through the rolling grassy plains.

For the next twenty minutes he ran, limp and spent, stumbling, falling. Each time he struggled back to his feet and continued running. When he managed a blurry look back at the hillside, although he no longer saw the rider, he knew the man was there, hunting him like an animal.

Dizzy, nearly mindless, his eyes watering in the chilled air, his breath pounding thick and tight in his chest, Jed felt almost relieved when he spilled headlong into the strong arms of who he thought must surely be his killer. "No, no!" he managed to say in a raspy, failing voice. He flayed out at Shepherd Watson with his powerless fists, convinced in his addled state that somehow the rider had circled around and found him.

"Whoa now, easy now, young fellow," said Shep, swinging the boy around effortlessly until he held him from behind. "Who are you running so hard from anyhow?"

Jed went limp and Shep lowered him into a sitting position. He turned to the colonel as Julie ran over from her horse with a canteen of water. "Colonel! I recognize this boy; he's one of the Shawlers. He's acting like the devil is snapping at his tail. What do you say we do here?" Shep asked, knowing beforehand what the colonel would do.

"I've never known any of the Shawlers to have trouble with anybody," said the colonel. "Get him off this trail, and keep out of sight." He looked off along the trail and up into the hill line, judging the distance. "My old soldier's nose tells me we'll be having company most any time."

Chapter 5

Goff Aimes knew that the distance between himself and the Shawler boy had grown less and less. From higher up on the hillside he'd seen the boy stagger, fall and pull himself up the side of a tree trunk a half hour earlier. The boy was too tired to have made it much farther, he thought, nudging his horse along beside the fresh boot prints in the dust. He gave a dark grin and jacked a round up into his rifle chamber. *Here goes* . . .

"All right, boy, the fun's all over," Aimes called out across the tall grass and into the sparse beginnings of a young woodlands alongside the trail. "I'd play some more if I just had the time."

He stopped his horse and listened closely for any sound from the wild grass or woodlands. Hearing none, he nudged his horse forward, slumped and comfortable in his saddle until he came to the spot where the Shawler boy's boot prints ran right into Shepherd Watson's.

"Whoa," Aimes said under his breath, looking around quickly. Seeing the hoofprints of the three horses a few yards to his right, he had bolted upright in his saddle and grasped his rifle with both hands. "I don't know who you are, but you are providing aid and comfort to an enemy of the Free Kansas Militia!" he called out, hoping to raise a target, a voice, something.

"An enemy?" the colonel called out from the sparse woodlands. "What has this boy done to incur the wrath of you buzzards?"

A dark sly grin came to Aimes' face, recognizing the colonel's voice. "Careful how you bad-mouth us, Colonel. This war is going more and more our way." As he spoke he nudged his horse around in the direction of the colonel's voice. "As for the boy, he's a livestock thief who has been slicking calves, chickens and anything he can get his hands on, and giving it to Southern Regulars."

"Bull!" said the colonel. "There's no Southern troops within a hundred miles of here; hasn't been all winter."

"Then you're taking this boy's side against our militia, are you, Colonel?" Aimes inquired coolly.

"I don't even know *his side*," said the colonel. "The shape he's in, nobody might ever know *his side*. I found him unconscious in the middle of the trail. I'll take him to Umberton, let the Union garrison commander decide if he's done any wrong."

"I just can't allow you to do that, Colonel," said Aimes, raising the rifle to his shoulder. He had listened to the colonel long enough to single out his position. He quietly pulled back his rifle hammer. "Step out where I can see you; maybe we can talk more about it."

"Shep?" the colonel called from behind his tree. Behind Aimes, on the other side of the trail in the tall grass, another rifle cocked, this one making no attempt at keeping quiet.

"I've got him sighted dead-center, Colonel," Shep called out in reply, "just awaiting your order."

"I didn't come here looking for a fight, Colonel," Aimes said, suddenly sounding nervous and pressed.

"I figured as much," said the colonel. "You came looking for easy pickings. But what you've found is a hornet's nest." He leveled his rifle against the side of the tree and centered it onto Aimes' chest. "Lower the rifle and drop it to the ground."

"Now, come on, Colonel," said Aimes. "There's no need in all this. Can't I just—"

"Sergeant Watson!" the colonel called out. "Prepare to fire!"

"Yes, sir, with pleasure," Shepherd Watson shouted back to him.

Sergeant Watson . . . ? Shep . . . ? Aimes began to sweat. These old fools were crazy. His eyes darted back and forth; his rifle lowered down the side of his horse and dropped to the ground. "All right, Colonel, see? I dropped it," he said, raising his hands chest high. "No harm done. I'm gonna just back this horse and head out of—"

"Now raise your sidearm from its holster and drop it too," the colonel commanded.

"Jesus!" Aimes protested under his breath, but he raised his pistol with two fingers and let it drop beside his rifle. "Colonel, this is a bad mistake. Captain Plantz ain't going to take this kindly."

"Get that saddle out from under you," the colonel demanded.

"What?" Aimes said in disbelief. "You're stealing my horse! You'll hang for this, Colonel."

"I'm not stealing it," said the colonel, watching Aimes step down grudgingly from his saddle. "It'll be waiting for you three miles along the plains trail."

"But, Colonel," Aimes started to protest.

"Start walking back the way you came, Aimes," the colonel called out, cutting him short. "You can head back this way once you know we're gone."

"You're going to hear from us, Colonel," Aimes warned him, stepping backward, his hands still raised.

"Keep talking that way, we'll shoot you where you stand and not have to worry about it," the colonel called out. Beside the colonel, crouched down beside the half-conscious Shawler boy with a wet bandanna in her hand, Julie looked up at her father with apprehension in her eyes. "Pa, is he going to bring the army or the rest of *his* bunch down on us?"

"Let him try," the colonel said. "I know this boy is no thief. I'll stake my honor on him. Whatever Aimes and the militia have done to him, I'm betting the last thing they'll want to do is take this run-in with me to a Union garrison commander."

"But what about the militia?" Julie persisted, reaching back down to the Shawler boy and patting the cool wet bandanna to his forehead.

"The militia could be a different story, Daughter," the colonel said, a troubled look coming to his weathered eyes. "They are a treacherous bunch. But they are cowards who ride at night, hiding their faces behind a flour sack. Give in to the likes of them, it won't matter who wins this blasted war; nobody on either side will ever live free again."

Julie nodded. "We best get this boy somewhere, cool him out and get some more water in him."

"Right you are," said the colonel, craning his neck, gazing out to make sure Aimes had begun walking away along the plains trail.

From across the trail, Shepherd Watson saw the colonel and called out, "He's leaving, Colonel. I can still see him. I'm keeping an eye on him."

The colonel turned and gave his daughter a proud look. "Old Shep and I still know how to raise our bark if need be."

"So I see," Julie said, returning his smile, yet not completely comfortable with her father and Watson letting the militiaman walk away. But then, what would she have done, she asked herself, not liking the harsh reality that her answer brought to mind.

Would she have killed him, had it been her choice? She considered it but only for a fleeting moment. No, she decided, dismissing the matter. She wouldn't have killed him. Julie knew she did not have it in her soul to deliberately pull the trigger and watch a man fall dead by her hand.

"Are you all right, Daughter?" the colonel asked, seeing her expression turn grim.

"Uh, yes, Pa," said Julie snapping out of her dark thoughts.

"I know this is all ugly and coarse," the colonel said in a softer tone. "These hooded riders are what a war spawns after a while." He stooped down beside her and added, "But don't worry. We'll soon be out of bloody Kansas. Once we're back east, we'll have put all of this madness far behind us."

Before the two had stood up from beside the

exhausted boy, Shep came walking toward them, leading their horses in one hand and carrying his repeater rifle in the other. "I watched Aimes till he was all the way out and over a low rise," Shep said. "It'll take him a while before he gets back here. We'll be gone by then."

"Good work, *Sergeant Watson*," said the colonel.

Shep beamed with pride and handed the colonel the reins to his horse. "Just following orders, *sir*," he said with military bearing.

Julie and Shep pulled Jed Shawler to his feet and pushed him up into Julie's saddle. Shep held the wobbling boy in place until Julie climbed up behind him, reached around and took her rein, letting Jed lie back in her arms. "Where— Where are you taking me?" Jed asked in a weak voice.

"Shhh, you just rest," Julie said. "We're taking you somewhere safe."

"But my family . . ." Jed's words trailed as he slumped against Julie and allowed himself to drift back out of consciousness again.

In the afternoon, Delbert Reese and Nez Peerly had reined their horses to a halt at a place where the hill trail began to spill out and down onto the plains when Peerly raised a hand and said, "There comes that sorry sumbitch, right there!" He pointed ahead across the tall wild grass at Goff Aimes as Aimes and his horse rose and fell on the rolling terrain, like a ship at sea.

"Good," said Reese, letting out a sigh. "I was afraid we'd be tracking him down long after dark. My horse ain't been feeling real spry of late."

"To hell with your horse, Reese," Peerly said

sharply, giving him a harsh glance, then looking back at the oncoming rider. "Aimes got some damn tall explaining to do," Peerly added, "causing me to have to ride out here after his sorry ass. It'll be dark before we catch back up with the others."

"Yeah, we've all got better things to do than traipse out across these plains," said Reese.

Peerly lifted a canteen from his saddle horn, un-capped it, took a swig of cool water, swished it in his dry mouth and spit it out. Glancing again at Reese, this time eying his tired-looking horse, he passed Reese the canteen, then said, "I meant no harm, saying what I said about your horse. I'm just plumb worn out." He plucked at the tunic of his wool uniform. "This gawddamn getup is hotter than a woodstove, even at this time of year."

"Yeah, it is sure enough." Reese pulled off his hat, lay it on his lap, lifted a swig from the canteen and spit it out. "I'd give anything for some whis-key." He raked his fingers back through his hair.

Looking the horse over again, Peerly said, "Why don't you do you and this plug both a favor, put a bullet in his brain?"

"Because he's been a damn good horse!" Reese said defensively. "Hell, he's only nine years old. He's got a couple good years in him. He just has his bad days, is all, just like some folks do."

"Gawddamn," Peerly chuckled darkly under his breath, "a fucking horse." He took the canteen back from Reese and said, "I'll down him for you, if your heart's a bit too tender."

"You worry about your *own* horse, Peerly," Reese said, getting prickly about the matter. "Anytime you think my *heart* is too tender, you're welcome to come try taking yourself a bite of it."

"I was just remarking, Reese," said Peerly, passing it off with no concern.

"So am I," Reese replied.

"Look, he sees us," Peerly said, nodding toward Aimes, seeing him wave his hand, but make no effort to kick his horse's pace up a little. "Don't get in no hurry on our account, you malingering son of a bitch," he muttered.

Reese chuckled. "You've got the red-ass at everybody today, don't you, boss?"

"Not everybody"—Peerly stared straight ahead as he spoke—"just turds like Aimes, making me have to ride out here . . ." His words trailed as the two watched Aimes bring his horse over the last low rise and slow down to a walk the last ten yards until he stopped and sat facing them.

"Boys, I have just been put through pure hell," Aimes said, taking off his militia hat and fanning himself with it.

"Where's your sidearm?" Peerly asked bluntly, seeming unconcerned with whatever had happened to Aimes out on the plains.

"That's what I'm *about* to tell you," Aimes said, giving Peerly a narrowed gaze. "I was ambushed back along the trail by—"

"Where's your rifle?" Peerly cut in. "I guess you lost it too?"

Aimes turned sharp himself. "I never *lost* a gawddamn thing, Peerly," he said. "As I was saying, I was put upon by Colonel Bertrim Wilder and that crazy old sumbitch that rides with him. They

ambushed me, stole my horse, my guns. Luckily I
managed to get my horse—''

Peerly interrupted him again, this time by breaking into a fit of laughter. "You let them two old
Injun war relics strip you down, guns, horse and
all?"

Reese also laughed, but unlike Peerly, he lowered his face and kept his laughter to himself.

"No," Aimes said in a chilled tone, "there were
others with them."

"Others?" Peerly stifled his laugh and asked,
"You mean a *young woman,* wearing a tall
Montana-style hat?"

Aimes gave him a hard questioning stare. "I
didn't see any young woman. What I did see was
three or four more rifles pointed at me from all
directions," he lied.

Peerly nodded and looked off as if pondering
Aimes' story. "All right, let's look at this," he said.
"You're saying Colonel Wilder, an old Union officer, who is on the same side as us in this war,
ambushed you, stripped you down and sent you
running?" He shook his head. "That's hard for *me*
to swallow, let along Captain Plantz."

"Yeah," Reese asked, "why would the old colonel do something like that?"

"Because he's old and crazy. That's why the
Union wouldn't put him back in the field, ain't it?"
Aimes said.

The two only shrugged.

"Anyway, he's got the Shawler boy I was chasing," Aimes said, giving them both a grim look.

"Damn," said Peerly. "Why didn't you say so to

begin with? Plantz is going to throw a straight-out fit when he hears that."

"I know," said Aimes, sounding worried. "I wish to God I didn't have to tell him."

"I bet you do," said Peerly. As he spoke, his hand instinctively rested on the butt of a large pistol holstered on his side. "But tell him you *surely* will, you sorry bastard."

"I was on my way to the old barn to tell him, Peerly," Aimes said defensively.

"Maybe you was, maybe you wasn't," said Peerly. "But you for damn sure *are* now." Nodding back along the trail leading up into the hills toward the Shawler house, he said, "Get around here and stay in front of us. I don't want you turning rabbit on us."

"Damn you, Peerly!" Aimes raged, yanking his horse around roughly by its reins and gigging it out ahead of them.

Following him, his hand still on his pistol butt, Peerly grinned and asked Reese, "So, tell me, Delbert, what have you got planned for yourself once this war winds down?"

Chapter 6

At dusk, Plantz brought his men to a halt at the sound of horses' hooves galloping up from along the edge of a thin trail leading into a dry creek bed. "Check it out, Macky," he ordered in a lowered voice. "If somebody is trailing us, I want to lead them to the crossroads barn."

Macky cut his horse away from the rest of the riders and gigged it out toward the sound of the horses. No sooner had he dropped out of sight over a rise than the galloping came to a halt and left Plantz and his men sitting in silent anticipation until finally Macky called out to them, "It's Peerly, Reese and Aimes, Captain."

Plantz and his men relaxed in their saddles. "All right then, all of you get back here," Plantz called out in reply.

As the four men came riding back into sight, seeing Aimes riding behind Macky, followed by the other two, Plantz said to the parson sitting close beside him, "I better see some proof that he killed the last of the Shawlers."

"And if he didn't?" the parson asked, his voice low, his eyes staring straight out at the four riders.

"Then I expect this is as good a time as any to start weeding out our fold," Plantz replied quietly.

As the three riders approached Plantz and the other men, Peerly spurred his horse forward. Passing Aimes, he said sidelong to him, "It's your ass now!" and raced into the lead until he slid his horse to a halt in front of Plantz. "Captain Plantz," he said quickly, "I want you to know this son of a bitch Aimes hasn't done a damn thing he was told to do! He deserves to be horse-whipped, sir!"

Plantz gave Peerly a narrowed gaze and said, "Keep you thoughts to yourself, Private. I'll be the one who decides who gets horse-whipped."

"Yes, sir, Captain," said Peerly. He quickly reined his horse to one side and sat watching as Aimes rode up to Plantz, followed by Delbert Reese.

"Captain Plantz," said Aimes, with a worried look on his bearded face, "whatever Peerly is saying about me is a damn lie!"

"Oh," said Plantz coolly, "then where is the Shawler boy?"

"Yeah," Peerly interjected, "and ask him where his damn guns are, Captain!"

Plantz slid Peerly a dark glance, then said to the parson who sat on his other side, "If he interrupts me one more time, Parson, I'd be obliged if you'd carve his tongue out of his face."

The parson nodded grimly. "I will do exactly as you ask when the next word leaves his mouth."

Peerly seemed to freeze under the parson's words.

"Now then, back to you, Aimes," said Plantz. "Did you or did you not kill the person I sent you to kill?"

"No, Captain," said Aimes in tone of dread and apprehension. "I was set upon by Colonel Wilder and some other gunmen. They have the boy now. I was on my way to tell you when I met Peerly and Reese. I figured you needed to know right away. I was headed to the old crossroads barn—"

Plantz cut the frightened man short with a brisk wave of his hand. "Get out of my sight, Aimes," he said in a tight angry voice, "and do so quickly."

Aimes turned his horse and, giving Peerly a dark glance, rode around the loosely formed column of men and sat at the rear, looking dejected and ashamed. The men deliberately averted their eyes away from him.

"All right, men! You all heard him," Plantz called out along the ranks. "You can count on us having trouble over this. We do the work that regular troops don't have the guts to do. But we will catch hell over this when the Shawler boy starts shooting off his mouth, especially when he's got a crazy old army officer by his side!" He looked from one grim face to the next, then continued. "I know I could have this wretch shot for dereliction of his duty," he said, pointing toward the rear at Aimes. Then he turned to the parson and said, "Parson, tell them why I won't."

The parson spoke up with confidence. "Men, with this war ending, the captain wants to be remembered as a fair man by his troops."

"There you have it," said Plantz in agreement. Taking over he said, "Aimes is one of us, and I'm not letting this come between us. Now, all of you remember this evening, and how I dealt fairly with him."

The men nodded solemnly and murmured quietly among themselves. "Now all of you go on home," the parson called out, "and God be with you." He watched the men's horses begin to move away from one another. "We've done good work on this ride. We can all be proud. As soon as we need to ride again, you'll be notified where to meet by one of our own."

"Keep Aimes and Peerly here," Plantz said quietly to the parson.

Smiling knowingly to himself, the parson gigged his horse forward and sidled up close to Aimes before the man could ride away. "The captain wants you, Aimes," the parson said in a lowered tone, while the rest of the men broke away and went their separate directions. Seeing the worried look come back to Aimes' face, the parson said in a soothing voice, "Don't make this any harder on yourself, Goff. We're all your brothers. Don't make yourself look bad."

"Am I going to get whipped?" Aimes asked in a shaky voice.

"Probably not," the parson said with a cold, blank expression. Watching Aimes closely, seeing that at any moment the man's self-control might snap and send him bolting away, the parson said, "But whatever happens, think about Caroline and your baby. I know you only want the best for them. Am I right?"

Aimes weighed the parson's words, understanding their dark meaning. He calmed himself and breathed deeply. "Will you see to them now and again, Parson?"

"You needn't have to ask, Goff," said the parson, giving him a coaxing nod toward Plantz, who sat as still as stone, staring at him. Off to one side of Plantz, Peerly sat slumped in his saddle, his head cocked curiously to the side.

"I hate giving that rotten little bastard the pleasure," Aimes said under his breath, his voice shaky but under control.

"Use your knife," Plantz said quietly to Peerly, watching the parson and Aimes ride toward him. "I don't want anybody hearing gunshots out here."

"Am I allowed to speak now, Captain?" Peerly asked, testing his standing. "I mean without the parson carving my tongue—"

"Speak," said Plantz, cutting him off bluntly.

"Since you want me to use the knife, can I stab him as many times as it pleases me?"

Plantz gave him a disgusted look. "Take him out aways into the woods. Kill him as slow as you like, but I better not hear any screaming."

"You won't, Captain," Peerly said, getting excited. "I promise you."

"The parson and I are going to ride on. As soon as you're finished, go get yourself some shut-eye; then go round up Kiley, Conlon, Macky, Evans and Muller. Bring them all to the old barn out by South Bluff."

"Hot damn," said Peerly, even more excited, "we're heading out again, ain't we?"

Plantz didn't answer. Instead, he stared straight ahead in silence, watching Aimes and the parson draw closer with each slow rise and fall of their horses' hooves.

Julie sat on the side of the small bed and wiped Jed Shawler's scraped and scratched forehead with a damp cloth.

Jed had recovered from his exhaustion, but he remained weak, not yet in full control of his faculties.

"It's the same as what us soldiers always called battle shock," Shep Watson had said earlier, leaning down close to Julie's ear as if to keep Jed from hearing him. "I've seen men act this way after their whole patrol had been slaughtered and they was the only one left alive."

Jed's eyes stared off at the flicking low flames of the evening fire in the hearth. Julie noted his blank eyes and asked Shep, "How long does it last?"

"It's a hard thing to predict," said Shep. "For some it lasts only a short while, maybe only a day or two. But there are others who never get all the way out of it."

"I'll— I'll get out of it," Jed said in an unsteady voice, surprising them both, his eyes still staring somewhere deep into the firelight. "I have to . . ."

Across the room, the colonel had stood lighting his charred briar pipe, but at the sound of Jed Shawler's voice, he shook out the long slim twig of burning white oak and pitched it into the hearth as he stepped in closer. He still wore his leather brush chaps and kept his hat in hand, ready for him and Shep to ride to the Shawlers' and see the carnage for themselves.

"Right you are, lad," the colonel said to Jed. "You have to get back on your feet for your family's sake, and see to it these men pay for what they've done."

"I *told* you about it?" Jed asked, looking confused. "I don't remember talking about it." He reached a hand to the side of his scratched, bruised head. "I don't remember much of anything . . . after what happened."

"Yes, lad, you told us the whole terrible story," said Colonel Wilder, "and you'll have to keep things clear in your mind so you can tell it to the military and before a judge once these murdering scoundrels are brought to justice." His voice softened as he added, "Shep and I are headed over right now to do what needs to be done for your family; then we'll ride into Umberton and report what happened. We'll instruct the Union troops to come here to talk to you and listen to your account."

"I—I should go to," said Jed, attempting to rise.

"No." Julie pressed him back down with her hand on his chest.

"But I—" Jed tried to state his reasons but the colonel would have none of it.

"No," the colonel said, cutting him short. "You're staying here with my daughter. She'll look after you until Shep and I return in the morning. We need you up and sharp when the army gets here."

Julie looked up at her father and asked with a tone of apprehension, "Pa, are you and Shep going to be all right, riding all that way after dark?"

"We'll be fine, Julie," the colonel reassured her. "Shep and I know our way."

"But, what if . . . ?" Julie let her words trail.

"Plantz and his men won't be anywhere around the Shawlers," said the colonel. "They've done their dirty work. Now they'll all crawl back under their rocks somewhere until the next time they strike."

"Mind what the colonel told you, Miss Julie," Watson warned her with a wary look. "Keep these doors and windows bolted . . . and don't let nobody in unless you see it's us."

"Come, Shep, let's be off," Colonel Wilder said. "Julie has both the ten gauge and the Sharps rifle. She and Jed can hold off anything a snake like Plantz and his rascals can throw at them." He looked at Jed and asked him pointedly, "I'm sure you wouldn't mind putting a bullet in these murderers, eh, lad?"

Jed's eyes lowered as if in shame. "I'll try, Colonel," he said.

"And try is the best any of us can ever give one another," Colonel Wilder said, knowing he had touched a raw and sensitive nerve in the boy.

"We'll use caution," Julie reassured her father, taking the focus away from Jed.

"Of course," said the colonel. He stuck his briar pipe between his teeth as he remarked, "This house was built to withstand the Comanche and the Cheyenne. I expect it will fare well enough against this Free Kansas Militia trash."

"But do be careful, Pa," Julie offered.

"That I will, and you can count on it," said the colonel, reaching down with his free hand and caressing Julie's cheek. "Now that I have my daughter here with me, I'll do nothing that might steal any more of our precious time together."

"And I'll see to it he doesn't forget that," Shep

said, rising to the colonel's side, staying a respectable two feet behind him.

Standing up from the edge of the bed, Julie followed her father and Shep out onto the porch. Colonel Wilder turned, kissed her on her cheek and said as he turned toward the horses, "Don't forget . . . Draw the bolt on the door as soon as you go back inside."

"I will, Pa," said Julie, still liking the sound of the word *pa* on her lips.

Placing his hat down firmly on his head, the colonel and Shep stepped into the saddle. Within a moment both turned their horses out of sight in the direction of the Shawlers.

Chapter 7

The first three hours after the colonel and Shep left, Julie had busied herself straightening up the house and preparing some dried elk shank and warmed-over hoecakes for her and the Shawler boy to eat. She'd set the plate of food beside him while he sat in silence staring once again into the flames. Moments later when she came back for the plate, the food had been untouched. "You should try to eat something," she said, "even if you're not hungry. You need to get your strength up."

When Jed made no reply, Julie left the plate beside him and walked away, leaving him alone with his thoughts.

In the crushing quiet, Julie felt a deep sense of foreboding begin to close in tightly around her. She looked all around at the windows, making sure the wooden bolts were in place. Through the shooting ports in each wooden window shutter facing west, the last rays of grainy sunlight stood slantwise across the plank floor. Were there eyes watching the house from the shadows along the woods line?

She started to walk to one of the shuttered windows and peep out, as if to see if eyes might be watching the house from within the dark woods. But catching herself in time, she stopped and let out a breath.

Stop it, she told herself, not wanting to let herself fall into the clutches of some unfounded fear. Her father and Shep knew she would be all right here; otherwise they never would have left her and the Shawler boy here alone. At length she stood up, but she did not go peep out through one of the shooting ports. Instead, she walked to the rifle leaning against the wall near the front door. She picked it up, checked it, then leaned it carefully back in its same position.

On her way across the floor to where the shotgun stood in a corner near a window, she heard Jed Shawler say in a quiet tone, "If they come while we're here . . . I don't know if I can help you defend us."

"They won't come here," she said, hoping she sounded confident. She looked over at him and saw his cheeks glisten with tears. She picked up the ten gauge and turned it back and forth in her hands. "You heard what my pa and Shep said about it. These men are back in hiding somewhere by now."

"I turned coward," Jed blurted out, seeming to pay no attention to her words. For the past few moments he'd sat silently recounting the grisly scene of his family dying in their front yard while he tossed away his squirrel rifle and fled to save himself.

"I'm sure you did all you could," Julie said, trying to console him.

"What I did was let everybody die," Jed said. His clenched fists trembled violently. Julie watched, not knowing what to do for him. "All the people who loved me . . . who trusted me," he continued. "I had a gun, I—I could have done something . . . but I didn't! All I did was drop my gun and desert them without even firing a shot!"

Julie interceded, saying, "You've been through an awful lot in one day. Maybe after a good night's rest, things will look a little better to you."

"Nothing will ever look better to me until the men who killed my folks are dead," Jed murmured, his voice turning bitter and hard.

"They will be," said Julie, seeing that only his rage for his family's killers seemed to keep him from breaking down and sobbing aloud. "My pa will bring the army and they'll see to it justice is done."

But her words didn't seem to console the boy. He turned his face away and stared into the flames, withdrawing back into silence.

Another silent hour had passed before Julie saw the boy move a muscle or utter another sound. When he finally stood up on unsteady legs and turned toward the rear door of the house, Julie walked toward him, seeing him lift the door's wooden latch. "Jed," she said quietly but firmly, "don't go out there. We're supposed to both stay inside until my pa and Shep return."

Without turning to face her, Jed replied in a flat, lifeless tone, "I'm going to the privy," and contin-

ued out into the darkness as if nothing she could
have said or done would have stopped him.

"Please hurry back," Julie called out, keeping
her voice guarded and low, walking over to close
and latch the door he had left standing wide open
behind him.

With the door shut and securely latched, she
leaned back against it and looked at the battered
wind-up clock standing atop a table in a corner of
the room, making it a point to keep track of time.
As she waited, she moved away from the door,
picked up the shotgun from its place beside a window and held it close across her stomach.

When the boy had not returned after a full ten
minutes, she cracked the door a few inches and
called out to him through the shadowy darkness
beneath a half-moon sky. Listening closely, hearing
nothing from the direction of the weathered plank
outhouse, she called out again. But this time when
she heard no reply, she could think of nothing else
to do but close the door softly, latch it and stand
there alone. *Pa,* she thought to herself, as if in that
ringing deathlike silence the colonel could somehow hear her, *I wish you'd taken us both with
you . . .*

Twelve miles away at the Shawler farm, all that
remained of the house were a few charred piles of
ash-covered timbers and bits of household scraps
that had been blown away from the flames by the
bellowing force of heat. In the flicker of a torchlight
that Shep held above them, Colonel Wilder shook
his head slowly and flipped the corner of a wool

army blanket over the faces of the dead they had dragged to one spot and lined up along the ground.

"The men who did this are no better than animals," the colonel said, standing back away from the dead and dusting his hands together.

"Colonel, there's not even enough rock or board around here to cover them with until we bring the army back," Shep commented, looking all around the dark yard.

"All the more reason why we must hurry, Sergeant," said Colonel Wilder, turning to the horses.

With his boot sole Shepherd Watson smothered out the torch's flames on the ground. "Yes, sir," he said, hurrying, joining the colonel at the waiting horses.

The two started to turn their horses toward the thin trail leading up across the stretch of low hills between the Shawler land and the wider main trail running toward Umberton. But before they could do so, they both halted abruptly, hearing the quick thunder of horses' hooves rush in close around them. "Steady, Sergeant," the colonel said to Shep, seeing the old soldier reach for the army Colt holstered on his hip. "Hold your fire . . . Let's see what we've got here," he whispered in a lowered voice.

In the thin light of the half-moon, they both watched the loose circle of horses draw tighter around them until directly before them, the colonel heard the familiar voice of Ruddell Plantz call out, "Who's there? State your business here, and be quick about it."

Colonel Wilder had an idea that Plantz already knew whom he and his men had ridden in on, yet he answered anyway, trying to keep his voice level and his temperament in check. "I am Bertrim Wilder, U.S. Army Colonel, retired, sir," he called out as a matter of formality. "To whom am I speaking?"

Plantz chuckled menacingly and nudged his horse forward until the colonel and Watson could see him clearly in the pale moonlight. "Oh . . . I think you damn well know who you're speaking to, Colonel," he said. He gave a broad gesture of his arm and brought the rest of his circled men in closer. "Now, the question is, what the hell are you and this old fool doing out here, traipsing around in the middle of the night?"

"We came to see your handiwork firsthand, Plantz," the colonel said with disgust.

"It's *Captain* Plantz to you, Colonel Wilder," Plantz said. "Being a former military officer yourself, I'm sure you want to extend the courtesy that a gentleman's rank demands." He grinned secretly to himself in the shadowy moonlight. "Even though as I understand it, your petition for a command was turned down on grounds of mental incompetence."

"Damn you! You are no officer, and certainly no gentleman, sir!" Watson blurted out, unable to control himself at Plantz's accusation. "Colonel Wilder's mental competence was never in question!"

"As you were, Sergeant," the colonel said to Shep in a firm tone, quieting him. To Plantz he said, "I won't argue trivial matters with you, Plantz. You have some serious explaining to do when I inform the army about the bodies of the Shawler family that you and these rats slaughtered."

"Whoa, now, Colonel," Plantz said. "It appears to me, you and Shepherd here are the ones with some explaining to do. *You're* the ones *we've* found riding away from this place. Perhaps I need to report this to the army and let them sort things out."

A dark chuckle went up from the circle of men.

"I realize that's ordinarily the way you operate, Plantz," said the colonel. "But this time you've slipped up. We have a living witness who will tell the army exactly what happened to the Shawlers." He nudged his horse forward confidently. "Now move aside! We're coming through."

"Easy, Colonel," Shepherd Watson whispered, even as he put his horse forward beside his commander.

"We have no choice, Shep," the colonel whispered in reply. "Stay close to me and sit boldly. This is not the first time we have had to buy a pot for ourselves."

"Indeed not, sir," whispered Shepherd Watson, sidling close beside him, rifle in hand, cocked and ready. "We'll be just fine."

For the first hour Julie had chastised herself for letting Jed Shawler go out into the darkness alone. She had given her word to her father to stay indoors no matter what, but she couldn't stand by idly, not knowing what had happened to the boy. Surely the colonel would understand, she thought, turning the shotgun back and forth restlessly in her hands. Finally she could wait no longer. She'd taken a lantern down from the mantel over the hearth, lit it and unlatched the door. *Here goes,* she'd told herself, walking out with the shotgun in her right hand.

Julie did not want to admit to herself that Jed Shawler had taken off into the night; however, when she'd held the lantern up along the path across the side yard, she chastised herself even more as she'd looked down at Jed's boot prints in the dirt leading out into the woods.

Hoping against hope, she'd called out his name in a guarded tone. At length she had no choice but to accept the fact that the Shawler boy was gone; her wandering around outside in the dark was not going to help matters.

Turning, she carried the lantern low at her side, hurried back inside the farmhouse and latched the door behind herself. "Pa," she murmured, slumping back against the closed door, "it looks like I've made a poor job of things here."

Throughout the night, even though she knew the boy had left, she'd tried her best to stay awake and keep her attention turned toward the outside, in the direction of the woods beyond the privy. But in spite of her best effort, she eventually leaned the shotgun against a wooden chair next to where she sat and laid her head down on the wooden table.

In the first silver-gray light of dawn she was awakened by the sound of a voice calling out to her from the far side of the yard. "Pa?" she said, snapping awake and batting her eyes as if it might have all been a dream. She sat tensed for a moment until she heard the sound of horses walking into the yard from the trail. Then, she jumped up from her chair, ran to the shooting port of a front window and peeped out.

At the edge of the yard the colonel and Shepherd Watson came into view, their horses walking slowly toward the house. "Thank God!" Julie said aloud, hurrying to the door, unlatching it and running out off the porch to meet them. "Oh, Pa!" she called out. "You can't imagine how glad I am that you've made it back so soon!"

As she ran to meet the two horses coming toward her, she noticed no change in either her father's or Shep's stoic expressions. "Pa?" she said, coming to halt, seeing for the first time the red blood stains on their chests, the paleness of their faces. "What's happened to you?" she asked, already feeling herself being overcome by dark realization.

The colonel's blank lifeless eyes stared straight past her as he wobbled slightly in his saddle. "I'm dead, you silly girl."

Julie gasped, hearing the voice, knowing it was not her father's, and realizing at the same time that her father was not seated in his saddle under his own strength. "Oh no!" As she stiffened in fear, ready to bolt back to the house, she saw her father and Shep both being flung sidelong to the ground by the two hooded men hidden behind them.

"My my, but don't *you* feel foolish!" said Nez Peerly, the nasty grin on his face hidden within the loose flour sack. All Julie saw were piercing eyes staring out at her through roughly cut eyelets.

Upon seeing her father's and Shep's bodies, Julie turned quickly toward the house. But it was too late. She'd been trapped. Between her and the open door three more hooded men had stepped down from their horses and stood blocking her way. She turned quickly to her right, but saw two more hooded men step down, facing her in the grainy dawn light. Behind her she heard a muffled voice call out, "We came for the Shawler boy. Give him to us!"

"He's—he's not here," Julie replied, keeping her voice steady even though her knees grew weak with fear.

Ruddell Plantz, whose voice she'd heard from behind his hood, stepped forward. "If you're lying to us, you'll get worse than the colonel or his flunky got."

Julie stood firm as Plantz came nearer, his eyes glistening from within the eyelets like those of a wild animal. "You can search the house, if you don't believe me," she said. "He left during the night to use the private house and never returned."

"Must've fallen in over his head," Peerly quipped behind his hood.

"Shut up, *Private!*" Plantz said in a strong tone, turning rigidly toward Peerly. Then to Julie he said, "We *will* search the house . . . and we *will* burn it to the ground if we find you're lying to us." He gave a hand signal to the men standing in front of the house, prompting them to turn and run in through the open door. After a moment of rummaging, the men came out, one of them carrying the rifle and the shotgun.

From near the front of the outhouse, another man called out, "There's boot prints here leading out into the woods, sir."

"Nobody in the house, sir," the one carrying the guns called out.

"Good work, men," said Plantz. Turning back to Julie he said, "So, maybe you *are* telling the truth.

He's gone, but that doesn't mean you haven't hidden him somewhere. Now, where is he?"

"I—I don't know," said Julie.

"Should we spread out and start searching for him?" one of the men asked.

"In a minute," said Plantz. "I think she's lying to me." As he spoke he stepped closer, peeling his leather riding glove from his left hand. "But I don't mind a little lying, because I *enjoy* getting to the truth." Before Julie saw it coming, he slapped her hard across her face with the glove, the impact and sting of it staggering her. But she only staggered for a second before the glove lashed back across her face, this time drawing blood from the corner of her mouth.

A small ivory comb slipped loose from atop her head and allowed her long, gathered hair to spill down around her face. Plantz quickly grabbed a handful of her hair and jerked down, causing her to bow forward as he dragged her back and forth in front of the leering men. "Getting at the truth can go on for *as long as it takes,*" he said, liking the feel of having this young helpless woman under his total control. "We can all take part in it, right men?"

The men moved forward in a tighter circle, nodding their approval.

"See, this is why *you* men were especially chosen to ride tonight, instead of some of the others," Plantz called out. Dropping his gloves, he swung Julie in such a manner as to step behind her and jerk her head back against his chest. His free hand reached around and ripped the front of her cotton riding blouse wide open, exposing her firm breasts in the silver morning light. "Some of them have no taste for this sort of work." He ran his rough gloved hand back and forth over her breasts. "But I'm betting *you* men do!"

Chapter 8

The last thing Julie clearly remembered was the cry of pain one of the hooded men let out when she sank her teeth into his cheek. She remembered the taste of his blood in her mouth; she remembered her red tooth prints—blood soaking through the flour sack—as he pulled back away from her and threw his hand to the side of his face. The rest of the men hooted and laughed, two of them holding her down, another holding her naked legs spread wide apart. The others stood watching, those who had already taken their turn with her, and those still waiting.

Once again Julie struggled against the men pinning her down, the same way she had each time before, even though she knew it would do her no good. She also knew that biting the man would not save her from him. In a moment he came back, dropping his loosened trousers down around his calves, exposing himself to her. This time she caught a glimpse of a pistol in his hand as he swung it hard sideways, cracking her across her jaw.

"Now spread her open, gawddamn it!" she heard

him say to the man at her ankles as her senses slipped away from her. She ceased struggling and felt her world turn black, and numb and mindless around her.

Hours later, as she awoke in the midmorning heat, recollection came back to her, but not clearly at first, only vaguely, as if seeping back to her through a thin, cloudy veil. "I'm not—" she rasped incoherently, unable to finish her words.

"Not *what?*" Peerly chuckled, pulling his flour sack back down over his face barely in time to keep her from seeing him. In his gloved right hand he held the silver rose on its chain, its clasp broken from where he'd grabbed it and ripped it from around her neck.

"I'm, I'm not—" she forced herself to say through her stiff aching jaw. But again her words failed her.

"Hear that, fellows?" said Peerly, adjusting his flour sack mask. "It's *not.*" He laughed and stuffed her silver rose necklace in his shirt pocket.

"Not what?" asked Conlon, leading both his horse and Peerly's over to where Peerly stood looking down at Julie. She lay bruised, battered and naked in the dirt at their feet.

Peerly shrugged. "Hell, I don't know," he laughed behind his hood. "But *it's not.*"

"I'm not . . . a whore . . . ," Julie managed to say in a strained distorted voice, still stunned, blood oozing from the deep gash in her purple swollen jaw.

"Oh, I understand!" Kiley laughed. "It's not a whore. You men remember that now. This *fine up-*

standing lady crawling around in the dirt is not a *whore.*"

"Like hell you ain't!" Peerly leaned down, raised the lower edge of his hood and spit on her. "If you wasn't before we started, you damn sure are by now!" He stepped back and gave her a sharp kick in her side. "You smell like one too."

"That's enough, men," the parson called out in his smooth, strong baritone voice. Without calling Conlon by name he pointed at him and said, "You, go torch that barn. Everybody else get mounted."

"What about the house?" Conlon asked. "Can't I torch it too?"

"Just the barn," said the parson. "It's bad luck torching a house in broad daylight."

Conlon shrugged. "Can I have another go-around with her?"

"No," said the parson. "You all had your turn. That's all you get." He walked over to where Julie lay gagging, rolled into a ball, trying to catch her breath.

"I—I'm not . . . ," Julie said, barely able to get the words out.

"Sure, I understand," said the parson. Stooping beside her, he clutched a handful of her hair and twisted her battered face around until she faced him. "We found the boy on our own," he said. "It looks like you wasn't lying after all. So we're not going to kill you." He shook her roughly by the hair, seeing that she was once again losing consciousness. "Listen to me! We're going to let you live. You'd be wise to leave this country. Do you

understand? There's nothing to keep you here, unless of course you're seeking vengeance." He stared
deep into her eyes as if he might discern something
from them.

Julie couldn't answer, but she nodded in reply
when he shook her again.

"Now, that's a smart girl," said the parson. "See,
this war is ending but we'll all still be here. Look
in any direction and there's we'll be, looking back
at you, remembering what we all did to you today.
We've all seen you, but you haven't seen us. Do
you understand?"

Julie nodded before he had time to shake her
head.

The parson smiled behind his hooded mask.
"That's it; you learn fast. Now, we don't want the
army to come looking for us, and we don't want
any act of vengeance from you or any of your kin.
If the army comes snooping around, we'll come
looking for you. Understand?"

She nodded again.

The parson reached around and patted her on
her bare behind. "Good girl . . . You know your
place. I like that in a woman." He looked around
at the other hooded faces, nodding, giving them
a smile they could not see. Then back to Julie,
he said, "There's a whole lot of Free Kansas Militia in these parts. Nobody will ever identify us.
As soon as you're able to ride, get the colonel and
Shepherd Watson buried and clear out of here."

"I will," she rasped as she nodded her head in
agreement with him.

The parson grinned to himself and said to her,
"And always remember, dear Julie, *'Vengeance is*

mine,' sayeth the Lord." He patted her almost affectionately on her naked breast.

Again she nodded, this time feeling him turn loose of her hair and stand up. She stared at his boots, his hand-tooled Mexican silver spurs covered with tiny engraved flying horses, their wings like those of angels. Then she quickly turned her swollen eyes away, and lay back on the ground, lest he see by the look on her battered face that she would never forget those tiny flying horses.

"Let's ride, men," Plantz called out from atop his horse thirty feet away.

The parson looked down and smiled to himself, seeing Julie lie back in the dirt as if resting on a comfortable bed. "That's the spirit, lie there and relax . . . Reflect on what I've said to you."

Julie did not answer or nod. She closed her eyes against the glaring sunlight and lay very still until she heard the sound of their horses trail off into the distance. A few more minutes passed before she ventured up stiffly onto her palms and sat in the dirt looking blurry-eyed all around herself. Sixty yards away the barn had already started to tremble on its frame, giving in to the high-licking flames, sending black smoke boiling upward across the clear Kansas sky.

To her right she saw the body of Jed Shawler lying in the dirt where the men had thrown him after finding him hiding in the woods a few miles from the house. "I'm . . . sorry," she said quietly, as if she might have saved him somehow. Looking away from Jed's body she saw her father and Shep lying where they'd been pitched to the ground that morning.

"Oh, Pa," she cried softly under her breath, forcing herself to crawl slowly and painfully to the colonel's side. "Why us? Why us?" she sobbed when she'd stopped and raised the colonel's lifeless head, cradling it to her dirty naked bosom. She turned her eye to the sky and said in a sobbing, broken voice, "All I ever wanted was to get to know my pa . . . to spend some time together."

Hugging the colonel's cold face against her, she noticed for the first time that her silver rose had been taken from around her neck. She turned her swollen eyes in the direction the riders had taken. "Oh, Pa," she sobbed, "look what they've done to us. They even took my rose necklace."

On the ground a few feet away lay a ragged wool blanket the men had used to drag items from the house and stuff them into their saddlebags. Julie crawled over, picked it up and threw it around herself and crawled back to the colonel's side. "I know you and Shep . . . need burying, Pa," she whispered painfully. "But let's just lie here . . . real quiet for a while." She'd hardly gotten the words from her mouth before the black silence overtook her once again.

On a wide stretch of grasslands, Baines Meredith stopped his big black stallion and looked all around as he lifted his canteen, uncapped it and raised it to his lips. When he lowered the canteen he made the slightest nudge with his knee. The stallion took the signal and made a complete turn, giving Baines an opportunity to gaze back along his trail through his dark wire-rim sunshades.

He saw no signs of being followed, but he would check again.

Raising his wide-brimmed hat, he ran his fingers back through damp gray-black hair that hung loosely past his shoulders. Lowering his hat back onto his head, he managed to look back again without appearing to check the trail. All right, that's enough, he told himself, knowing that too much caution could be as deadly as no caution at all.

"Let's go, Joseph," he murmured, giving the slightest touch of his knees to the stallion's sides. Joseph moved forward once again, as if on his own, the rising drift of black smoke from the Shawlers' place reflecting in his caged eyes.

No one had seen Baines Meredith cross the dry winter grasslands, but had someone been watching they would not have guessed he'd even seen the black smoke drifting eastwardly on the high thin air. If he had seen it, he'd certainly made no effort to rush toward it. Instead, he deliberately kept the stallion pointed straight ahead in the direction of Umberton, and only eased the big animal over gradually until he'd reached the stretch of bare woodlands separating the Shawler homestead from the open plains.

Inside the shelter of woodlands, Baines turned the stallion off the worn path and stared back along his trail once again. The horse scraped a restless hoof on the ground.

"Settle down, Joseph," he said in a whisper, patting a gloved hand on the stallion's powerful withers. "Let's not get in a hurry and forget ourselves."

The stallion settled reluctantly, blowing out a hard breath. Baines swung down from the saddle, took a short stick of hard sugar candy from his saddlebags and broke it into two pieces. "The only place hurrying ever takes a man is to his grave," he whispered, holding the first piece of candy to the stallion's warm muzzle. "Now, you remember that, my friend."

The second piece of candy he stuck into his own mouth, and sucked on it while he watched the trail and listened to the stallion chomp his treat into a sweet mush and swallow it. Rubbing the stallion's muzzle for a moment, Baines worked his piece of candy over into his jaw, then swung back into his saddle. Satisfied that no one lurked along his trail, he nudged the stallion forward and did not stop again until he reached the edge of the woods looking out upon the yard.

"What have we here?" he whispered to the stallion, seeing the collapsed barn still burning. He saw the bodies of the two elderly men, and the woman, only partially covered by the ragged blanket, lying slumped over one of them.

Baines expertly slipped his repeating rifle from the saddle boot and laid it across his lap, his thumb cocking the hammer quietly as he heeled the stallion forward. Looking around closely, he stopped the stallion a few yards away, stepped down silently, walked over and looked down at the three corpses. He'd already gotten an idea of what had happened from the many fresh hoofprints in the dirt.

Rifle in hand, he reached down, took the edge of the blanket and raised it carefully, seeing Julie's nakedness, her cuts and bruises. But more importantly, he saw her breasts rise and fall slightly, and he heard a soft moan escape her parched, blood-crusted lips. With a dark grimace he looked again at the many hoofprints as if judging how many men had been there. He didn't have to wonder what the men had done. The signs were obvious, he thought, looking back at the naked woman for a moment as if unable to keep himself from doing so. He saw the thin cut along the side of her throat where her rose necklace had been ripped away from her.

"Damn it, young lady," he said under his breath with a sigh. "If you only knew how bad I hate doing a good deed for *anybody* . . ."

But here goes, he thought. He gave the stallion a hand signal, bringing the big animal forward toward him while he stooped down, scooped Julie into his arms, blanket and all, and carried her to a bare-branched oak tree a few yards away. Julie came to just long enough to look into his face with blurry swollen eyes and ask in a broken voice, "Who—who are you?" She shivered, even in the warming sunlight.

"I am your hero for the day, young lady," he replied. But feeling her tense up as she began studying his rough rawboned face, he continued in a more somber tone, "Don't worry, ma'am; I am not out to do you harm."

He felt her go limp in his arms as he lowered her onto the ground and leaned her back against the tree trunk. Even though he knew she couldn't hear him, he said to her battered face, "You've taken worse than just a bad beating, ma'am. I believe we better get you to a doctor as soon as I take care of things here." He turned and walked to the bodies of the colonel, Shep Watson and Jed Shawler while he rolled his shirtsleeves up past his elbows.

Against the bough of the tree, Julie drifted in and out of a stupor, at one point hearing a faint sound of rocks clicking as Baine piled rocks atop the three bodies, and at another point feeling herself lifted upward and settled onto Baines Meredith's lap, atop the stallion. Moments later when she reached another foggy state of consciousness, she felt herself cradled in his arms, the blanket falling loosely from around her.

"Who are you?" she asked in a weak voice, struggling with the blanket, trying to raise a loose corner in order to cover herself.

Without answering her, Baines Meredith said, "I put a spare shirt on you before we left, ma'am. You're dressed, sort of, anyway."

Julie realized that beneath the blanket she remained naked from the waist down, but she felt herself slipping away again before she could do anything about it. "Water?" she moaned.

"Of course," said Baines. With his free hand he lifted a canteen from his saddle horn, uncapped it and held it to her cracked, bruised lips. She sipped sparingly. When he took the canteen away from her lips, he judged her state of consciousness and asked, "Do you feel like telling me what happened?"

"No, not now. My jaw . . . feels broken," she said stiffly. She touched her fingertips to the side of her battered face.

"It's up to you," Baines said, understanding her reluctance.

"They wore masks," Julie said in her broken voice, a trickle of bloody water running down from the corner of her mouth. Her swollen eyes took on a cautious look as she searched Baines Meredith's rough, weathered face. "I—I promised I'd move on, and I will, as soon as I'm able."

"I expect it's up to you, ma'am, whether or not you move on," Baines said. "But don't figure you owe the men who did this any promises."

Julie gave him a cautious, questioning look.

Baines read her look and said, "No, ma'am. I can understand your fear, but believe me, I had nothing to do with any of this. I'm Baines Meredith, all the way from Denver. I saw the smoke from the barn burning and rode in to see about it. As soon as I get you to a doctor, I'll see to it someone comes back with a shovel, to do some burying.

Having little choice but to trust him, Julie forced her suspicions aside, let out a breath and looked closer at his face as recognition came to her. "Baines Meredith, the manhunter?" she asked, her jaw throbbing in pain, her entire body aching and trembling beneath the blanket.

"The same, ma'am," said Baines, staring straight ahead, sunlight glinting off his wire-rim sunshades. "Now, try to rest some more and not let yourself think about anything. We'll be in town before you know it."

Chapter 9

In Umberton, Baines Meredith rode straight to the sheriff's office and slipped down from his saddle with Julie half-asleep in his arms. Heads turned toward him along the mud-crusted board-walks, watching curiously as he reached out with a gloved hand and knocked soundly on the rough plank door. He waited for a response from inside, but none came.

"We don't have a full-time sheriff," said an old man who appeared as if out of nowhere, a short pocket knife in one hand and a whittled stick in the other. "We have a sheriff who rides between here and Spotsworth . . . comes through here about once every week or so, unless he goes on to Rulo." As he spoke he studied the sleeping girl curiously, seeing her sore and battered condition.

"What about a doctor?" Baines asked. "Last time I came through here there was a doctor named Addison. He treated me two years ago when I rode through here."

A light came on in the old man's eyes. "You

must be Baines Meredith! I remember now. Old
Doc cut a rebel bullet out'n you."

"Right you are," said Baines, a bit hurried.
"Where can I find Dr. Addison?"

"I'm afraid old Doc took ill himself and went
back to Louisville, to die among his kin," the old
man said. "But we've got a young doctor who rides
circuit out here. He's due through here most anytime now."

Baines looked all around without expression, his
dark shade lens hiding his eyes. "Who should I best
take an injured woman to until the doctor gets here?"

"What happened to her?" the old man asked,
taking a short, curious step forward.

Baines gave him a flat cold stare from behind
the shades.

The old man got the point. "Sorry, I reckon I'm
just too nosy for my own good." He pointed the
whittled stick toward a white clapboard two-story
house sitting back a few yards from the mud-rutted
street. "Constance Whirly's boardinghouse is about
the best treatment a body can get in Umberton.
Constance runs it by herself now that her husband
is dead. She's also birthed most babies around here
since Doc Addison left."

"Obliged," said Baines.

"Want me to—?" The old man stopped short of
asking if Baines needed help, seeing him turn, walk
back to his horse and step smoothly up into his
saddle without disturbing the woman asleep in his
arms. "Well, anyway," the old man said, "I'm Merlin Potts . . . If I can be of any assistance, just
holler out."

Baines rode the stallion at a slow pace to the white clapboard boardinghouse, his hidden eyes looking back and forth from behind his shades at the faces of curious onlookers. At a hitch rail out front of the boardinghouse he stepped off and walked along a plank walkway toward a wide porch. To Julie's sleeping face he whispered, as if she might not really be asleep, "You can wake up now; they're all behind us." He studied her closely, yet he saw no change in the bruised, battered face lying cradled in the crook of his left arm.

Ahead of him, a tall woman wearing a long gingham dress, sleeves rolled up to her elbows, stood on the porch in the open doorway, her hands on her hips. "Death rides a black horse," she whispered under her breath, seeing the young woman lying limp in the rider's arms.

Her bearing and attitude turned bristly toward Death; however, upon seeing Julie's swollen face as Baines stepped down from his saddle and up onto the porch with her, Constance relented and said, "My Lord! What's happened to this poor child?"

"Where to?" Baines said, walking past her through the open door, into the cooler shaded house.

See, Constance told herself, taken aback, *Death waits for no invitation . . .* Yet, hurrying alongside him, she said, "Downstairs here." Then she moved past Death and directed Baines to a room just off the entrance foyer. "This will be more convenient for her than the stairs, once she gets up and around."

"Obliged," Baines said sincerely, seeing the

woman had already taken on the responsibility of looking after the injured woman, in spite of the strange looks she'd given him.

"Lay her down here for now," Constance said, gesturing toward a small sofa. "I'll have a regular bed brought from upstairs this evening. I rarely use this room for boarders, except when I get too crowded with stockmen and drummers."

"I'll pay extra, ma'am," Baines said, his expression revealing nothing.

"Now, you just hush," the woman scolded him, indignantly, suddenly putting Death out of her mind. "I didn't say that to gig you for more money. This poor woman is hurt. What kind of person would I be to charge extra for a person in need?" Looking more closely at him, Constance saw something familiar in his face.

"Sorry, ma'am," Baines said flatly. He laid Julie down gently on the sofa, her lower half still wrapped in the blanket.

"I should say so," the woman went on as she bent over Julie, brushing her hair from her face with a wince. "I get fifty cents for the room. Any nursing care I do is just me doing what the Lord requires of us." She gave Baines a sharp sidelong glance. "You're Meredith, the man-killer, aren't you?"

"Man-killer is not a name I prefer," Baines said, denoting her critical tone. "But that is what some call me."

"I remember you riding in here a couple years back, bowed over your saddle, bleeding like a stuck hog. Doc Addison saved your life."

"That is true, ma'am," said Baines, watching her

draw back the blanket carefully from around Julie's
waist. He took off his hat, held it at his side and
ran his fingers back through his long hair.

"Stop calling me ma'am," she said, again with
the sharp tone. "My name is Constance Whirly."
Her words stopped in a short gasp as she saw the
dark purple bruises, the cuts and whelps on Julie's
ribs, stomach and lower abdomen. "My God! Who
did this to her?"

"She won't say much about it," Baines said
softly. "But I expect it was night riders. She said
they wore hoods. They killed her father, a hired
hand and a young boy."

"Oh my goodness, no," said Constance. "This
must be Colonel Wilder's daughter! I heard about
her from the livery man. Then Colonel Wilder and
Shepherd Watson are both dead?"

Baines nodded. "That's what I make of it," he
said. "She wasn't in any condition to do a lot of
talking about it, even if she wanted to."

Constance Whirly gave him a look.

"Stop right there," said Baines, seeing her mind
race with possibilities. "I'm only doing what I figured I should do . . . no different than yourself."

"He—he saved me," Julie said in a faint voice.

Constance turned to her, seeing her try to rise
up onto her forearms. "There now, child, you lie
still," she said to Julie, pressing her gently back
down. "Don't be moving around; I'm afraid you've
got some broken ribs here." She grimaced, looking
at Julie's flattened broken nose, and added, "I wish
to God I could get my hands on the animals who
did this to you!"

"They're gone . . ." Julie murmured, seeming to

not want to even think about it, let alone talk about it. She lay back flat, trying to let her pain subside. She closed her swollen eyes.

Turning to Baines, Constance said in an angry voice, "I hope you're going to get the animals who did this to her."

"No," said Baines. He took her by the arm and guided her away from Julie's hearing before saying under his breath, "I believe she's afraid to do or say anything. She's lucky to be alive. Maybe that's all she gets for now." He lowered his face and gazed at her over the top edge of his sunshades. "Maybe that will be all she gets *period*. She said she's headed back east."

"And let this terrible thing go unpunished?" said Constance in disbelief. "If she doesn't report this to the army, I will!"

"I'm sure she'll report everything to the army," said Baines. "But let's allow her all the room she needs to do things her way." He stared at her again from above his sunshades. "Don't forget, the men who did this come from around these parts. They saw her, but she didn't see them."

"And they made threats," said Constance Whirly, understanding the matter more clearly.

"That's my speculation," said Baines. As if dismissing the matter, he drew a pocket watch from his black vest, checked it and said, "Who is the livery owner in this town?"

Constance gave him a quick stare. "Why do you want to know?" she snapped. "Were you headed this way anyway? Do you have business here?"

"I do," said Baines, plain and simply, with no offer of apology.

"Then, you are badly mistaken this time," Constance remarked. "Our livery man is Davis Beldon. He's as fine and decent a man as I've ever known." She tilted her chin upward in the livery owner's defense. "He's never harmed a living soul. Can you make such a claim for yourself?"

"I make no claims, ma'am," said Baines. As he spoke he reached inside his black brush-scarred riding duster, took out a stiff wanted poster and unfolded it in his gloved hands. "I do what I'm paid to do. In this case my employer is the government. Is this the man you know as Davis Beldon?" He turned the poster and put it into her anxious hands.

Her tense face turned slack in relief as her eyes went over the face on the poster. "No . . . thank God," she whispered. "This isn't Mr. Beldon. This is the man who works for him. His name is Virgil Tolan."

"No," said Baines, "he's a cold-bloodied killer by the name of Tom Heilly. He's been on the run for the past two years for sabotage of a Union armament shipment and killing two civilians and three soldiers in the process." Baines studied her eyes for a moment, then said quietly, "If you judge me, at least judge me against the kind of men I'm hunting."

"I am not judging you, sir," Constance said firmly, folding her arms across her bosom. "Take your leave whilst I look after this poor child."

"I will take my leave," said Baines. "I'll go about my business . . . and I'll come back to check on the woman afterward."

"I understand," said Constance. "But what

makes you so cocksure you'll be *coming back,* if this man is the killer you say he is?"

"I always come back," Baines said flatly, turning to the door.

Inside the livery barn, Davis Beldon stood in the cover of large wooden grain bin and watched the front door swing open slowly. He saw the dark silhouette of Baines Meredith in his long riding duster fill the incoming slice of sunlight. A long Dance Brothers pistol hung down in Baines' right hand. Before Baines' eyes could have possibly adjusted to the darkness, Beldon felt a cold chill go up his spine when he heard the man-killer call out, "Tom Heilly. This is Baines Meredith. I've come to hold you accountable for the murders of—"

"He's not here!" Davis Beldon cried out from behind the wooden grain bin and stood at its edge. "I'm—I'm the owner. I'm Davis Beldon. We saw you ride in. Tolan—that is, Tom Heilly, told me you would be coming here for him. He lit out of town, probably headed west. There's no telling how far he's got by now."

Baines waited almost a full minute before calling out in a calm flat tone, "Step out more, so I can see your face."

Davis Beldon stepped out sideways, but it was only one short, grudging step, in spite of having the whole center of the straw-covered floor to stand in. He held his shaky hands up over his head. "Mister, I don't know what he's done, but he's been a good hand since the day I hired him."

"You're lying, barn-keeper," Baines said flatly.

"Oh no! It's the truth," said Beldon, his brows rising at Baines' accusation. "He kept this place collected, kept the stalls mucked!"

"I mean about him heading out of town," Baines said, cutting him off.

Davis Beldon swallowed a hard knot in his throat and replied, "Listen, Mr. Meredith. I don't want no trouble here."

"Then quit trying to throw me off, Mister," Baines said in a demanding tone. "Where's Heilly?"

"I don't know, Mister," said Beldon. "And I don't know what he's done or who he might or might not have killed. But I believe he's a good man. And I believe a good man deserves a second chance."

"I see," said Baines Meredith as if having come to an understanding about the livery owner. Seeing Beldon's arm lower an inch and lean slightly toward the hidden corner of the grain bin, the man-killer raised the big pistol from his side and fired a single shot through Beldon's heart.

Beldon hit the straw-covered floor flat on his back, dead, his right boot toe jerking in reflex for only a second before it fell limp to the side. Baines slid a searching glance back and forth in the darkness as he punched out the spent round, replaced it and walked forward, the big Dance Brothers' back at his side.

Around the edge of the grain bin, he picked up a sawed-off ten gauge shotgun, cocked it and laid it out on the middle of the floor near Beldon's dead hand. He stepped back away from the body and stood on the same spot where he'd stood moments earlier, while outside, boots and voices hurried toward the sound of the gunshot.

"Stupid move," Baines murmured to the body on the barn floor.

In a moment, he stood to the side when three townsmen stepped through the door and looked all around warily.

"My God! He's killed ole Davis!" one of the townsmen said. He started to step forward to the body, but then stopped and gave Baines Meredith a suspicious look. "You're the man-killer? Baines Meredith?" he asked.

Baines only nodded.

"Davis pulled this scattergun on you?" another townsman asked.

"That's correct," Baines said with resolve.

"But why did he do something like that?" the third asked.

"He was trying to protect a wanted murderer who works for him," Baines replied, gazing straight and steadily into the man's eyes.

"Tolan? A murderer?" the first man asked as if in disbelief.

"His name's not Tolan; it's Tom Heilly," Baines said flatly. "And if any of you has seen him, I'm obliged to know his whereabouts."

"He's—"

"We haven't seen him all day," said the first townsman, giving the other one a hard look before the man could finish what he'd started to say. "I'm afraid we can't help you, Mr. Meredith."

Baines gave a slight shrug. "It's your town. I'll go from one door to the next if I have to. Heilly is going out of here with me, faceup or facedown."

"Now, just a minute, Meredith," the first townsman said, stepping closer. "You can't ride in here and start pushing folks around!"

"What's your name, Mister?" Baines asked in a calm but firm tone.

"I'm—I'm Herbert Wright," the townsman said, giving the other two a look as if seeking their support. "These men are Bill Wilmens and Oscar Bales. We're all three sort of the *acting* town board."

"Then act wisely," said Baines. "I carry a marshal's commission from the government. I have every right to arrest this man."

"That may well be. But you don't wear a marshal's badge, and your commission might not amount to a hill of beans once this war is over," said Herbert Wright.

"But until that time," said Baines, his thumb sliding easily over the hammer of his Dance Brothers pistol, ready to cock it, "I'll be about my job, with or without your cooperation."

Herbert Wright started to protest further, but Oscar Bales stepped in and said in a nervous, worried voice, "All right, he's hiding in the back room of my barbershop. But I didn't know he was a wanted killer! I swear I didn't!"

His eyes went to Davis Beldon's body on the floor. "I don't think poor Davis knew it either!"

"Which way to your barbershop?" Baines asked.

Bales pointed a shaky finger off toward the far end of town. "At the striped pole," he said. "The front door is standing wide open."

Herbert Wright cut in, saying, "The man came here showing us nothing but honorable intentions.

We took him at face value. Does that make us wrong?"

"No," said Baines, stepping away from the three and turning toward the door. "But hiding him doesn't make you *right* either." Before leaving the barn he warned them, saying, "If you show up in the midst of this, I'll have to figure you're taking sides with a wanted man."

"Meaning what?" Herbert Wright asked indignantly.

"Meaning I'll kill you if you get in my way," said Baines.

The three townsmen looked at one another with shocked expressions and scurried out of the barn behind Baines Meredith, then disappeared as he walked purposefully away from the barn along the rutted dirt street. Along the street, other townsfolk saw their three town leaders hurrying away. They too began to duck through shop doors and behind cover, watching the man-killer walk with his eyes focused sharply on Bales' barbershop.

Chapter 10

——

From the front window of the boardinghouse, Constance Whirly watched Baines Meredith walk toward the barbershop. She'd also seen the worried look on Bales the barber's face as he and the other two town board members hurried away, also wearing worried expressions. For reasons she could not explain, she smiled slightly and murmured to herself, "You are one *big, long* slow-moving cat, aren't you, Baines Meredith?"

Her faint smile lingered for a moment as she toyed idly with the top button at the throat of her gingham dress. But when Julie's voice called out to her, she quickly put her smile and her thoughts away.

"Mr. Meredith?" Julie called out in a weak voice from the other room.

"He's no longer here," Constance Whirly replied, walking toward the sound of her voice as she touched her hand to her hair as if to make sure it hadn't somehow gotten out of place. "I'm afraid Mr. Meredith is out in the street this very moment, no doubt prepared to do his killing."

At the doorway, Constance saw that Julie had gotten up from the sofa and stood facing her, steadying herself with one hand on a lamp table. "Please . . . help me to the window, to see him?" Julie asked.

The two heard Baines' muffled voice, out on the street, call out to the barbershop, "Tom Heilly! Come out with your hands up."

Constance said to Julie with a pointed expression, "Are you *sure* you want to see him just now?"

"Yes, please," Julie asked in a strained voice, reaching out a hand to Constance.

From the street they heard another muffled voice, this one calling from inside the barbershop, "I know who you are and why you're here, Meredith! You're not taking me back alive!"

"Suit yourself, Heilly," Baines Meredith replied.

Constance looped Julie's arm over her shoulder and walked her to the window where the two stood watching as Baines walked cautiously sideways, keeping an eye on the barbershop until he had a good view down a narrow alleyway toward the rear of the whitewashed clapboard building.

"Child, this is going to get ugly very quick," Constance said to the battered young woman standing beside her. "Are you sure you want to see this?"

"This man saved my life," Julie murmured in her weakened voice, almost to herself. "I don't know how I will ever repay him."

Constance studied her closely, seeing beyond the swollen eyes and the bruises and welts. "I'm sure he'll think of a way," she said under her breath, giving a short sigh.

But Julie Wilder appeared not to have heard her. Instead she stared intently out the window until

suddenly she gasped at the sound of gunfire erupt-
ing from the doorway of the barbershop.

"Oh my, he's dead!" Constance said in a short
painful squeal, at the sight of a bullet slamming
into Baines' chest so hard it gave off a puff of dust
and sent him flying backward off his feet. "Oh no,
oh no!" She squeezed Julie's hand hard, Julie
squeezing equally hard in return.

From the door of the barbershop, Tom Heilly
came running, gun in hand, aimed and cocked, his
gun belt and holster hanging over his shoulder. "I
told him I wasn't going back alive!" he called out,
sidestepping quickly toward a horse standing at a
hitch rail. "Listen up, everybody! This town has
been good to me! That's the way I want to leave
things here!" He looked all around as he unhitched
the horse. "So don't nobody try to stop me! I'm
going somewhere far away and live out my life in
peace. Everybody forget you ever saw me!"

"Oh no, stay down!" said Constance, hearing
Heilly talk to the town, yet at the same time seeing
Baines Meredith push himself up onto one knee,
then stretch upward onto his feet.

"I've got—I've got to help him!" Julie cried out,
trying to pull herself free of Constance's hand in
hers.

"No, wait, please," Constance insisted, squeezing
harder on Julie's hand, refusing to let her go. The
older woman seemed to have come to a realization,
watching Baines walk toward Tom Heilly with his
gun still in hand, ready to fire. "I have a feeling
Mr. Meredith has all the help he needs."

On the street, Heilly only then saw Meredith
walking toward him, seemingly unharmed by the

bullet he'd taken in his chest. "What the fu—?" Heilly's words stopped short as Baines' big Dance Brothers bucked high in his hand and sent a loud blast resounding along the silent street.

Baines' first shot hit him dead center, spinning him backward in a fast circle. Heilly's gun hand came up, struggling to get off a last shot as a thick ribbon of blood rolled out of his chest and slung around with him. He stared wild-eyed and malevolent, shrieking loudly until the second shot hit him in the center of his thick mustache, sending a spray of blood, pulp, teeth and bone matter out the back of his head and pitching him backward dead on the street.

"Oh, that poor dear man," Constance exclaimed. She turned loose of Julie's hand and clasped both of her hands to her bosom.

"You mean Heilly?" Julie asked, standing on her own now but feeling faint from her effort.

"Oh no," said Constance, catching herself and giving Julie a startled look. "I mean, thank goodness Mr. Meredith is alive . . . but it is a shame Mr. Tolan, or whatever his name is, had to die."

"It looked certain that Heilly had killed Baines Meredith," said Julie. "What happened?"

"I don't know," said Constance, taking on her more rigid, tough attitude. "It seems all men are interested in is either how to *kill* someone or keep someone from killing *them*. I've washed my hands of the lot of them. If you are wise, you'll do the same." She turned Julie from the window and guided her back to the other room to the sofa. As they made their way there, she asked, "You haven't fallen for this man-killer, I hope?"

"No," said Julie, "it's nothing like that. He saved my life, though, finding me, bringing me here. I owe him for that."

"Careful what you owe a man in this life, child," Constance whispered near her ear, helping her down onto the sofa. "They always find a way to collect."

"Will you be going to check on Mr. Meredith," Julie asked, "to make sure he's all right?"

"Oh, I doubt if I need to go see about him." Constance smiled with reserve. "I expect he'll come this way soon enough."

No sooner than Constance had gotten the words out of her mouth, the brass door knocker tapped soundly. "See?" she said, knowingly. "There he is now." But before going to the door, she raised a small pitcher of water from a table beside the sofa, filled a drinking glass with tepid water and handed it to Julie. "Now, you relax, honey, and drink this."

"Thank you," Julie replied, her eyes going toward the sound of the door knocker when it tapped again, this time a little louder.

"Oh, don't worry about him," said Constance, "he'll wait." She brushed a hand gently along the side of Julie's bruised and tender face, then added with a wince, "Every time I look at what's been done to you, child, I start hating men all over again."

The third round of door knocking had started by the time Constance had left Julie's side and walked to the front door. "Yes, I'm coming," she called out, lightly touching her hair with her fingertips and opening the door before Baines Meredith finished his third knock.

The gunman stood silently, only staring at her for a moment, as if he knew of nothing more to say now that his killing was finished. Finally he stated in a flat, hardened tone, "He's dead."

"Yes, we saw," Constance replied, trying to look detached and only mildly interested. She stood firmly in the half-opened door, making no gesture for him to enter. "I suppose you are through here in Umberton and eager to get under way?"

"I might stay here a few days," he said. Then he stood in silence.

Looking him up and down Constance noted how his face had turned pale, drained, as if indeed the bullet hole in the middle of his shirt might have gone through him and struck his heart. A bloodless heart, she thought upon close observation. "I have no empty rooms," she said, "if that's your question."

Baines Meredith only stared at her.

Nodding at the bullet hole in his shirt, she said in a tone of veiled disgust, "Are you some sort of fiend, some ghoul who kills, but can't *be killed?*"

"That's me all right," Baines replied almost in a whisper. Constance saw that in spite of his toughness, her words had affected him. She watched him try to mask the hurt in his eyes as he spread his shirt open enough to show her the thick quilted canvas vest he wore beneath it. Imbedded in the army blue canvas lay the flattened lead bullet from Heilly's gun. "I'm bulletproof, compliments of the Union army."

Constance shook her head and said with an almost bitter snap, "What will they think of next?"

Baines only nodded, closed the front of his shirt and said, "Knowing the young woman to be in good hands . . ." He let his words trail, stepped back with his fingertips to his hat brim and turn to walk away.

"What the hell," Constance cursed under her breath. Then, raising her voice a bit, she said, "Wait," and watched him turn back to her. "I suppose I can make room for you here . . . for a short time."

"But you said you are full." Baines gave her questioning look. "Will I be sharing a room?"

"Will you be staying or not?" Constance said flatly, as if they both knew they were talking about more than just a sleeping room.

"Yes, ma'am." Baines Meredith smiled to himself beneath his thick drooping mustache and looked away along the dirt street to where three men carried Tom Heilly's body back inside the barbershop. Turning his eyes back to Constance Whirly, he saw her step slightly aside, giving him entrance. Removing his hat, he stepped inside and narrowed a gaze into her eyes. "You are a fine handsome woman, Miss Constance."

"Go on," she said shyly. "You don't have to say that."

"I know I don't, but it gives me pleasure," Baines said under his breath, aware of Julie on the sofa in the other room. "I regret you having to see what happened out there in the street. I know it's unpleasant for a lovely lady like yourself."

"Stop it now, and come along," she said, fanning him aside with a light hand. "I knew how to look away."

Five full days had passed before Julie's face

began to return to its proper shape and color. During those five days, Baines Meredith had ridden out to the army encampment twenty miles east of Umberton and told them what had happened to Julie, and about the deaths of the Colonel, Shep Watson and the Shawler family.

Once Julie's swelling had gone down sufficiently, Baines helped hold her in place for Constance Whirly, while Constance used both thumbs to reshape Julie's shattered nose cartilage. He loosened his hold a little as Constance finished pressing the nose back into alignment and packed the young woman's nostrils with clean white cotton to hold the shattered cartilage in place until healing began.

Baines had given Julie a strong double shot of rye whiskey a few minutes before they started. By the time Constance had finished packing her nostrils, Julie had stopped resisting and lay back in her own sweat, in a stupor of dulled pain.

"The poor thing," Constance whispered sidelong to Baines as the two stood over Julie's bed, wiping their hands on a towel. "I had to rebreak the cartilage before I could reset it properly. I don't know if she'll ever look *right,* after all this."

"Young flesh heals well," Baines offered, slipping an arm around Constance's narrow waist. They stood looking down on the sleeping young woman for a moment; then Baines whispered, "But there's more healing needed here than just the flesh."

Constance nodded. She stared down in contemplation for a moment longer; then, as if coming to a decision, she gestured Baines out of the small room, into the foyer, and said, "She suspects little

Jimmy Buckles of being one of the men who did this to her."

"The boy who does your odd jobs around here?" Baines asked. "She told you that?"

"Not in words," said Constance. "But I saw how she watched him when he moved the bed down from upstairs and set it up for me. It's the same anytime he comes to the house."

Not ready to dismiss Julie's suspicions out of hand, Baines said, "How do you know she's not right about him? She didn't see their faces, but maybe something else about him stuck in her mind."

"Not Jimmy," said Constance shaking her head. "He was right here during the time this would have happened. I had him doing some painting upstairs and he spent three nights in a spare room to keep from riding all the way from his father's farm."

"I see," said Baines, considering the situation. "So, you think she's going to have some trouble getting over this?"

"Wouldn't anybody?" Constance asked.

"I expect so," said Baines. "It might have been easier for her had she seen their *real* faces that day. As it stands she could go through her life seeing their *imaginary* faces every time she closes her eyes—the cowardly sonsabitches." He ended his words with a bitter tone, his right hand closing instinctively around the bone handle on the Dance Brothers pistol on his hip.

Taking note of Baines' hand on his pistol, Constance said in a firm voice, "This is not your fight, Baines Meredith. You brought her here . . . You notified the army. The rest is up to her."

Baines eased his hand away from the pistol butt and let it fall to his side. "I know it," he said. "These are her own devils . . . She'll have to fight them the best she can."

Constance glanced toward the doorway to Julie's room, then said in a lowered voice, "These *devils* have scared this child into a dark corner. I'm afraid she might never come out of it." She paused and shook her head. "What on earth is going to become of her?"

"We'll just have to wait and see," said Baines, staring off across the room and out the window, toward the empty plains beyond Umberton's town limits.

Reading the distant look that had suddenly come over his face, Constance changed the subject away from Julie Wilder. "We said for a *few days,* didn't we?"

"Yes, I expect we did," Baines replied, his gaze still fixed on the endless land.

"It'll soon be a week." She moved close enough to rest her face on his wide chest.

"Yes, it will." He took an envelope from inside his shirt and pressed it into her hand. "There's a hundred dollars in there."

"We don't owe one another a thing, Baines," she said, nudging the envelope away from her.

But Baines persisted, pressing it into her fingers and folding her hand over it. "Keep it for Julie. She arrived broke and naked here in Umberton. It'll help her some."

Constance nodded and rested her head against his chest, the envelope in her hand. "Yes, for Julie I'll take it," she whispered.

Baines reached a hand up and stroked her soft gray-streaked hair. "No regrets?"

"None here," said Constance. "And you?"

"None here either," said Baines Meredith. He shook his head slowly in reflection and added, "None except the leaving."

"You could stay," Constance suggested.

"No," Baines replied, "if I stayed, it wouldn't be what it is." He smiled down at her raised face. "There's nothing sweeter than a sad good-bye."

"Go on with you, Baines Meredith," Constance said with a trace of a tear forming in her eye. "I'm starting to suspect that you are a lady's man."

"It all depends on the lady, ma'am," he replied, holding her against him.

PART 2

Chapter 11

April 1865

"Well, it's about damn time," said Constance Whirly.

A week after Baines Meredith had left Umberton, a Union army major, accompanied by a Free Kansas Militia officer and three of his militiamen, rode up to the hitch rail out front of Constance Whirly's boardinghouse and stepped down. From the window both Constance and Julie stood watching. Constance could feel the young woman's grip tighten on her hand as the men walked up to the front door.

"Don't you worry," said Constance, patting her nervous hand. "You tell them whatever you're comfortable telling and get it over with." She led Julie beside her to the front door.

"No! I can't!" Julie said. "You saw how long it took for the army to even send someone! And you see who's riding with him! For all I know these could be the very ones who did all this!"

Constance stopped and searched her eyes for a

moment, then said, "Then tell the major just enough to send him down the road. There's no denying that your father and Shepherd Watson are dead. . . . So are the Shawlers. You'll have to tell the army something, or else you'll be in the wrong."

"I know," said Julie, with a troubled expression. "I'll tell him what the killers told me, that I better keep my mouth shut and clear out of here. He'll just have to understand." She gave Constance a troubled look. "So will the killers, until I'm well enough to travel."

"Whatever you feel is best, child," said Constance Whirly, helping Julie along, realizing the young woman's dilemma. "Let's get you seated in the parlor. I'll see them in."

In the small parlor Julie eased down onto a cushion-backed chair, carefully keeping her weight shifted away from her healing ribs. She tried to compose herself as she heard voices at the open door, followed by the sound of the door closing and footsteps across the wooden floor coming toward her.

But in spite of her efforts she knew hadn't been able to hide the fear in her eyes when Constance led the four men into the parlor. "Miss Julie, this is Major Gerrard. He's brought along four members of the Free Kansas Militia." Gesturing politely with her hand, she said to the major, "Major Gerrard, this is Miss Julie Wilder, the late Colonel Bertrim Wilder's daughter."

Julie saw only kindness and concern in the major's eyes as he stepped forward with a slight bow, his cavalry hat tucked into the crook of his arm and said, "Miss Wilder, I can't tell you how sorry I am about the colonel's and Shepherd Watson's death." He reached down, chivalrously took Julie's hand for a second, then released it.

"Thank you, Major Gerrard," said Julie, hoping she'd managed to keep any traces of fear or unsteadiness out of her voice. She breathed a bit easier, at least for that moment. But when the major turned and introduced the three men to her, she knew they had to see the shock, the fear and the desperation in her dark eyes.

"This is Captain Ruddell Plantz, of the Free Kansas Militia," said the major, sweeping a hand toward Plantz.

"An honor, ma'am, in spite of the circumstances," said Plantz, giving what Julie thought to be a smug grin and a short bow at the waist. Plantz made no effort to step forward and take her hand, something that Julie was thankful for as her eyes moved away from the indiscernible look on his face. Turning to the other three men Plantz said, "Please allow me to introduce Parson Preston Oates, and Privates Kiley and Peerly."

"Ma'am," said the parson, speaking for the three of them. The men made short bows, of courtesy without moving toward her. But Julie didn't hear the parson's voice; she hardly saw his lips move. Instead she sat stunned, staring at the three but hardly aware of them being in the room. A moment earlier, her eyes had gone to Plantz's boots as she'd looked away from his face. And there her gaze had riveted for just a second on the tiny winged horses engraved on his Mexican spurs. She'd had to force her eyes away in order to recapture her breath.

Seeing the tense silence set in, Major Gerrard took control. "Mr. Baines Meredith reported what happened, and I must say we were all shocked at his implication toward our Free Kansas Militia. That is why I insisted that Captain Plantz and some of his men join me here this morning."

"Implication?" said Constance, giving Plantz and his men a harsh stare, a hand planted firmly on her hip. "It was the work of the Free Kansas Militia, plain and simple."

"Please, Mrs. Whirly," said the major in a conciliatory tone, "let's allow the young lady to tell us what she knows."

Julie felt all eyes on her. She had barely recovered from the shock of seeing Plantz's silver Mexican spurs. Did he realize she might recognize the spurs if he wore them here, she managed to ask herself. Or was he wearing the spurs here simply as a test, to see if she would dare say anything? "I—I didn't see anyone's face," she said grudgingly, not about to mention the spurs or make any accusations against Ruddell Plantz.

"But according to Baines Meredith, you and your father found a Free Kansas Militiaman chasing the Shawler boy," said the major. "Didn't you get a look at his face?"

"No," Julie lied, without raising her eyes to face the major.

"But he was wearing a militiaman's uniform?" the major prodded. "The same type of uniform these four men are wearing?"

"Yes, I believe so," said Julie, "but I can't be certain."

"You mean you cannot attest to it under oath, in a formal statement?" the major asked.

"Yes, that's what I mean," said Julie. "I can't attest to it in a formal statement." As she said the words she raised her eyes and looked at Plantz, letting him know that she wanted no trouble with him and his men.

"I see," said the major, rubbing his bearded chin in contemplation. Noting her reluctance even to discuss what had happened, he asked, "Do you wish to file a statement of any sort, to assist us in finding the persons who killed your father, Shep Watson and the Shawler family?"

"There's nothing I can tell you that would help you find the Shawler family's killers." Julie faced the major as she spoke. "It was still early morning dark when the men who assaulted me brought my father and Shep Watson to the house and dropped them in the dirt."

"So you did not witness your father or Shep Watson's death firsthand?" the major asked. "For all you know those men might have found the two bodies along the trail and brought them home?"

"That's right, for all I know," said Julie with resolve, seeing that the law would have been of little benefit to her even had she chosen to confide in them and seek their help. "My pa is dead. Nothing is going to change that," she said, again letting herself face Plantz long enough to see to it he got her message. "I took a beating, but I'm alive and getting over it. All I want is to get out of here and go live in peace—try to forget this ever happened."

"I understand," said the major, "and I sympathize with you. But a terrible crime has been committed, and according to Mr. Meredith, it involved the Free Kansas Militia—"

"If I can say something here, Major," said Plantz, cutting in. "As ashamed as I am to admit this, I'm afraid our militia has a share of bad apples." He smiled at Julie as he continued. "A scoundrel by the name of Goff Aimes has only recently proven himself unworthy of wearing our uniform. He has mysteriously disappeared, but . . ." He let his words trail.

"Go on," the major encouraged him.

Plantz continued. "The fact is, it might very well have been him and some other ne'er-do-wells who committed these crimes. If that's the case, I want the young lady here to feel confident that as soon as this man can be found, if he had anything to do with this, he *will* be punished most severely."

"There then," said the major, looking at Julie, "I hope that is of some consolation to you, Miss Wilder. This matter will not go unattended. It will be pursued until we have caught the guilty parties."

"Yes, indeed," said Plantz, giving Julie the same smug grin, "you have our word on that."

Seeing the same smug grin on the other three faces, Julie did not respond. Instead she stared back down at the floor and felt Constance's hand rest on her shoulder as the older woman stepped over beside her.

"Gentlemen, this poor woman is still healing, and I'm afraid it's too upsetting for her to talk about right now. You heard her. She just wants to leave here and get on about her life.''

Knowing he had won, Plantz took a step forward toward Julie and said to Major Gerrard, ''Since a militiaman might have been a party to this, Major, I feel responsible for looking after this young lady's well-being as long as she's in Umberton. That is, provided the army has no objections?''

''I see no problem with you making such an offer, Captain Plantz,'' the major said. ''Of course it's up to Miss Wilder whether or not—''

''No! Please!'' Julie said, hoping her voice didn't sound as desperate and frightened as she felt at the idea of having these men around her.

But both her words and the words of the major fell lost beneath several random blasts of gunfire from the middle of Umberton's main street. ''What the—?'' Major Gerrard hurried to an open window, his hand already unsnapping the flap on his army sidearm holster. Plantz and his men followed suit, snatching pistols from their holsters and gathering near the window.

From the street, amid the gunfire, came loud cheers and applause. ''It's over . . . It's over . . . It's over!'' an old man shouted joyously, as he danced an excited jig in the dirt.

A young boy came racing barefoot past the front yard in a wide circle, leaving a cloud of dust in the air behind him and waving a stick above his head. ''Lad! What is all the commotion out there?'' Major Gerard shouted.

''It's over! The war is over! General Lee just

surrendered his army!" the boy shouted back without slowing down. "My pa is *coming home!*"

"Oh my," the major said with a gasp, turning away from the window, all color gone from his face. "Dear God, can it be so?" he whispered, looking back and forth between Plantz and his men and Constance and Julie. A second passed before the women saw the great welling of tears come to his eyes. "I—I must excuse myself, with your permission of course," he said to Julie, sounding dumbstruck. "It's—it's over."

"Yes, it's *finally* over," said Constance, left equally tearful by the unexpected good news.

"I will have to confirm the information right away, of course," said Gerrard. He pulled a folded handkerchief from inside his tunic, pressed it to his eyes, recomposed himself and said, "So, I must get back to the camp. There will be an emergency meeting of staff officers, I'm certain." He paused, then said to Julie, "Rest assured, young lady, this atrocity will not go unattended. With the war over, it may even mean we have more resources to pursue this matter."

Constance accompanied the major to the front door. The other militiamen followed a couple of feet behind. Peerly and Kiley gave Julie a sharp knowing glance and a faint scornful smile, confirming for her that each of these four had been involved in her assault.

"Yes, wouldn't that be great?" said Plantz, turning to look back at Julie, who had stopped and stood at the doorway of the parlor. Giving her a guarded glance while the major opened the large oak door, he said, "You can go on to where you're headed, and know that we're all back here giving this matter our undivided attention."

Julie looked away, avoiding Plantz's grin as he, Peerly and Kiley followed the major and Constance out through the front door onto the porch.

"And, until you *do* leave here," the parson said, lingering behind the others and speaking to her in a low sinister voice, "we'll remain close behind you, watching every move you make, whether you're awake or asleep, just to be on the safe side."

Julie gave him a stunned look, knowing no one else had heard him.

"That's the least we do for our dear old colonel's daughter," he grinned slyly and winked. Then his smile vanished and he added in a harsh whisper, "Don't count yourself more wronged than you are. I know you are nothing but the bastard daughter of an army camp whore." With a dark, critical stare he stepped past her and out the door.

Julie's knees went weak beneath her, to think that this man knew so much about her. She clung to the parlor door casing, catching her breath, feeling trapped here by these men, into some sort of cat-and-mouse game. "I've got to get out of here," she whispered desperately to herself, realizing that her ribs, her face and, more important, her spirit still had a lot of healing left to do.

Outside, the revelry had begun to grow, with more gunshots, cheers, wild laughter and music swelling along the dirt street. While Constance stood on the porch and stared off at the growing celebration, Julie made her way to her small room, sat down on the side of her bed and buried her face in her cupped hands. She cried silently,

and in doing so she told herself to get all the
weeping out of her system. After today, there
would be no more tears. Not for herself or for
anyone else.

Chapter 12

In spite of her pains and soreness, at first light, Julie arose from her bed and looked at the clothes Constance Whirly had foraged for her from among items left behind by countless guests over the years. Holding a modest gingham dress up against herself in front of a dressing mirror, Julie saw that the clothes were not a perfect fit, nor were they the type of garments she would have ordinarily worn. But she would make do with them until she purchased some more suitable trail clothing with the hundred dollars Baines Meredith had left in the envelope for her.

Looking closer into the dressing mirror, she touched her healing nose cautiously, noting the tenderness still even though the swelling was all but gone. "You weren't that pretty to begin with," she sighed, whispering to her face in the mirror.

She unwound the length of gauze binding from around her mending ribs and stood naked for a moment, looking herself over before stepping into the clean, soft cotton undergarments. Satisfied that her bruises, cuts and scrapes were healing steadily, she cupped her tender left breast, examining three purple bruises made by one of her attackers' knuckle prints. *By Plantz himself . . . ?* She wondered. Or by Parson Oates, or one of the other two, Peerly or Kiley?

Stop it . . . ! She demanded of herself, seeing each of the four men's faces staring knowingly at her. The mental image of them made her skin crawl. She had to force the smug leering faces from her mind, pick up the dress, slip into it and button it up the front, hurrying, busily, in order to keep both the faces and the dark images of her ordeal from overwhelming her.

When she'd finished dressing, she seated herself on the side of her small bed. She put on a pair of ladies' shoes, buttoned them, then stood up stiffly, smoothed her clothes down and stuck the envelope with the money in it down into a dress pocket.

In the kitchen at the back of the house, Julie found Constance Whirly taking a pot of freshly boiled coffee from atop the black iron cookstove. The smell of hot biscuits, eggs, pork and gravy filled the air, awaiting the arrival of the four other boardinghouse guests. "Are you sure you feel up to this, child?" Constance asked, seeing Julie steady herself with a hand on a chair back. "Maybe a day or two more, before you try to ride? My home is your home. I won't even charge you board."

"Obliged," Julie said. "But I'm going to be all right. You've done a fine job taking care of me." She offered a brave smile. "I'm good as new."

"I have my doubts about that," Constance said, eying her closely. "Careful you don't overpush yourself. You still need some healing time."

"I'll be careful," Julie said. She liked the way the older woman had taken to mothering her, even though Constance could at times be a little abrasive.

"I should hope so," said Constance. Stepping closer, she pushed aside a loose strand of her graying auburn hair and wiped her hands on her long white apron. "I saw how those men looked at you, Julie Wilder," she continued in a lowered tone, glancing around as if making sure no one heard her. Her hand slipped into the apron pocket and came out holding a small pocket revolver. "I want you to carry this in case anybody tries to harm you today."

Julie took the pistol and slipped it into a dress pocket. "Hopefully things won't go that far," Julie replied. "If I can get myself a good fast horse today, I'll ride away unnoticed."

"Listen to me," said Constance, insistently, taking her firmly but gently by her shoulders. "Don't you hesitate to use that gun if you have to."

"I won't, Constance," said Julie. "But I don't want to have to shoot anybody if I can keep from it. There are too many of them; I have no idea who they are."

"I understand." Constance wanted to give more advice, yet realizing the difficult spot Julie was in, she could only shake her head and say, "Child, just be damned sure you shoot to kill."

"I will, Constance," said Julie, patting her dress pocket. "I can promise you that."

"Will you be coming back today, before you leave?" Constance asked. "I'll make you up some food for the trail."

"I'll try," said Julie, "if things feel peaceable enough."

Leaving the boardinghouse, Julie walked through spent cartridges and empty whiskey bottles left over from a night celebration. She went first to the livery barn, where she found old Merlin Potts pitching hay over a rail into a stall. Seeing Julie, Potts leaned slightly and looked past her toward the street. "Young lady, you are the first sober person I've seen all morning." He grinned; then as if he remembered something unpleasant, his grin vanished. "The Free Kansas Militia has told me I *better* let them know straightaway if you come here looking to buy a horse," he said grimly.

"So, you're going to tell them?" Julie asked.

"Hell no!" said Potts. "Nobody tells me what I *better* do!" His crooked grin returned. "They said I better not sell you a horse either. But just watch me, if a horse is what you want."

"A horse is what I want," said Julie. She gave a look around over her shoulder as she spoke. "I want one that's about half-green, spooks easy and is faster than a skyrocket."

"You can handle a horse like that?" Potts asked, noting the bruises on her arms and throat, and the stiff way she had walked into the barn. He remembered the condition she'd been in the day Baines Meredith carried her in his lap; like everyone else in Umberton he had since heard what had happened to her.

"Yes, I can," said Julie, confident in spite of her sore condition. "Can I count on you picking out such a horse for me and having it saddled and ready when I return later today?"

"Whoa! I'm no keen judge of horse flesh, young lady," said Potts. "I've just been looking after this livery since Davis Beldon got himself killed—I'm doing sort of a public service you might say, until the town decides what's to be done with this place." He chuckled and shrugged. "But you don't want me picking a horse for you."

"All right," said Julie, "then show me the corral stock; I'll pick one for myself."

She followed the old man to a corral behind the livery barn and looked at the string of horses milling amid a pile of fresh hay that Potts had thrown in only moments earlier. Looking them over, some of them the same horses her father, Shepherd Watson and she had brought to town, Julie's gaze went to the other side of the corral where she spotted her buckskin bay standing saddled, at a hitch rail beside a silver gray. Her heart seemed to stop for a second. Then, composing herself, she forced herself to say with no expression in her voice, "These are all good-looking horses, Mr. Potts." Nodding across the corral toward the other two horses she asked, "What about those two horses? Are they for sale?"

"No, ma'am," said Potts. "They belong to a couple of militiamen, Nez Peerly and a fellow they call Kid Kiley. I doubt they'd sell them. Peerly just acquired the buckskin since last I saw him in town."

"I see," said Julie, feeling her blood boil at the sight of her horse—a horse her father had given her—in the hands of one of the animals who'd killed her father and assaulted her. *Easy . . . ,* she cautioned herself, realizing that under the law

Peerly could say he purchased the buckskin almost anywhere, and probably produce a set of phony papers to confirm it.

This was the Free Kansas Militia's home ground, she reminded herself. Now wasn't the time to step forward boldly and start making legal charges against these men. This was the time to stick to her plan, to get out of town and out of the reach of these killers. "Forget I asked," said Julie.

Potts saw something in her eyes, and heard something in her voice that gave him pause for a second. He gave her a questioning look, then said, "Yes, ma'am, I'll forget you asked."

Julie looked back at the horses in the corral, away from her buckskin, trying to swallow yet another mouthful of hurt and outrage. After a moment, she pointed out a black rawboned Spanish barb that seemed to stand itself off away from the other horses, its ears perked as if trying to hear what she and the old man had to say. "That one will do."

"Are you sure, ma'am?" asked Potts. "He's out of the old Comanche breeds. He might be *too* green for anybody to ride right away, let alone . . ."

"Let alone a woman?" said Julie, finishing his words for him.

Potts looked embarrassed, but then covered it over, saying, "I'm no horse expert, but that black barb is wilder than a spring antelope. I expect he spends over half his life with no saddle on his back."

"He'll do," said Julie, unable to keep her eyes from going back to the buckskin. "How much?"

"Well," said Potts, "like I said, I'm new at this

livery business. I'm told horses are selling for eighty dollars and up—"

"I'll give you fifty," said Julie cutting him off, seeing he wasn't as new to dickering over horses as he pretended to be.

"I'll take sixty," said Potts.

"After telling me he's too green for anybody?" said Julie. "I'll give fifty-five, and another ten for a used saddle and some usable tack that's not dry-rotted."

"Done," said Potts with a broken-toothed grin. "I'll get him saddled and papered and ready for you."

"Thank you." Julie managed to smile. "I'll be back for him this afternoon." She turned slightly, lifted the envelope from her dress pocket and counted out fifty-five dollars. As she started to close the envelope to put it away, she found it peculiar that someone—Baines Meredith? she wondered—had written directions on the underside of the flap. *Never mind* . . . She closed the envelope and attended to the business at hand.

Upon paying for the black barb, Julie left the livery barn and walked along the empty boardwalk toward her father's attorney's office. A few yards ahead of her, out front of the office, she saw an open-topped buggy pull up to a hitch rail. Before she reached the office, she saw a large man wearing a stovepipe hat and a wrinkled swallow-tailed coat step down from the buggy, his left arm cradling stacks of folders, a battered book and a bulging attaché case.

Julie walked closer as he hitched the horse and stepped up to the door of the office, pulling a key from his baggy trouser pocket. "Excuse me, sir," Julie called out, seeing the door open and the large man start to walk inside.

He stopped and turned, facing her. "Yes?"

"I'm Julie Wilder," she said, keeping her voice lowered and guarded, lest there be militiamen around. She gave a quick glance along the nearly empty street, but saw only farmers arriving early in their wagons, merchants tidying out front of their stores.

"Oh my! My *indeed!*" said the large man. He shuffled to the side and gestured his thick free hand toward the inside of his office. "I'm Horace Freedman, attorney-at-law, at your service!" He reached up and adjusted a pair of wire-rims on the bridge of his wide nose. "I have been meaning to come see you, Miss Wilder . . . being your late father's attorney." He paused as Julie stepped past him and into the office, taking a last quick glance along the street. "I—I'm terribly sorry, both for your father's untimely demise and, of course, for having heard what has happened to you." He offered a detached smile. "I trust you are feeling better?"

"Thank you, Mr. Freedman. Yes, I am feeling much better," said Julie, entering and following the attorney's directing hand to a short wooden chair across the desk from his high-backed leather chair. She seated herself stiffly and waited for the large man to walk around the desk and sit down in his leather chair.

"My father told me he had hired you to work on having me officially become a *Wilder*."

"Yes, that is correct," the attorney said, looking more comfortable now, behind his desk. "The papers have been filed and accepted in Topeka. It is now only a matter of waiting until they return to me by mail."

"Then I am now legally a Wilder," Julie said, relieved. "That's all I wanted to know."

She started to stand up, go buy herself some trail clothes and get ready to leave. But the attorney stopped her, saying, "I'm sure you want to know about your father's estate, don't you? After all, you are his closest surviving kin . . . his *only child* as it were?"

Julie looked at him curiously. "Yes, I suppose I am, at that."

"In that case I must assist you in filling out the papers—"

"I don't have time to fill out any papers today," Julie said, cutting him off. "I have some things planned that I have to do."

"—for the transfer of the deed to the farm," Freedman continued as if he'd never stopped. "And for the acceptance of his money from the colonel's account at the bank."

"You mean, the col—that is, *my father* left me everything, his farm, his money?"

"Yes, indeed he did," said the attorney. "Shepherd Watson would have had an interest in the farm and a modest set-aside amount of cash. But owing to these unfortunate circumstances, poor Shep is out of the picture. It's all yours."

Julie sat staring at him. "How much money is in the account at the bank?"

"Quite a tidy sum," said the attorney, licking his large thumb and leafing through a stack of papers inside a folder he'd spread open on his desk. "Yes, here we are." He picked up a sheet of paper and adjusted his spectacles. "In the Umberton bank, the Colonel—that is, *you*—have forty-two thousand, seven hundred thirty-one dollars and four cents." He looked back at her across the top of the sheet of paper with a smile. "Will you please reconsider and make some time to get this estate properly transferred today?"

"My goodness," Julie whispered. "Yes, I will."

Chapter 13

———

At the livery barn, Kid Kiley watched, grinning, while Nez Peerly backhanded Merlin Potts across his face for the third time. "You better tell him something quick, old man," Kiley warned. "He gets tired of smacking you around, he'll turn you over to me . . . Hell, I'll just gut you with a pigsticker and hang you over a stall rail."

"One more time," Peerly said to Potts. "What did she want here?"

"Nothing!" said Potts, smelling the strong odor of whiskey on both men's breath.

Holding the helpless old man out at arm's length, Peerly shook him, then drew back his rawhide-gloved hand. "All right, here we go."

"Wait!" said Potts. "Don't hit me again! I've held out as long as I could. I'll tell you what you want to hear."

Kiley chuckled. "See, it's the ole pigsticker story that gets them every time."

"Start talking, old man," said Peerly. "I'm ready to beat your face in with a shovel."

"All right, she wanted to buy a horse," said Potts.

"Yeah? What kind of horse?" Peerly asked.

"A buggy horse," the old man lied, just to be defiant. "She wanted to buy a buggy and a horse, but I told her there's no buggy around here, for sale, rent or anything else."

"A damn buggy horse?" Peerly gave Kiley a puzzled look. "What would she want with a horse and buggy?"

"Beats me." Kiley shrugged. "But all this jawing is cutting into my drinking time. We're not through celebrating, are we?" He looked longingly out the open front door in the direction of the saloon a hundred yards away. A drinking crowd had formed all the way out onto the boardwalk.

"We are until this old buzzard tells us what we want to hear," said Peerly, shaking the old man roughly.

"Maybe she don't ride so good," the old man offered, trying his best to throw Peerly off.

"Or maybe you're lying, you old son of a bitch," said Peerly. He drew back his hand, feigning another slap in Potts' face.

But the old man stood firm. "Why the hell would I lie now?" he insisted. "You think I enjoy getting the shit slapped out'n me? I said I'd tell you what she wanted, and I did. But I can't explain why a woman wants what a woman wants! If I could, I'd have died years ago, worn to a frazzle with a smile on my face!"

"Why you . . ." Peerly started to hit him, but Kiley cut in.

"Hold it, Nez. The old man's right, gawddamn it. He's got no reason to lie to us. Let's go get a couple drinks, talk about what the buggy is all about . . . see if we can figure what this woman's up to."

Peerly shoved the old man away from him, saying, "I better not find out you're lying to me, you old buzzard."

"I'm not, I swear I'm not," said Potts.

"Whoa now! Look at this; here she comes!" said Kiley, seeing Julie step down off the boardwalk in front of the mercantile store and walk toward the livery barn with a bundle wrapped in brown paper under her arm. He gave a sly grin. "She must've known we was thinking about her."

Potts stepped away, ran his hand across his bleeding lower lip and watched Peerly join Kiley near the open door. "Damn, Kid, she looks good all over again," Peerly said in a lowered voice, seeing the soft sway of the yellow gingham dress as Julie walked closer.

"Yeah," said Kiley, "to tell the truth, I never got all I wanted of her in the first place."

"Well, you poor mistreated man," Peerly teased.

"Go to hell, Nez," said Kiley. He grinned and chuckled. "But you've got to say, there's something appealing about a woman you've had your way with, and she don't even know who the hell you are."

"Meaning it's worth doing all over again?" Peerly asked, watching Julie intently.

"Meaning, hell yes it is," said Kiley. "Captain Plantz told us stay close and keep her worried. I can't think of anything that would worry her worse than you and me taking want we what, any damn time we want it."

Peerly looked over his shoulder at Potts, who stood just out of hearing range. The old man had dipped a bandanna into a bucket of cool water and pressed it to his stinging face. "When she gets here, old man, you best keep your mouth shut," Peerly warned.

Outside, Julie walked on toward the livery barn, thinking over what the attorney had told her. She realized that suddenly, after her years of drifting, she finally had a home of her own. Though the house had burned to the ground, she at least had land on which to build a home, after things settled for her. *Someday maybe*, she told herself. Right now, her thoughts had to be on Plantz and his men, and on her getting out of Umberton alive, in one piece.

Thinking of Plantz and his militiamen, Julie gave a guarded look back and forth along the street before she stepped into the livery barn through the open doorway. In the dark interior of the big barn she saw Merlin Potts standing at a stall door, holding the wet bandanna to his lips. "Mr. Potts?" she asked, growing suddenly cautious, seeing the strange look on his face.

When the old man only stared at her, wearing a troubled look on his weathered face, she walked forward to the stall door where he stood and said, "What's the matter with you? You look as though you've—"

Her words stopped cold as she saw Kiley step forward out of the shadows of the stall, his pistol in hand. "He looks like a man who's been told it's

time to die, don't he?" Kiley said, giving her a
dark grin.

Julie stopped suddenly and half turned toward
the open door. But as she stood on the verge of
bolting away, she realized that even if she made it
safely out of the barn, she was afraid of what would
become of Merlin Potts. As the thought ran
through her mind, she heard the door swing slowly
shut and saw Peerly walk out of the darkness
toward her. "You hesitated too long, sweet Julie,"
Peerly said. "Now you have to pay a price for not
acting quickly enough."

Julie looked back and forth wildly, seeing herself
trapped between the two men, seeing the look on
Potts' face as he said, "I'm sorry, ma'am!"

Julie jerked the small pistol from her pocket and
aimed it point-blank into Peerly's face as he closed
in on her. "Stop right there! Don't take another
step! I'll shoot, I'm warning you!"

"Aw, come on now," said Peerly, spreading his
hands in a show of peace, but making no effort to
stop. "There's no need in violence. All me and my
friend want is what any red-blooded man wants
from a pretty young woman."

"One more step and I'll shoot!" Julie cried out.
But before she could cock the pistol, Peerly was
upon her, knocking her gun hand sideways and en-
closing the pistol in his gloved fist before she could
swing it back and shoot.

"Too late, harlot!" Peerly shouted at her. Her
wrapped bundle of clothes flew from under her arm
as Peerly's free hand balled into a fist, snapped forward and punched her hard in her already-injured
face. The impact of the blow caused the gun to come

out of her hand and into his grip. "When it's time to shoot, you have to shoot, not make stupid threats!" he said, seeing her fall backward onto the straw-piled floor.

In her fall, her gingham dress flew up to her waist, revealing her inner thighs, her pale white legs, her clean white cotton undergarments. "Oh my *my!*" said Kiley, stepping forward, seeing Julie flounder for a moment, unable to collect herself. "I'll just have myself some of that while it's warm!" He dropped his gun belt to the floor and stepped forward, loosening his trousers.

"Not until I do, you randy dog!" said Peerly, laughing, grabbing him by his loosened belt and yanking him backward.

In an instant while the two struggled back and forth like schoolboys, Julie managed to clear her head, spring up from the floor and leap over a rail into a stall. From there she scrambled around an excited roan and over a rail into another stall, closer to the rear door.

"Damn it, Nez, now look what you've done!" Kiley shouted, quickly closing his trousers and snatching his gun belt from the floor.

"Come on, Kid! Don't let her get away!" Peerly shouted in reply. He hurried along the center of the stalls, seeing Julie race frantically over one rail after another, until she managed to scramble over the last one and out the rear door of the barn. "Gawddamn it! There she goes!" he shouted in defeat, seeing Julie race away along an alley behind a row of buildings. "You've got a lot to learn about cornering women, Kid!"

Kiley ran up beside him. The two stared off after

Julie until she disappeared in the long alleyway. "Let's go get her, Nez," Kiley said, panting, wiping his hand across his lips.

"Hell, you could sooner catch a jackrabbit, than you could her," said Peerly. "She ain't in near the bad shape she appeared to be. He grinned, looking Kiley up and down, seeing his gun belt hanging from his free hand, his other hand holding his loose trousers bunched up at the waist. "Hell, you couldn't run with something like that swinging in the wind anyway."

"What're we going to tell Plantz?" Kiley asked, catching his breath.

"We'll tell him the damn truth," said Peerly. "He wanted us to keep her spooked. By God, we spooked her, proper like." He slapped Kiley on his back and chuckled as he turned and looked all around for Potts, who had slipped out the front door and made a run for it himself.

"That old sonsabitch got away too," said Kiley.

"He didn't get away," said Peerly. "We was finished up here anyway, far as Plantz has to know."

Julie reached the rear door of the boardinghouse, out of breath and clutching her aching ribs. Constance Whirly met her on the back porch and helped her into the house and into a kitchen chair. "My goodness, child! What has happened to you?" she exclaimed. Brushing Julie's hair from her eyes, she saw bits of straw still clinging to her.

"The two . . . militiamen cornered me in the livery barn," she gasped, out of breath, still clutching her sore rib cage. "I don't know how I . . . got away from them."

"Oh, dear Lord!" said Constance. "Those bastard sons of a bitch!" She turned and hurriedly stuck a dipper into a water bucket and handed it to Julie to drink. "You mean two of the militiamen who were here yesterday?"

"Yes," Julie said, breathless, sipping water, still panting hard, "the privates, Peerly and Kiley. They tried the same thing all over again. Luckily . . . I got away."

"It'll be a wonder if you haven't harmed yourself, running that way." She reached down, removed Julie's arm from across her ribs and prodded her gently. "Are you feeling all right, I mean except from being winded?"

"I think so," Julie replied. She took another sip, then said, her breath coming back to her, "They took your gun from me."

"Before you got a chance to draw it and use it?" Constance asked, wiping her sweaty hair from her eyes.

Julie looked ashamed. "I drew it . . . One of them knocked it from my hand."

"Umm-um," Constance murmured, shaking her head. "Those bastards wouldn't be doing this out in the open this way, unless they were told to by their captain. They wouldn't dare. The army would have them in irons before they could say their names backward."

"I know," said Julie, "Plantz and his whole militia band are against me. I don't know why. All I want is to leave, get away from them and try to forget this ever happened."

"I expect that's what they find hard to believe," said Constance. "Fact is, I have a little trouble understanding it myself." She paused, studying Julie's dark eyes. "After all, they killed your pa. It seems only natural that you'd want vengeance."

"What I wanted was justice, within the law," Julie said. "But the more I look for justice, the less I see of it ever coming about. At first I had no idea who the men were who killed my pa and did this to me." She thought of the flying silver horses on Plantz's spurs and decided to keep it as her personal secret for now. "But I'm beginning to see who did it. They seem to think that because they forced themselves on me against my will, that I somehow belong to them."

"As long as you allow them to keep knocking you around and frightening you, they'll have power over you. They own a part of you. The only way you'll ever get yourself back, is to stand up and fight back, take a piece off their lousy hides."

"I can't, Constance," said Julie. "I pulled your pistol on them today, but when it came to pulling the trigger, I couldn't make myself do it." As she spoke, she recalled Jed Shawler telling her almost the same thing the night he died. The thought of it sent a slight chill up her spine.

"You'll have to," Constance insisted.

"All I want is to get out of here alive," said Julie. "I'm hoping with the war over, I can come back soon and take over my pa's place. I found out from Attorney Freedman today that Pa left it to me."

"Well, that's some good news, Julie," said Constance.

"Yes, I now have some land to build on," Julie informed her. "Pa also left me some money, enough to build a home, with plenty left over." She paused in contemplation. "But I can't live here in peace as long as these men are running free and think they can do whatever they want to with me."

Constance started to say more on the matter, but a knock at her front door caught her attention, "Sit right here and rest yourself while I get the door."

Julie listened to Constance walk quickly to the front door, open it and say some words that Julie could not clearly make out. In a moment, the door closed; Constance walked back into the kitchen carrying Julie's bundle of new clothes. "That was Merlin Potts," she said. "He brought the clothes you purchased today." She plopped the bundle down onto the table and said, "He told me that Kiley and Peerly are drinking at the saloon. Said he's bringing your horse around back for you."

Julie stood up and opened the brown paper wrapping, as if expecting some sort of trick. Taking a pair of boots from between a wool trail shirt and a pair of soft canvas trousers, she sorted out a flop hat, a bandanna, riding gloves and a folded up rain slicker. She sighed and said to Constance, "It looks like everything is here."

"Which way will you be headed?" Constance asked.

"I'm not sure, just away from here," Julie replied. After consideration she said, "West, maybe."

"Baines' address is on the envelope flap," Constance said, matter-of-factly.

"I saw it there . . . and I have thought about it," Julie said.

"He *is* a gunman," said Constance. "If you go to him and tell him you need his help, he'll help you." She gave Julie a knowing look. "Tell him you have money . . . and that you want these men dead. If I know Baines, they will be before you finish asking him."

Julie did not answer; she only nodded, took the envelope from her dress pocket and looked at it. Then she folded the envelope, stuck it into the pocket of her new wool shirt and buttoned the pocket.

Constance walked away shaking her head, saying, "I'll gather you up some food and a nice clean blanket for the trail."

Julie carried the bundle of clothes to her small room and changed quietly. When she returned to the kitchen, Constance handed her a small canvas bag and a rolled-up wool blanket. "There's two pounds of dried beans, some fresh cornbread, dried pork and some coffee beans in here, not enough to last you as far as Colorado. But there's places where you can resupply yourself along the way." She stopped, seeing the look on Julie's face. "Listen to me going on," she said. "You've made this ride before, haven't you?"

"Yes," Julie replied, "and it's a long lonesome ride. I'll need these staples to get me from place to place." She took the bag and blanket. "I'm much obliged," she said. The two walked out onto the back porch. Julie gazed all around before stepping down from the porch and walking over to the horse. Constance stayed close beside her. After looking the animal over thoroughly, Julie tied the blanket and bag of food behind her saddle, turned, gave Constance hug and said, "I can never repay you for all your kindness."

After a short embrace, Constance dabbed at her

eye with a small handkerchief. "I can't help but feel like you're leaving here in shame, even though I know damn well you shouldn't be. I think you've had enough hard knocks in this life. It's time something good came your way." She touched the handkerchief to her eye again.

Julie stepped up stiffly and adjusted herself in the saddle. She offered a brave smile. "Don't go feeling sorry for me. I've had my share of ups and downs, but I'm not complaining. I've got a good horse under me and an open road. I've even got a real home to come back to as soon as I get things settled."

"Promise me you will come back," said Constance, seeing a tear glisten in Julie's eye as well.

Julie nodded, lifted the hat from her lap and pulled it down onto her head. "I'll be back, Constance; I promise you," she said. She turned the black barb with a touch of her boot heels and left Umberton unnoticed, taking a long alleyway out of town.

Chapter 14

When Kay, the youngest of the Wright girls, didn't reply when her mother called out several times for her, Herbert Wright stood up from the kitchen table and took off his reading spectacles. "Do you see her?" he asked his wife, Margolin, who stood staring out across the yard toward the tree line, her hand visoring her eyes against the bright rising sun.

"No," said Margolin. "What could be keeping her? I need the bucket of water for scrubbing." She looked concerned, but not yet worried.

"We all know that Kay is at that dawdling age," said Herbert. "The others went through it; now it's her turn." He sighed, folded his reading spectacles and slipped them into his shirt pocket.

"I don't want to impose . . . ," said Margolin, squinting, searching the long woods line above the creek bank.

"I suppose you want me to go find her? Encourage her dawdling," he said, not sounding imposed upon in spite of a slight frown.

"If you would, please," said Margolin. "That big

oaken bucket full of water is awfully heavy for—"
She stopped with a short gasp.

"What is it?" asked Herbert, seeing his wife's
face suddenly drained of color.

"Herbert, get out there quickly," Margolin said
in a shaken voice, staring out across the yard
toward the tree line.

Hurrying to the door, Herbert saw what had his
wife upset. At the woods line, four riders stepped
their horses out slowly from within the trees. On
the first horse sat Ruddell Plantz; on his lap sat
twelve-year-old Shirl Kay Wright. Behind Plantz
came the parson, followed by Clement Macky and
big Clarence Conlon. The four still wore their militia uniforms.

"Hunh-uh! I'm not standing for this!" said Herbert, shaking his head. "Plantz has gone too far
this time."

"Don't start trouble with Kay on his lap! For
God sakes! Just get her away from him, Herbert!"
Margolin demanded, her voice trembling in fear.

Herbert gazed toward his shotgun above the
hearth, but then thought better of it. He walked
quickly out the front door and down off the porch.
Seeing the angry expression on Wright's face,
Plantz called out, "Uh-oh, men, it looks like Councilman Wright must have woke up with a mouthful
of horseshoes this morning." He gave Herbert a
tight smile, riding in closer without loosening his
arm from around the young girl. "Why so cross
today, Councilman?" he asked.

"Shirl Kay, climb down here this minute," said
Herbert in a tight but controlled voice, ignoring
Plantz's question.

"I can't, Pa, he's holding me," said the young girl, offering a slight struggle, then ceasing to resist.

"He's holding me, Pa, this bad ole man!" said Plantz in a mock childlike voice. "Ain't that the most precious thing you ever saw." He rustled Kay's silky yellow hair. "I could just eat her!" Before Herbert could say anything more, Plantz lifted the girl out away from him and down to the ground. "Conlon, bring the young lady's bucket of water up here," he called back over his shoulder.

Herbert Wright breathed a sigh of relief as his daughter stepped away from Plantz's horse. He watched as big Clarence Conlon rode up, leaned down and handed Kay the oaken bucket dripping fresh water from its rim. "Hurry inside with that water, Kay; your mother needs it," Herbert said, keeping his voice even.

When Kay stepped inside the house, Plantz sat staring after her for a quiet moment. Herbert Wright glared at him, smoldering. Finally, Plantz said, "Councilman, you are truly blessed, having not one, not two, but *three* beautiful young daughters around you!" He grinned, looking all around the yard and asking, "Pray tell, where are the other two darling angels?"

"They're at their Aunt Madeline's house," Herbert said grudgingly.

"Ah, Aunt *Madeline!*" said Plantz, as if in fond reflection. "Yet another beautiful Wright woman! A schoolteacher, isn't she?" Plantz squinted as if trying to remember. "She's out toward Topeka, or thereabouts?"

"What can I do for you, Plantz?" Herbert asked, not wanting to make small talk with Plantz or his men. He looked the four men over, noting their frayed and faded militia uniforms. No one in Umberton believed for a moment that Plantz and his men had nothing to do with murdering the colonel, Shep Watson and the Shawler boy, and raping and assaulting Julie Wilder.

"We've got a little problem, Councilman," said Plantz, suddenly losing his smile and turning to business. "We're hoping we can count on you, Wilmens and Bales to help us out."

"What's the problem?" asked Wright. "I thought the army issued orders for the militia to disband and stop wearing those uniforms."

"Yes, the army did issue such an order, and *that's* our problem right there," said Plantz. "See, me and the boys here don't mind giving up these uniforms; they're about spent anyway. But it strikes us that this is a bad time to be disbanding." He gave a stiff grin. "We think this is the time to be unifying."

"Unifying?" said Wright, getting an unpleasant feeling in his stomach, the way he always had when standing this close to Plantz and his men. "What exactly are you proposing, Ruddell?"

Plantz's mock smile vanished. "To start with, you still call me Captain, Councilman," he snapped. "This war is over, but by God let's show some respect for them who protected your family, your home, your possessions!" He nodded toward the house.

"Yes, you are absolutely correct, *Captain* Plantz," Wright said quickly, realizing that the war's ending hadn't changed a thing when it came to these men. "I apologize, most sincerely."

"Hear that, men?" Plantz said over his shoulder.

"He apologizes, *most sincerely.*" He stared hard at Wright, then said to him, "It's a good thing you do. We've been starting to think folks around here don't appreciate all we've done for them these bitter years."

"Of course we do!" said Wright. He was nervous, knowing how ruthless these men could get. "What is there I can do for you?"

"So, you still support our cause?" Plantz asked pointedly.

"Yes, as always, sir," said Wright.

"Now that the Union has won this war, they're going to forget what me and these boys done for them. We're going to need help in order to keep up with the business of protecting Umberton and all the outlying areas."

"Help?" Wright stalled.

"Yes, help!" said Plantz, raising his voice. "Am I talking to myself here?" he demanded. "I'm talking about money, gawddamn it! We need money! Else we'll be limited to sticking around Umberton and hereabouts. You know my boys get rowdy and restless in one spot too long."

Knowing where the conversation was headed, Wright said meekly, hoping his fearful voice didn't sound too shallow, "I'm afraid any funds from Umberton would be out of the question right now. We've had difficulty managing to—"

"Hear that, boys," Plantz called out to his men. "He's giving us the old political runaround speech. Going to tell us all the important spending the town council has done, instead of going ahead and telling us to straight-out go to hell, like he wants to do!"

"No, no, please, Captain Plantz, that's not what

I'm wanting to do at all," said Wright. "I only wish I had all the money in the world to give you brave men," he lied. "But the fact remains that financially, Umberton is going to be strapped for a while, until we—"

"Five thousand dollars, Wright!" Plantz shouted, cutting him off. "To let us know that this town really is grateful for all we've done." He swung an arm toward his men in their ragged uniforms to help make his point. "Look at us bunch of scarecrows. Our lives have been torn apart serving this community. You won't just sweep us away from your doors like beggars. Will you?"

"God no!" said Wright. "But, five thousand dollars! Captain, this town doesn't have that kind of money, I assure you."

"You can raise it," Plantz said. "There's four councilmen and a president. That's only a thousand dollars each, if you five wanted to take on the cost yourselves."

"Gracious sakes, Captain!" said Wright. "That's a staggering amount of money for only us five to come up with. I don't think I could even come with my share of it!"

"Can't or *won't?*" Plantz asked harshly.

Wright sweated. "Well, I suppose I can come up with it, but it's going to just about gut me. It's certainly not going to be easy."

"Easy?" Plantz looked all around. "It's a hell of a lot easier for you to raise your thousand than it will be for you to raise a new barn, a new house, maybe even a new family." His stare bored into Wright's eyes. "That's exactly the way you need to tell it to the council. Are you hearing me, Mr. Councilman?"

"I hear you, Captain," said Wright, looking crestfallen and weak.

"Then you will have that money raised for us in two weeks when we ride back in here? So we won't have to camp in your front yard?" Plantz asked, although it was really not a question.

"I— Yes, I'll *certainly* try," said Wright, swallowing a knot in his throat.

"Try?" said Plantz, his hand going to the butt of his holstered pistol.

"No, I mean I will. *I will!*" said Wright. "I'll go immediately to the other councilmen on your behalf."

"Good." Plantz grinned again and dropped his hand from his pistol butt. "Look at it this way. You're speaking to those folks on our behalf. We're not telling them five thousand is our figure. You can tell them any figure you come up with. It's all right with us. Far as we're concerned, you can pass your part of any cost on to the others." His grin widened. "Hell, you can even *make* yourself some money on this deal, if you're a good *convincing* talker."

Wright wiped a hand across his sweaty forehead. "Of course I would never—"

"Shut up now, Councilman," Plantz interrupted. "Don't start lying to us. Save your lying for the townsfolk and the council."

"I'll do everything in my power to raise the five thousand you men need to get your lives back in order and get farther away from here," said Wright,

seeming reenergized by the talk of passing his cost
along to the other townsmen. "But can I have your
word, sir, that no one will ever know the exact
amount you asked for?"

"Are you trying to insult us, Councilman?" said
Plantz, wearing his grin.

"No, please! I wouldn't dare, Captain," said
Wright, sorry he'd opened his mouth on the matter.

"The *true* amount will go with us to our grave,"
said Plantz. "We are all honorable men."

From inside the front door, Margolin Wright
stood watching, clutching her youngest daughter
against her side, the loaded shotgun down from the
wall and leaning close at hand. "He touched me,
Mama," the girl whispered, cradled in the crook of
her mother's arm.

"Shhh, child, no, he didn't," Margolin whispered
urgently in reply.

"Yes, he did, Mama," Kay insisted. "He touched
up here, and down there, too."

Margolin Wright stood in a tense nauseated silence for a moment; then she struggled to keep an
even tone to her voice, asking, "With his *hand,*
Kay? He only touched you with his *hand?*"

"Yes, Mama," said the child, sounding confused.

"Thank God," she breathed. "All right, darling,
you couldn't help it," Margolin said to her. "Keep
quiet about it. . . . Don't ever tell Pa about it,
promise me?"

The child only nodded against her mother's side.
Margolin looked down at the loaded shotgun,
trembling. But then she lifted her eyes back out
through the window, having fought off the urge to
grab up the gun and run screaming out the door

and empty it in Ruddell Plantz's face. She stood in silence, stroking her daughter's hair until Plantz and his men turned and rode slowly back the way they had come.

At a crossroads a mile from the Wrights' farm, the parson rode up beside Plantz and said with a short dark laugh, "That was almost too easy, wasn't it?"

Plantz smiled, staring straight ahead. "If he wasn't convinced when we left, his wife will convince him for us."

"What have you done, you dirty dog?" the parson asked with a sly grin.

"Nothing worth mentioning," said Plantz. "But Margolin Wright will make sure her husband does everything he can to get us away from here."

The parson nodded, staring straight ahead. "And leave we shall, for a time anyway."

"Yeah, for a short while," said Plantz. "This is going to be our home stomping grounds, just like before. Only now that the war is over we'll spread out in any direction we please, do our raiding, then come back here where we know we're safe."

They rode on for the next two hours until they reached an abandoned barn in a stand of trees near a crossroad. Stopping a few yards away, Plantz and the parson looked down at two fresh sets of hoofprints leading to the barn door. "Everybody back," Plantz said quietly.

The parson and the other two men started to rein their horses off the thin path, but before they could do so, the sound of an owl resounded four times from inside the barn. "Hold it," said the parson, stopping his horse. The other two men followed suit. After a short pause, four more owl hoots resounded from the barn. The parson and the men breathed more easily.

"All right," said Plantz with a short chuckle, "it's Peerly and Kid Kiley. Nobody but Peerly gives that bad of an owl hoot."

The four rode closer to the barn, watching Peerly swing the big door open for them. Once inside, the four riders stepped down and handed Kiley the reins to their horses. While Kiley led the animals aside for a short rest and some water from a rain barrel the militia kept there for that very purpose, Plantz stretched his back and said to Peerly, "All right, Nez, it's been a busy day and it's still not over. Give me some good news."

"We scared the hell out of the woman, Captain," Peerly said with a firm smile. "Just like you told us to."

"Enough to make her keep her mouth shut and send her packing?" Plantz asked.

"I would say so, Captain." Peerly beamed.

"Because I don't want no trouble from her right now. Nobody has ever been able to pin any murders on us. Let's keep it that way."

"But she couldn't have done that anyway," said Peerly, still beaming. "She had no proof."

Plantz's attitude turned sour. "Are you a gawddamn lawyer now, Nez? You know what will or *will not* get us hung from a gallows pole?"

"Well no," Peerly said, quickly deflated, "but I always heard you say the same thing."

Plantz gave him a cold stare, then said in a quieter tone, "You've talked enough to everybody to know who is with us and who's not?"

"Oh yes, Captain, I've done all that," said Peerly, regaining his confidence.

"Good work," said Plantz. "You can forget about the woman for now. Let's wait and see what she does. We've got more important matters to attend to right now."

The parson cut in, asking Peerly in an accusing tone of voice, "You and Kid Kiley didn't do anything to her, did you?"

"No, hell no!" said Peerly. "We did just what we was told to do. We hung around, made our presence felt, scared the bejesus out of her, then rode here!"

"Satisfied?" Plantz asked, a bit cross over the parson cutting in.

"Sorry, Captain," said the parson. "I just get bad feelings about this woman. I've been getting them ever since we left the boardinghouse."

"Bad feelings how?" Plantz asked. He was always interested in hearing the parson's premonitions.

"It's not all clear just yet," said the parson, slightly closing his eyes as if for a better look into some netherworld inside his mind, "but I see her holding a hangman's noose."

Plantz thought about it for a moment. Not wanting to look too superstitious, he shrugged, grinned and said loud enough for the others to hear him, "Hell, she's just a woman. One hard stare from us and she'll fold like a house of cards. She's weak, I saw it in her eyes."

"A woman doesn't have to be all that strong, if she manages to get the law on her side," said the parson, defending his premonition.

"Law or no law," said Plantz, "she's not going to be a problem, right, Peerly? Right, Kiley?" He looked back and forth between the two.

"Not at all," said Kiley, standing aside with the horses.

"No problem," said Peerly. To the parson he grinned and said, "I expect even the best of us can have a wrong vision now and then."

The parson gave him a sharp look.

"Forget the woman," said Plantz, to both Peerly and the parson. To Peerly he said, "Go bring everybody together, tonight!" He turned back to the parson. "It's time we ride away from here long enough to make some fast money. When we get back, there'll be five thousand dollars waiting for us," he said with bold confidence.

Chapter 15

Being familiar with the trail west, Julie traveled quickly and efficiently, putting Umberton and the Free Kansas Militia out of her mind as best she could. At night she made her camp off the flatlands in any trees, gulches or bracken she could find. She banked her fire and made sure the flames were down low on a bed of glowing coals before darkness set in. This she would have done regardless of her encounter with Plantz and his militia.

Having traveled the high northwest, Julie was no stranger to the perils of the trail. Riding down from the high country to her father's farm, she had swung wide of buffalo hunters, trappers, roving Indian bands under paint, and any other traveling parties that her intuition might have warned her against.

These were not gentle times, she warned herself, on her third night out. She sat idly poking a stick around in the low-glowing coals of her campfire. These were times of restlessness, and uncertainty, she recalled her father having told her not long before his death; now with the war over, she speculated that both the restlessness and the uncertainty would only grow worse before they grew better.

"This nation has wounded and lost itself," she recalled the colonel saying, when he'd seen that the war was about to come to a close. "Like anything lost and wounded, it will prowl about in its pain, until it finds itself a place to settle, lick its wounds and heal."

Oh, Pa . . . Julie raised her free hand and wiped her shirt cuff across her eyes. She stared down into the coals, feeling the warm glow somehow draw tears from her. Don't do this, she had told herself, remembering how she had vowed there would be no more tears. She laid the stick aside, picked up her warm tin cup of coffee and stared upward, out across the deep purple sky, her eyes finding a wide track of glittering diamond stars and following them farther out, deeper into the endless universe.

How long had she been alone now, she asked herself. *Jesus, how long?*

She spent her nights wrapped in the wool blanket, lying close to the warm glowing bed of embers. Before dawn she would awaken, feed some dried twigs and larger bits of kindling into the dying embers and stoke up enough fire to heat the remains of coffee from the night before. Then she would prepare herself a small breakfast before saddling the horse and getting back on the trail.

The black barb gelding was what she had asked for and what she'd expected. He was green, and more than a little skittish. The powerful half-wild plains horse stood constantly alert, as if eager to bolt out of control at the slightest provocation. Ordinarily these would be considered bad traits in a riding animal. This was not the horse for a weekend trip to town, or to hitch to a family buggy for a picnic outing.

But Julie knew that such an animal would have not only speed, but also razor-sharp reflexes, and a lightning-fast start. It was up to her to bring the horse to accept her commands on instinct and come to accept her upon his back as if she were a part of himself.

Time and patience, she'd told herself, rubbing the barb's muzzle, the day she'd let him run himself out on a long stretch of flat trail a day west of Topeka. Afterward, while the two of them rested in the shade of a cottonwood tree, she could see that the horse had wanted to run that hard and that far for a long time.

"You're sweating out fears and shadows, aren't you, boy?" she asked, supposing correctly that for the rest of the day and for an undetermined number of days to come, the powerful animal would be as tame as a lapdog. She pondered her words for a moment, still rubbing the black's muzzle, and said quietly to herself, "I reckon I'm doing the same."

After a week on the trail, Julie rode into the small but growing town of Abilene, a place that she had passed through on her way to her father's house only weeks earlier. Among log cabins and sod-roofed dugouts stood newer homes, and bare frames of houses still under construction. The sound of hammers resounded out across the open land.

Passing alongside a creek, Julie noted the large difference only a few weeks had made in this city of the plains. A tinny piano sang out through the open doors of one newly built saloon standing on a street amid three other such establishments. Boardwalks ran back and forth from one doorway to the next across a wide dark mire that served as the main street. Julie kept the black barb to one side of the odorous thoroughfare and slowly walked the animal along.

"Hey, you-hoo! Julie!" a voice called out, causing Julie to look around and see a young pale-skinned woman her own age plodding along through ankle-deep mud. She held up her cheap gaudy saloon-girl dress with both hands, revealing her unstrung hobnail boots. "Stop! It's me, Ruthie! Remember me?"

Julie brought the barb to a halt and looked down at the painted face and at the ace of hearts with an arrow through it tattooed above the woman's thin left breast. "Yes, I do, Ruthie," Julie said, recalling their meeting on her trip down.

But before Julie could say another word, the young saloon-girl spoke quickly, as if still desperate to make Julie recognize her. "You and me ate supper together at the hash house? I just had got here? You were riding through? We talked about why didn't you stay and go to work for Daniel, like I did? Remember?"

"Yes, Ruthie, I remember," Julie said, offering a cordial smile. "How are things going for you?"

"Me?" The pale-skinned girl shrugged her thin shoulders. "Oh, I'm doing *real* good, you bet I am! Couldn't be better!" She swished back and forth as far as the mud-stuck boots would allow, showing Julie her gaudy gold and red striped dress. "Just look at me! Daniel has these trappers and drovers

and buffalo hunters treating me like a princess!"
She laughed melodiously; yet Julie could tell the
laugh was not authentic. She'd grown up hearing
that sort of laughter. She'd always thought of it as
laughter to cover a cry of pain.

"That's good, Ruthie," Julie said.

"Yeah, ain't it though," the young woman said.
"And how about you, Julie? Did you come back
to go to work for Daniel . . . Because if you did"—
her voice lowered—"it would sure look good on
me, if I told him you're a friend of mine, and that
I sent for you."

"No," Julie said patiently, taking no offense, "I
didn't come here looking for work. Once again, I'm
just passing through." She didn't want to confide
in the young woman. "I'm taking on some trail
supplies, on my way back up north." She paused
for a moment, then said, "But it's good to see you
again . . . to hear you're doing well."

"Yeah, *real* well," said Ruthie. But Julie saw her
clouded brow. "It only takes about a minute or so
for these randy ole trappers to peter out. Half the
time the drovers pass out drunk before they even
get it in me." She grinned and giggled mischie-
vously. "All I've got to fear is that I don't get the
sickness from them, you know?" She patted her
flat lower belly. "But I've been lucky so far, and I
wash down there and attend myself afterward almost every time."

"Take care of yourself, Ruthie," Julie said, about
to give the barb a nudge forward.

But Ruthie continued, stepping heavily alongside
the horse, needing to talk. "Mostly, they never get
rough, these trappers, surveyors and whatnot. If

they do, Daniel cracks their head for them!" She grinned, but in doing so looked closer at Julie, seeing the fading bruises about her eyes and cheek. "Did they get rough with you where you worked?" she asked. "Is that why you're headed back this way?"

"No," said Julie, still patient. "I told you that's not my line of work. I ran into some bad characters. But I'm getting better now."

"I remembered you said you wasn't one of us," said Ruthie. "But I thought maybe you used to be, and had stopped being. Because you seemed like you were." She looked to Julie for an answer.

"I have to go, Ruthie."

"And because you look like one of us, sort of," Ruthie said, "no offence intended." She plodded along again as Julie nudged the barb slowly forward.

"No offence taken, Ruthie," said Julie. She stepped up the barb's walking pace.

"I hope you'll change your mind," Ruthie called out, stopping and standing in the mud. "There's talk that this is going to be railhead. Now that the war's over there's going to be a lot going on here! Think about that! There's going to be more cattlemen here than a hundred girls can handle!"

Julie raised a hand in farewell without looking back, and rode on to where three men stood atop ladders, nailing a long wooden sign reading MERCANTILE above a new clapboard storefront. A smaller sign on the entry door read OPEN FOR BUSINESS. The three workmen barely gave Julie a glance as she stepped down from her saddle, spun her reins around a wooden hitch rail and walked inside.

But a hundred yards away, out front of the saloon where Ruthie walked laboriously back through the mud, two pairs of eyes had been watching Julie like hawks. Once Julie had stepped out of sight into the mercantile store, a pimp named Daniel Tandy in a dirty gray swallow-tailed coat and a dingy derby hat said insistently to Ruthie, "Who was *that?* Where do you know *her* from?"

Ruthie, having learned to look out for her own advantage, replied, "Oh, she's a friend of mine. We came here together. I told you about her. She rode on over past Topeka . . . to see about her father, I believe."

"You believe?" said Tandy, with skepticism. "If she's a friend of yours, you ought to know for sure."

"Well, I do know," said Ruthie. "That's what she told me she was doing . . . going to see her father, that is."

"Is she a whore?" a man three feet tall and missing an arm asked bluntly. After he'd spoken, he glanced straight up at Daniel with a thin crooked smile.

"She's on her way north, I think," said Ruthie.

"Ruthie, you heard the dwarf, gawddamn it," said the pimp. "Is your so-called *friend* a whore?"

"Don't call me a dwarf!" the man fumed, staring up at the pimp. "My name's Thomas!"

Daniel chuckled and shrugged. "All right," he said to Ruthie, "you heard *General Tom Thumb;* he wants to know if she's a whore."

"She says not," Ruthie said, "but she seems to know about the life . . . Seems like she's either been one or been around plenty. I'm talking to her about coming to work with us."

"What did she say?" he asked.

"Said no," Ruthie replied. "But she could change her mind, right?"

"Yeah, right," said Daniel. "It makes no sense, a woman out here, alone. What the hell is she going to do?" He shrugged again. "Why wouldn't she sell it? How does she make a living for herself?"

"Maybe she's selling it and keeping on the quiet about it," Thomas speculated.

"Maybe she's a swabber," said Daniel, staring off at the mercantile store. "Yeah, that's it. She's probably been a swabber at a big whorehouse somewhere. Cleaning up after them with the guts enough to sell it." He winked and grinned at Ruthie. "Like our Ruthie here."

"Yeah, a swabber," said Thomas. "That figures." He gave a sour expression. "I hate those bitches. You always see them sneaking around and about like a cat, an arm full of towels. It's unnatural, them cleaning up other people's messes, I say."

"Or, maybe she's a *manly* woman," Daniel said, still going through his mental list of possibilities.

"Yeah, maybe," said Thomas. "I hate them too. I'd like to smack them in the face every time I see one." He curled his thick upper lip at the thought of it. "Fact is I don't care much for any woman who *ain't* a whore. A whore is the only woman a man can trust."

"Amen to that," Ruthie said in proud agreement, standing in the mud in her saloon dress.

The three stood in silence for a moment longer; then Daniel said to Ruthie, "Are you asleep out there?"

"Huh, what?" Ruthie said in surprise.

"You've let one on horseback and three in a buckboard ride right past you. Are you taking the day off?"

"Oh! Sorry," Ruthie said, looking fearful. She knew how quickly Daniel's mood could turn dark, and how suddenly his easygoing charm could turn ugly and violent.

Turning back to the mud street, she pirouetted like a marionette on strings and called out sweetly to a passing horseman, "Yoo-hoo. Did you come here to see me? I sure hope you did!"

On the short boardwalk, Daniel and Thomas watched her for a moment with faint smiles on their faces. "Show him something," Daniel said to Ruthie, keeping his voice lowered.

Ruthie quickly raised her dress up past her waist, exposing her pantaloons to the horseman, who slowed down, made a wide circle in the mud street and nudged his horse back toward her.

"Dumb whores," Daniel said under his breath. He gave another glance toward the mercantile store and said, "What would any of them ever do without us?"

"Yeah, what would they ever?" said Thomas with a cocky swagger as they both turned and walked inside the saloon.

Chapter 16

Colorado Territory

Baines Meredith reached out with a gloved hand and gave his stallion, Joseph, a slight nudge on the rump. The big horse galloped away quickly into a tall stand of pines clinging to the sloping hillside. Walking slowly forward, his eyes scanning across a low ravine to a rocky slope facing him, Baines raised the brass rear sight on his newer-model Winchester repeating rifle and turned the screw tight with his fingertips.

"Bobby Bantree!" he called out into the thin chilled air. "Lew Kerns!"

No reply resounded across the ravine.

Baines waited another silent moment, watching a hawk circle high and effortlessly on an updraft of air. "Lucky bastard." He grinned to himself. To the other side of the ravine, he called out, "Bantree! Be a man about this. There's nothing left for you out here, not with me dogging you everywhere you go. One of us has to die before the other can go on about our business. Come out and get it over with."

Baines looked surprised when a voice called out, "He ain't afraid of you, Meredith!"

Baines tracked the sound of the voice with his eyes and raised the rifle to his shoulder. Under his breath, he whispered, "Much obliged, Lew." He scanned the slope through his rifle sights until he caught a glimpse of a horse's mane move back and forth behind a stand of rock. He held the position for a moment, then drifted all around it, searching intently.

Across the ravine, Bobby Bantree could barely control his anger. "Gawddamn it, Kerns! Why did you shoot your mouth off that way? That's all he was trying to do was to get one of us to say something!"

Lew Kerns stared at him with a dull expression. "You ain't, are you?"

"Ain't what?" Bantree asked, his anger growing by the minute.

"Afraid of this bounty dog!" said Kerns, nodding in Baines' direction.

"What the hell difference would it make if I was?" said Bantree. "You've just seen to it I'm going to have to face him down! You and your gawddamn big mouth!"

Kerns shrugged. "Hell, I'll face him. I've been wanting to face him one-on-one to begin with. I ain't afraid of the sonsabitch."

Bantree stared at him coldly. "If you've been wanting to face him, why the hell didn't you do it three days ago, save us all this trouble?"

Baines spotted the horse's man again through his rifle sight. Watching closely, he saw the top of a hat move from right to left. He watched, his finger across the rifle trigger. "We're coming out, Meredith!" Kerns shouted across the ravine. "Hold your fire!"

"Step out slow like, with your hands up where I can see them," Baines shouted in reply.

Taking a close aim down his rifle sight, Baines watched first Kerns, then Bantree step out from behind the rock, their hands chest-high. "You're the one taking the lead on this, Lew. Don't freeze up on me," Bantree said quietly to his pal, although there was no way Baines could have heard them from such a distance.

"I've got this all worked out in my mind," Kerns whispered in reply. "Just make sure you're there if I need you." He stared hard toward the other side of the ravine, but saw no sign of Baines Meredith.

"Don't worry about me, pard," said Bantree. "I'm backing your play on this."

"Start walking down this way, slowly," Baines called out.

"What about our horses?" Bantree asked.

Baines half smiled to himself, seeing what Bantree was up to. "We'll come back for them directly, Bobby," Baines replied. "Are they hitched good and sound?"

"Yeah," said Bantree, "they'll keep."

Kerns called out, "Baines! Don't worry about the horses. As soon as we're in pistol range, I'm calling you out, one-on-one!"

"Ah, Jesus!" Bantree said to Kerns under his breath.

"Why?" said Kerns. "I ain't afraid of telling him what we're going to—"

Bantree had already dropped his hands and made a dash back behind the cover of rock when a bloody hole appeared in Kerns' chest, followed by the loud blast from Baines' rifle. Kerns crumbled backward onto the rocky ground and began sliding limply down the slope over rock and low, dry brush.

Baines wasted no time. He levered a fresh round into his rifle chamber and sighted it along the edge of the rock, ready for Bantree as two horses bolted into sight.

But Bantree had thought ahead. Instead of sitting upright in his saddle, he'd dropped over onto his horse's side, using the two animals as his shield. "You could have done better than that," Baines said, quietly shaking his head, then taking aim.

Knowing Bantree couldn't make it far riding that way on the rough sloping ground, Baines waited until he saw the fugitive drop off the horse's side and scramble for the shelter of trees, thinking Baines could not see him. "End of hunt," Baines said to himself. He fired a shot that dug up a clump of rock and dirt in front of Bantree's head as the man clawed and scratched his way toward shelter.

Knowing the shot had been a warning and that Baines was just telling him that the next shot would be dead center, Bantree stopped scrambling on the ground, jumped to his feet, threw his hands up and shouted, "All right, I'm done! I give up! See? My hands are up! I surrender!"

Baines took close aim, dead center at Bantree's chest. He took a breath and held it, ready to squeeze the trigger and put an end to the matter. But then, on second thought, he let out his breath, lowered the rifle an inch and looked left of Bantree where the two horses had come to a halt, then slowly made their way down into the ravine, their muzzles already down, searching for graze. "What the hell," Baines said. He lowered his rifle more, stood up from behind the rock and gave his stallion a hand signal, bringing the animal to him from within the trees.

"I'm not going to shoot him, Joseph," Baines said to the black stallion, as if the big animal understood him. "I should though, the way he was about to jackpot his partner." Together, Baines and the stallion walked down the slope.

"Obliged, Meredith," said Bantree, when the two men reached the bottom of the rocky ravine at about the same time.

Without a reply, Baines stepped forward, his rifle cocked and aimed at Bantree's chest. He reached out and jerked the pistol from the holster on the outlaw's hip. Shoving the pistol down into his belt, he gave Bantree a harsh stare. "Shame on you, Bobby. That poor fool didn't have to die." He made a twirling gesture with his gloved finger.

"Yeah," said Bantree, turning slowly in a full circle to show he had nothing behind his back, "if that poor fool had enough sense to keep his lip buttoned, me and him both would have given you the slip and been out of here."

Baines stared at him coldly. "What you mean is, if he'd kept quiet, you two would have ambushed me when I started up the hill."

Bantree gave a shrug. "Well, that too," he said.

"But then Lew said he wanted a fair standoff, just you and him. I saw no reason not to."

"And while him and I shot each other all to hell, you'd be making yourself a run for it up the slope with both horses?" Baines asked, although it was really not a question.

"Somebody was going to kill him sooner or later, Baines," said Bantree. "Tell the truth, did you ever see a more stupid sonsabitch in your life?"

Baines gestured him toward the horses standing a few yards away. "I have to admit he was awfully damned stupid," Baines said. He kept six feet between himself and Bantree, following him to the grazing horses. "The fact is, he wasn't even wanted for anything that I know of."

"You're kidding," said Bantree, giving a half glance back in surprise.

"No," said Baines. "It looks like he was just standing up for you . . . his *pard*," he added in a critical tone.

"Damn," said Bantree. "I reckon I ought to feel bad then, jackpotting him that way."

"That's for you to decide," said Baines. "My job is just to take you in. Least move you make to get away, I'll put a bullet in you and tie you facedown over your saddle. Do you understand me real clear?"

"I'm done, Baines," said Bantree. "You win, I lose. To hell with it." He paused, then asked, "Where are we headed though, just for curiosity's sake?"

"First we're stopping by my place, then on down to Donaldson," Baines said.

"Are we going to bury ole Lew first?" Bantree asked.

"I've got a shovel," said Baines. "You feel like digging in this hard ground?"

"Naw," said Bantree, walking on, "it was just a thought."

Two more weeks passed before Julie turned her horse onto the trail leading to Baines Meredith's house on the eastern outskirts of Denver. Having left Umberton at the war's end, Julie had passed through town after town of celebration until at length the festivities had worn thin and stopped by the time she had crossed over into Colorado Territory. At a stage stop and supply settlement along the trail, she stepped down from her horse while an old man and a young boy stood folding a large flag they had taken down from over the door of a sod and log trading post.

"What can I do for you, ma'am?" the oldtimer asked, stepping toward her, slipping the folded flag into a canvas bag and handing it to the young boy.

"The war is over!" the boy called out to Julie before she had time to answer the old man.

"Hush up, Imus," the old man said, waving the gangly boy away.

"I'm looking for Baines Meredith," Julie said. "His place is north along this trail, isn't it?"

"Baines Meredith?" The old man took on a serious look. He leaned slightly and gazed along the trail behind her as if making sure she was alone. "I haven't seen Baines Meredith for the longest time, ma'am." He looked her up and down, seeing the faded traces of bruises still lingering on her face. "No offence, but you don't look like most of the women who come looking for Mr. Meredith."

"Oh," said Julie, a bit taken aback by his words. "You make it sound like many women come looking for him."

Remaining elusive, the old man said hesitantly, "I've seen one or two maybe."

"Then I am headed in the right direction?" Julie said.

The old man only stared at her.

Realizing he wasn't going to say much more on the matter, Julie shook her head, and swung back up into the saddle. "I'll tell Baines how helpful you were," she said, giving the horse a turn back onto the trail.

"All right, ma'am," the old man said. "You're headed in the right direction. Stay on this trail another fifteen miles are so, turn onto a smaller trail where a big rock's lying beside a hulled-out freight wagon. You better not be up to no good," he warned.

"Don't worry," Julie said, offering a short smile. "I've come as a friend."

"Yeah," the old man called out as she nudged her horse forward, "I once had a fellow tell me that, then ride out and try to shoot Mr. Meredith! Don't you disappoint me, young lady!"

Julie rode on.

By midafternoon, she came to the spot where the skeletal remains of a freight wagon sat lopsided and half-sunken into the ground. A large rock lay against one of the broken wheels. Without stopping she turned the horse onto the smaller trail and rode for another half hour until a dull tin roof rose up in the distance.

When she reached the small half-clapboard, half-log house, she stopped a few yards away and called out to the closed door. After a moment of silence, she gazed all around at the yard, at a small barn, at an empty corral, its gate wide open. Then she stepped down, led the horse to a hitch rail, spun his reins and walked up onto the short porch.

The horse stood and watched her step inside through the unlocked door, and less than a minute later step back out, leaving the door open. Walking back down beside the animal, she untied her canvas supply bag and her blanket and took them down from behind her saddle. She stood for a moment looking out in each direction across rough rocky ground. Fifty yards to the west stood a woodlands along the edge of a shimmering creek. In the other three directions lay open land as far as the eye could see.

"It looks like we've got the place to ourselves," she said. She carried her bag and blanket inside and dropped them both onto a battered wooden table in the center of the room.

Chapter 17

Four days passed before Baines Meredith and his prisoner rode into sight across the open land. When Julie spotted them through the kitchen window, she dropped her dishcloth into the water pan and dried her hands quickly on a clean towel. She shoved her shirttails down into her trousers on the way to the door.

Outside, on the trail, Baines Meredith smiled slightly to himself after seeing the strange horse in his corral. He stopped where the trail ended at his front yard and brought Bobby Bantree's horse and the spare mount to a halt beside him. At the sight of the three horses approaching, Julie's black barb began cutting back and forth along the rail, eying them suspiciously. Baines noted the saddle, tack and blanket lying atop the fence, and said to his prisoner, "Looks like you'll be sleeping in the barn tonight, Bantree."

The prisoner shrugged, his cuffed hands resting on the saddle horn. "I've slept in barns before. It makes no never mind to me."

Baines looked him up and down. "Some men

would look at sleeping in the barn as an opportunity to see if they can break loose and get their knees in the wind."

"I can't say the thought wouldn't cross my mind," Bantree replied.

Baines nodded. "Here's something else to let cross your mind. . . . You're worth about the same to me dead as you are alive. The difference is, I save a little by not having to feed you." He tugged on the lead rope to Bantree's horse and nudged his stallion toward the house.

"I'm not going to try to run, Meredith," said Bantree. "Far as I'm concerned, I'll go in and face what's coming to me."

"That's a refreshing attitude," said Baines, watching Julie step out onto the front porch, her hands in the rear pockets of her canvas trousers. "Oh my, Julie Wilder!" he whispered to himself, seeing her raise a hand and wave at him. "What a fine strapping young woman you are."

Bantree sat quietly, looking all around the countryside idly, judging the distance to the rise of mountains on the far northwest horizon.

Stepping the horses' pace up a little, Baines turned wide in front of the house, putting himself between Bantree and Julie as she stepped down off the porch. "My my," Baines said, sweeping his wide flat-crowned hat from his head. "To what do I owe this honor, young lady?"

"Don't act too surprised," said Julie. "I know the man at the stage stop told you I'm here."

Without commenting on the matter, Baines asked, "Did you have a good trip up from the plains?" He gestured Bantree down from his saddle, then stepped down himself.

"Cool nights, but warmer days," Julie said. She stuck out her hand. Baines looked down at it, smiled as if he would have preferred something more, but then shook hands and half turned to the prisoner.

"This is Bobby Bantree," he said to Julie. "I'll be taking him to the fort to turn him in."

Bantree reached his cuffed hands up and touched the brim of his hat. "Ma'am."

Julie only nodded a short courteous response, not liking the way Bantree gazed into her eyes.

Baines noted Julie's clouded brow. "Bantree here has never been over in Kansas that I know of, have you, Bobby?"

Bantree shrugged. "No, why?"

"Never you mind *why,*" said Baines, looking at Julie as he spoke to the prisoner.

Julie got the message. "I'm all right with things now, Baines."

"Oh, are you?" Baines smiled wisely, as if to imply that he didn't believe her. "Then what brings you to my home?"

Julie started to speak, but before she could, Baines cut in, saying, "We'll discuss it later." He reached out with a gloved hand and patted her forearm. "Right now, just let me look at you." He smiled admiringly. "You certainly wore a much different face the last time I laid eyes upon you."

"I'm doing much better," Julie said.

"And I can see that plainly," said Baines. He gestured Bantree in front of him and led all three horses toward the barn. Julie walked along beside him.

"How is dear Constance Whirly?" Baines asked.

"Constance is fine," said Julie. "She sends you her best."

"No, she doesn't," Baines chuckled, "but much obliged for your thoughtfulness." At the barn he stepped around in front of Bantree and opened the door. Gesturing the prisoner inside, he ushered Julie and closed the door behind them. In the shadowy gloom, he picked up a lantern, lit it and trimmed the wick to a bright glow.

"Jesus," said Bantree, looking disappointed at the iron-barred cell standing before them, next to one of the stalls. Inside the cell a set of shackles lay attached to a long, heavy chain that ran out through the bars and connected to a barn post ten feet away with a thick anchor bolt.

Baines gave him a flat stare. "Like you said, you're not going to try running anyway, eh?"

"Yeah, but damn." Bantree stared down at the floor as Baines unlocked the cell door and motioned him inside.

Once he'd relocked the cell door, Baines walked over and hung the lantern on a post in the center of the barn. "There's a Bible and some reading material in there," he said, pointing at a small table beside a cot in the corner of he cell. Looking back at Julie, Baines smiled and said to Bantree, "Ordinarily, I help a prisoner pass the time with a stirring game of chess or checkers. But this isn't ordinarily."

Baines held his crooked arm up for Julie. "Now if you'll join me, dear lady, we'll have ourselves a cup of coffee and I'll hear what brings you to visit this lonesome old gunman.''

They walked to the house and within minutes Julie had set out two china cups and saucers from a small cupboard and poured each with coffee from a pot she had prepared earlier. Seating themselves at the kitchen table, Baines took out a briar pipe, filled it and lit it while Julie talked.

Over coffee, Julie told him everything that had happened to her since he'd left her in Umberton. She told him about the visit from the major and how Ruddell Plantz's men had accompanied him. She told him how the men appeared to treat the matter as a private joke among themselves. She finished by telling him about the two men in the livery barn, and how she couldn't bring herself to pull the trigger to protect herself.

Baines sat in a silent smolder for a moment, then shook his head. "I'm the one who saw firsthand what they did to you, Julie." His gaze turned grim in reflection. "If killing them for you would help, I'd be riding out today to get it done." He paused, then said quietly, "But that's not what you came here to ask of me is it, darling?"

"That's what Constance told me to ask of you," Julie said. "But no, that's not what I want. What I want is justice, for these men killing my father. What I want is to be able to tell the innocent faces I see every day from the men who did this to me."

"You want to rip those hoods from their faces," said Baines. "I don't know if that's ever going to happen for you."

She turned her face away and gazed out through the window. Tears glistened in her dark eyes.

"What I want," she continued, "is to live in peace, in Umberton, on the ground my father wanted me to have."

Seeing she did not want to weep, Baines gave her a moment as he sipped his coffee and blotted a white linen kerchief to his thick graying mustache. "You'll have to kill them to do that," he said with gentle resolve.

"I've tried not to tell myself that," Julie said, collecting herself. "There are too many of them for me to go up against."

"And yet you don't want me to go up against them with you?" Baines offered a tired thin smile. "What a puzzling woman you are, Julie Wilder."

"Puzzling?" said Julie. "I can't bring myself to kill the men who *I know* killed my father. I call that *lost.*"

Baines shook his head, and said, "You don't *know* they're the ones. And not knowing is your problem."

"I'm certain of it," Julie offered. "There is no doubt in my mind."

"Yes there is," said Baines. "You might be *certain* of it, you might *know in your heart* that they're the ones. You might even go to court and *swear on a Bible* that they're the ones. But there is a thing inside you that still gives humankind the benefit of a doubt." He gave the same tired smile. "The thing is a *conscience,* Julie. Some call it a *piece of God* in each of us. No matter how strong you feel that Ruddell and his men did these terrible things, all you see are the hoods on their faces. You don't see the faces themselves."

"I saw Plantz's boots," Julie murmured. "He was there; I saw his silver Mexican spurs."

"Yes," said Baines, "and today that is all you need to make you go for his throat. But take a gun in your hand, cock it and aim it at his heart, and your conscience starts whispering, *'What if someone else owned those spurs, or a pair just like them?'* You sure don't want to kill a man, then find out you were wrong, do you?"

"No," said Julie, in dark contemplation.

"And that's exactly why men like Plantz and his riders wear their hoods. It keeps the decent folks, like yourself, from even knowing *how* to fight back."

"What about you, Baines," Julie asked. "What about *your* conscience? How do you deal with it?"

Baines shrugged and puffed on his pipe. "I told my conscience to shut up and stand in the corner long ago. It's still standing there as far as I can tell." He gave her a curious gaze. "But who said I'm one of the decent folks, anyway? I stepped away from the rules and confines of decency a long time ago."

"That's not true," said Julie. "Look what you did for me. I see a goodness in you. Constance Whirly must have seen it too. I saw how the two of you took to one another."

"What Constance saw in me was *need* . . . a need in me and a need in herself—nothing nearly as important as the matter of killing. It was not goodness she sought. It may have even been my *lack of goodness* that attracted her."

"I don't think that's so," said Julie, "and even if

it were, *I* see goodness in you. If I didn't, I wouldn't have come here asking your help."

"Any goodness you see in me is the goodness of pretense," Baines said with resolve. "You came to ask help from the devil, in order to do the work the devil does best."

"But I—" Julie started to speak; Baines cut her off with an upraised hand.

"No, please, darling," he said. "You came to the right place." He drew on the pipe and blew a thin stream of gray smoke toward the ceiling in contemplation. "I will teach you how to tell your conscience to shut up and go stand in the corner. But you'll have to be careful not to leave it standing there too long." He eyed her closely. "Is that what you want me to do?"

After a silence, Julie whispered, "Yes, teach me to kill."

Baines laid his pipe in a tin ash tray beside his coffee cup and stood up from the table. Walking to the cupboard, he reached up atop it and took down a locked wooden box that lay out of sight. He blew a fine sheen of dust from the box, then walked back over, laid it on the table, unlocked it and opened the lid.

"A gun maker all the way over in Connecticut made this for me. Along the barrel he engraved, 'A job well done.'"

As he stepped back and put the key in his trouser pocket, he gestured Julie toward a large bone-handled revolver that lay shining on a bed of black velvet. "Pick it up," he said. "Look it over . . . Handle it. Get used to it." He watched her reach out toward the box, then saw her stop and hesitate for just a moment as he said, "Let's call it the devil's gun."

Baines stared at her. She looked as if she needed him to say something, some sort of coaxing to get her to pick up the gun after hearing what he'd called it. But Baines offered no such coaxing. Instead he took a step back, as if to say that she either picked up *the devil's gun,* or the whole matter stopped right there.

Julie's eyes took on a determination. She grasped the revolver and raised it from the box, turning it back and forth in her hand. She read the engraving to herself. "I am a pretty good shot, you know. This isn't the first gun I've ever held."

"I realize that," said Baines, "but this will be the first gun you ever held for the sole purpose of killing a man."

Julie looked at him as he stepped in closer. She held the Colt out to him when he raised his hand for it. Taking the gun, Baines took six bullets from his belt behind his back and loaded it. Clicking the chamber shut, he handed it back to her. "We'll find you a holster this evening and get started drawing and shooting tomorrow morning."

"But I already know how to draw and shoot," said Julie.

"Yes," said Baines. "But it's not second nature to you. Until you can draw fast and shoot straight, kill a man without thinking about it, all a gun will do for you is get *you* killed."

"I'm in your hands," Julie said. She realized that the day she'd pulled the gun on Peerly and Kiley, she hadn't done so with the intent to kill. She had only done so hoping the sight of the gun would make them leave her alone. "Tell me everything I need to learn."

"First things first," said Baines. "Come with me."

They walked from the house to the barn, Julie with the gun in her hand. At the barn, Baines swung the door open quickly and stepped inside, motioning Julie in behind him. They walked over to the cell. The prisoner stood up quickly from a spot in the far corner where he had stooped down to test the iron bars for any weaknesses that might be worked to his advantage.

"Shoot him," Baines said to Julie in a somber tone.

"What?" Julie looked appalled. So did Bantree.

"No! Please, Meredith!" the prisoner called out, seeing that Baines Meredith meant it. "I wasn't doing anything! I swear to God I—"

"Shoot him!" Baines demanded. His tone and demeanor became so intent that Julie raised the gun quickly in the prisoner's direction. Her thumb went over the hammer; she almost cocked it.

"No, please!" Bantree shouted. "Ma'am, I'm begging you! Don't kill me this way!"

Baines watched as Julie caught herself. She shook her head as if to clear it. Then as if snapping out of some deep state of mind, she sighed and lowered the gun. "No, Baines, I'm not killing him. This is murder. I'm not going to commit murder."

Bantree's knees went weak; he sank down onto his cot.

Baines stood still, studying Julie closely. "Not even if I tell you this is what you have to do in order to go back to Umberton and take care of the business at hand?"

"No," Julie said, "not even if it means I never go to Umberton. I can't tell my conscience to stand still for murder."

"I see," said Meredith, an indiscernible look on his face. Turning to Bantree, he said sharply, "This is your lucky day. Had I come alone and seen you looking for a way out, I would have shot you dead. Think about that for a while before you test my patience again."

The two turned and left, Julie carrying the gun with both hands now. On the way to the house, she said with a troubled look, "You—you knew he would be trying to break out? You used that as a reason for me to kill him?"

Without answering, Baines looked at the way she held the gun and said as they stepped onto the porch, "The devil's gun seems to have taken on some weight." He swung the door open and stepped inside behind her.

"Are you disappointed that I didn't kill him?" she asked.

"Disappointed, no," said Baines. "But it does give me some idea of what I can and can't expect from you." As he spoke he gestured a hand toward Julie's saddlebags and blanket lying on a braided Indian rug in front of the fireplace. "You're going to be staying here with me for a while; move your things over to the bed."

"To the bed?" Julie asked. "Where are you going to sleep?"

"In the bed. We both are," Baines said flatly.

"The two of us, man and woman. Is that unreason-able for me to ask, for a beautiful young woman to sleep with me, in exchange for teaching you how to kill?"

"Baines, I don't know what to say." Julie shook her head slowly, looking disillusioned by someone for whom she had such high regard. "I can't— That is, *I won't* sleep with you. You've misunderstood me . . . I'm sorry."

"Or, you've *misunderstood* me," said Baines. He walked over to her blanket on the floor, picked it up and carried it over to the bed in a corner. "For what I'm going to teach you, I have to get some-thing in return." He offered a thin smile. "Call it the devil's due." He dropped her blanket onto the bed and stood beside it, as if expecting Julie to come to him.

"No, Baines," said Julie. "I'm grateful for all you've done for me. But I'm no whore. I won't sell myself, not now, not ever. Not to you, or any-body else."

"Then you have traveled all this way for nothing, darling," Baines said, his voice taking on a cruel tone.

Julie walked to the bed, picked up the blanket and turned to walk away. "Yes, I suppose I have. I'll just gather my things and go."

"Wait, Julie," Baines said, his demeanor sud-denly changing again. Something in the sound of his voice caused her to stop and turn to him. "I had to know what kind of person I'm teaching," he said. "You've passed your first two tests."

Julie considered it, then said, "You mean, in the barn?"

Baines nodded. "I had to know if you would. Those are blank loads in the pistol. If you had fired, nothing would've happened. You were right; I did hear about you from the stage stop attendant. I had a pretty good idea why you were here. I prepared."

Julie looked at the blanket in her hands. "Sleeping with you? You didn't mean it?"

"I wouldn't turn you loose on the world if you'd sell yourself that cheap," said Baines. "I had to see some character behind the hand that carries death."

Julie gave him a thin, knowing smile. "It was a test? You wouldn't have gone to bed with me, if I had agreed to it?"

"Oh, yes indeed," said Baines, returning her smile with a crafty one of his own. "We would have gone to bed. But I would have taken the gun back and never taught you to kill."

Julie stared at him for a moment, then said, "No matter what you teach me, how will I ever fight men who wear hoods? Who mask their faces?"

"By doing what you've been doing, wearing a mask of your own," said Baines, walking closer to her.

"I've been wearing a mask?" Julie looked confused.

"I think so," said Baines. "What have you been saying, that you want to live in peace, that you want no trouble?" He grinned. "We both know better. Oh, you want to live in peace all right. But once you know who these men are and how to kill them, that mask will come off." He paused, then said, "For now, keep wearing it. It's the best weapon you've got on your side. Don't let them know what you're doing until it's done. It'll keep you one step ahead of them at all times."

Julie just stared at him, not sure she understood, but willing to listen and learn.

"Don't worry, we'll talk more about it tomorrow," said Baines. "I'll also show you how to use a couple of *quiet* weapons I recommend for the kind of fight you're getting yourself into."

"Quiet weapons?" Julie asked, studying his weathered face, his dark fathomless eyes.

"Oh yes, *quiet*," said Baines. "There's more ways to kill a man than with a gun, you know." He gestured toward the door before she could respond. "But enough. Right now, let's sit out on the porch where I can look at you in the light." He paused abruptly and asked in a playful tone, "It is all right that I *look at you*, isn't it, darling? An old man like me . . . I want to look upon your face and yearn."

Julie gave a shy nod. "Oh, Baines. If I was looking for a man in my life, I expect I could do a lot worse than you."

"That's the kind of talk I like to hear," Baines replied.

PART 3

Chapter 18

Wakeland, Missouri

Plantz and his men rode into the small town in the middle of the night. They rousted the sleeping citizenry to their feet with blasts of gunfire. Some fired wildly into the darkness overhead; others aimed deliberately at shop windows and doors. A total of eleven shots had been fired into three townsmen who had been awakened from their sleep and grabbed their firearms on their way outside. Their bodies lay bleeding in the dirt. The riders carried flaming torches, for both light and sinister effect. They had shed their hoods and ragged militia uniforms.

"Everybody outside! Let's go! Let's go, folks!" the parson bellowed, firing his pistol straight up and watching the men who had scrambled from their horses as they kicked down doors and began dragging people out onto the street.

Circling wildly on his horse beside the parson, Plantz laughed through his mask and said, "Mister!

I believe you have taken on a new calling in life! You love this, don't you?"

"I love the *cause*," the parson replied, also laughing. He circled his horse as well and fired another round amid the screams and shrieks of women and children. "God help me, I do love it so!"

Looking up from his belly in the dirt a stocky man with a pencil-thin mustache and a two-day beard stubble caught the parson's eye.

"What are you looking at, you fine-trimmed *dandy!*" the parson shouted. Without taking close aim, he fired a quick shot at the man. Luckily for the man the shot only struck the dirt, two inches from his head. He pressed his face straight down into the dust and kept it there.

"Damn, that was close!" Plantz said, chuckling, the two of them keeping their restless horses moving back and forth and in short circles.

"Close?" The parson's eyes showed surprise. "I thought I nailed him!" He started to turn back toward the cringing man.

But Plantz stopped him, saying, "He'll keep. Let's see what we've got here."

The militiamen jostled the townsfolk roughly into a line along the edge of the street. Men, women and children stared blurry-eyed and stunned at what could well have been an army of some sort.

With the extortion money Plantz had raised from the Umberton town councilmen, he and his men had purchased long riding dusters—uniforms of a different sort. Their hats, boots and shooting gear varied, but each wore around the neck a bandanna, convenient to pull up over the bridge of their nose and hide their faces at will.

"Everybody listen up!" Plantz shouted, settling his horse now, looking down on the helpless townsfolk. "We're going through your houses, and your businesses! We're taking anything of value! You can't stop us! You can only *die* trying! Any questions?"

"Yes, who *are* you people?" a young business owner asked, stepping forward boldly, having to pull his wife's clinging hand off his forearm. "Why are you doing this to us? We're trying to build a town here! We're not trying to crowd anybody . . ."

Plantz shook his head in disgust while the young man rattled on. He raised his big pistol and shot the man through the heart. "Any other questions?" he asked, holding the smoking pistol pointed up, smoke curling from its barrel. When no one dared open their mouth, Plantz grinned to himself behind his bandanna mask and said, "Good! Then I must have made myself clear!" He nudged his horse closer to the woman whose husband he'd just killed, seeing her wrench herself from Nez Peerly and fling herself to the ground by her dead husband's side. She cried out painfully.

Peerly jumped forward to drag her to her feet, but Plantz waved him back. "She's already proven to be too strong for you, *Mister,*" he said to Peerly in a cold, dry tone.

"I can handle her, Mister!" Peerly said in his own defense. "She just slipped away from me is all!" He spread his hands, as if asking his leader

for some understanding. His eyes widened when
Plantz lowered the pistol and leveled it at him.
"Jesus!"

But Plantz lowered the pistol downward away
from him and said above the woman's loud sobbing, "Since you can *handle* her, *handle* her right
up here to me. I'll shut her up." He stepped his
horse forward while the town looked on in horror
and uncertainty.

Struggling and sobbing, the woman fought
against Peerly as he raised her from her dead husband's bloody chest and pitched her up to Plantz.
"Damn, she's worse than a wildcat!" Peerly said,
staggering back, touching his fingertips to three
long scratches down his cheek.

"So I see," Plantz said, struggling with her until
he forced her across his lap. "But a damn pretty
little heifer!" He drew his pistol butt sideways and
swiped it across the side of her head, not knocking
her out, but stunning her into silence. In her struggle, the cotton gown she wore had ridden up, partially exposing her thighs. Plantz ran his free hand
up under the gown, then pulled it out and said,
"And hotter than a woodstove." He jerked her
gown into place as if to keep the townsmen from
seeing her, and asked them, "What's her name?"

Behind the line of townsfolk, Plantz's men ran
from business to business, and house to house,
coming out with jewelry, cash, items of gold and
silver. When no one dared speak, the parson called
out, "Folks, make sure you understand how this
works; when one of us *Misters* ask you something,
you'd be wise to answer."

"What's her name, gawddamn it!" Plantz shouted.

"It's Mrs. Paiges," a woman said hesitantly. "Her name's Shelby Paiges. They just got here!" She nodded at the dead man on the ground. "He's building an apothecary. She's going to teach school to our children."

"All right; that's enough!" said Plantz. "I didn't ask their whole family history." He chuckled, looking at the parson.

"Put her down, Mister," said the parson, in a cautioning tone of voice.

"Like hell," said Plantz. He patted the stunned woman's buttocks. "A schoolteacher? Named *Paiges?* Not if my life depended on it. I never had me a pretty little schoolteacher. Always wanted one though."

"Just so's you know, I'm all against it," said the parson, looking away as if he'd said his piece and would speak no more on the matter.

"I can see that," said Plantz. He called out to the townsfolk, "Where's the schoolhouse?"

The same woman who'd spoken before pointed toward the end of the street without opening her mouth.

"You catch on quick, old woman." Plantz grinned behind his mask. "Take over, Mister," he said to the parson. "I'm going to school."

Watching him turn his horse and ride away, the parson cursed under his breath, then turned to the men who stared after Plantz. Then they turned their eyes to the parson with hopeful anticipation. "What do you say, Mister?" Kiley asked him.

"Damn it," the parson whispered, knowing what Kiley asked. He looked along the line of townsfolk, seeing two young women clutching their mother's side in fear. Farther along the line, a middle-aged woman stood holding a blanket around herself, her hair hanging wet down past her shoulders, as if she'd been awake and caught in the midst of bathing. "It's slim pickings here," the parson called out to Kiley.

"We'll make do," said Kiley, straightening his mask on the bridge of his nose.

"Finish up first, then have at it." The parson turned his horse toward a darkened tent that had a hastily painted sign reading SALOON stuck to its front center pole. "You know where to bring everything," he said, nodding toward the big ragged tent. Before riding away, he appraised the seven men at a glance. He and Plantz had been right. The ones riding with them were the very same six they had both predicted would stay with them after the war was over.

The murder of the colonel, and even more so, the raping of Julie Wilder seemed to have formed a tight bond among the men. To their surprise, Delbert Reese, who had been with them that night, had also stayed with them after the war.

"Nine of us," the parson grinned and said aloud to himself, kicking his horse toward the tent. "Enough to raise hell above ground."

As the first sliver of daylight slipped over the horizon, Nez Peerly and Delbert Reese counted out money onto a long wooden table in the ragged tent saloon. "Most of this ought to be ours," Peerly whispered under his breath. "We're the ones who did all the work." His bandanna sagged down below his nose, partially exposing his face if anyone happened to be looking. "Now he's telling you and me to ride on back to Umberton; *'keep an eye on things,'* he tells us. What gawddamn things?" Peerly demanded of Reese.

"Hell, don't ask me." Reese shrugged. "I expect it's because we've been gone so long this time. He wants me and you to scout things out at home before he gets there."

But Peerly didn't seem to hear him. "Who are we, his personal servants?" he asked. "I can take only so much . . . then I'll blow up. I blow up, I'll kill somebody. That's a natural fact."

"That's dangerous talk," Delbert whispered in reply. He touched his own nose for an example and said, "Fix your mask, Nez."

"Aw, hell, who's looking anyway," said Peerly; but he adjusted the bandanna up all the same. He gave a quick glance around the shadowy dark tent outside the glow of the lantern sitting atop the table. In a far corner one of the two younger women who'd been pulled away from their mother's side sat shivering, naked, except for a dirty wool blanket pulled around her.

At another table a few feet away, also holding a ragged blanket around herself, the woman who'd been caught in the middle of her bathing the night before stood up and walked toward the front fly of the tent. Her swollen left eye had started turning purple during the long, torturous night.

"Yeah, maybe it is *dangerous* talk," Peerly said. "But I'm getting gawddamned tired of being yelled at in front of everybody, and getting a gun pointed at me. You saw that, didn't you?"

"Yeah, I saw it," said Reese. "I can't say I blame

you much there. I always believe when you point a gun at a man, it's because you mean to kill him."

"That's what I always heard too," said Peerly. "You don't think he means to kill me, but he just hasn't realized it yet?" Peerly asked Reese.

"I don't think I'm the one who can say," Reese replied. But before he could say any more on the matter, Peerly turned quickly toward the woman as she attempted to exit the tent. "Hey, bathing lady!" he called out. "What's this? Where the hell do you think you're going?"

"Back home, to what I was doing," the woman said in a weak flat voice. "If you assholes haven't burnt it down yet."

"You're not going anywhere," said Peerly, yet he made no move to stop her.

Battered and half-drunk from the whiskey she'd been forced to drink, she winced from the pain in her swollen face and said, "Look at me. You got what you wanted. You're through with me. What good am I now?"

Peerly chuckled, "Hell yes, *I'm* through with you anyway. You wouldn't look so bad if you hadn't tried to be so tough. You was asking for a beating."

"Fuck you sonsabitches," said the woman, turning away and heading on for the front fly.

"Did you hear that?" Peerly asked Reese, appearing shocked.

"Sounds like she ain't learned nothing through all this," Reese said, looking surprised.

Peerly raised his pistol and cocked it, aiming at the center of her back. "Stop right there or you're *dead,* so help me," said Peerly.

In the far corner the young girl sat shivering and

whining aloud, raising her hands over her eyes to keep from seeing what was about to happen.

"Go on and shoot," the woman said without even looking back. "I don't really give a damn." She continued on out of the tent.

"I hate hearing a woman using foul language that way," said Peerly, chuckling again. "It's not at all becoming." He raised the gun, uncocked it and put it away.

"Yeah, me too," said Reese. He looked back down at the money on the table. "Where was we?"

"We were finishing up counting the money so's we'll know what our shares come to before we head on back to Umberton, gawddamn it," he said, angry at the thought of having to ride back ahead of the others and wait for his cut of the spoils.

At the end of the block, the parson walked into the one-room school, still under construction, and looked at Plantz, who sat staring at the naked woman lying on the rough wooden floor in a dark pool of blood. Upon a closer look, the parson saw the wooden handle of a wood chisel standing between her breasts.

"My my," said the parson, taking off his hat and running his fingers back through his long hair. "What have you done here?"

"Nothing, Parson," said Plantz. "She got ahold of it from those tools." He gestured a nod toward a pile of tools sticking up from a carpenter's wooden tool tray. "Before I could stop her, she held it against herself with both hands and lunged forward."

The parson stood in silence for a moment, then said, as if dismissing the incident, "Well, it's turning daylight. We're through here . . ." He let his words trail.

"Pretty gawddamn insulting," said Plantz, his eyes pinned on the naked lifeless body. "A woman does something like this, just when you're getting ready to enjoy yourself on her."

"You mean you didn't even touch her?" the parson said, looking more surprised. "You've been sitting here all this time, just staring at her?"

"Yes, that's what I've been doing," said Plantz, keeping his eyes on the woman's body. "Don't tell anybody."

"Of course not; I wouldn't," said the parson.

"You saw this coming, didn't you?" Plantz asked.

"No, I didn't see this coming . . . not *this,*" the parson replied.

"You saw something," said Plantz. "That's *why* you said *what* you said, that you were against me doing this. You saw something bad happening."

"That was about something different all together," said the parson, shaking his head slowly. "I've been seeing a woman from a long ways off bringing trouble down on us. But now that this has turned out the way it has . . . I don't think this is the woman I've been seeing."

"Then what *the hell* woman have you been seeing?" Plantz asked, getting impatient. "This is a *long ways off* for all of us."

"But this *ain't* her, because none of us died tonight," said the parson.

"So, you've seen some of us die, because of this woman from a long ways off?" Plantz pried. "How many of us?"

"I don't know," said the parson, clearly not liking to talk about it. "Maybe one, maybe all; I just don't know! I can see death in my premonition, but I can't see the ending." He paused, then put his hat back on. He tugged it down and looked again at the body lying on the rough plank floor. "Do you know what that means?" he asked with a grim expression.

"No, what does it mean?" Plantz asked, staring at the dead woman.

"If I can't see the ending, it means I'm the one who's going to die," said the parson.

Chapter 19

Julie noticed a difference in herself when she'd headed back for her farmland near Umberton; yet she could neither identify nor understand that difference. It was something she felt deep inside, something that Baines Meredith had made her see. *Baines Meredith . . .* She smiled to herself thinking about the aging gunman. Over the past few weeks she'd come to realize that Baines tried hard to be exactly the kind of person he admitted to being.

Baines didn't claim to be good, she'd come to understand. He only claimed to be right. He was a gunman, a hired killer, no more, no less; yet, in the darker matters of life and death, she found his logic to be sound. Somewhere deep in her core, she had hesitated to shoot Peerly that day in the barn, because her conscience had not given her permission to do so beforehand. Baines, as if speaking to her as a wise, all-knowing father, had given her that permission. He not only permitted her to kill, for her own sake; he demanded it of her.

She had gone into the livery barn armed, she

recalled, seeing clearly the picture of Nez Peerly taking the gun from her hand. "Armed but unprepared," Baines had pointed out. That was one mistake she would never make again.

She stopped long enough to look at the burnt remnants of the barn, and the deserted looking homesite from seventy-five yards away. "I'm home, Pa," she whispered, gazing over to the right of the house at the three wooden grave markers standing in the sunlight. Then she gave her horse a nudge, pulled the pack mule forward by the lead rope and rode on to the colonel's headstone.

Moments later she left the graves of her father, Shep Watson and her father's beloved wife, Laura Nell. She walked the short distance to the house, leading both animals to the hitch rail. At first she avoided looking at the burnt barn, or at the place on the ground where Plantz and his men had flung the bodies of her father, Shep and the Shawler boy.

But then she coaxed herself to look closely at that terrible spot, and even take a long look at the other spot a few feet away, where the militiamen had forced themselves upon her. For a chilling moment she could hear their voices, smell them, feel their rough cruel hands upon her tender flesh. An illness began to stir low in her stomach.

"It's only dirt," she told herself aloud, feeling her breath grow labored in her chest; yet, looking at the ground, the burnt barn, the many boot and hoofprints still thinly visible in the dirt, she wondered if she would ever be able to live here without the past haunting her day and night. *This might have been a mistake,* she heard herself telling

Baines Meredith in her mind. But Baines' image
only stared at her, his unyielding expression telling
her to stick tight to her plan and not waver.

She nodded and walked away, her fingers going
to her throat for a second, idly seeking to touch
the necklace that was no longer there. At the hitch
rail, she took down her saddlebags, drew a Winchester repeating rifle from the saddle boot and
patted the black's withers when he blew out a
breath and tried nudging her with his head. Beside
him, the pack mule scraped its hoof in the dirt and
swung its ears back and forth. "Don't worry," Julie
said to the restless animals. "You'll both get your
grazing in before nightfall."

Inside the house, she'd found things in good
order, the way Baines had left them when he'd
returned and buried her father and Shepherd Watson. The chairs were back around the table. The
furniture had been righted and the cupboard stood
back up against the wall. The broken china had
been swept up and discarded. Only those who knew
otherwise could say that anything had happened
out of the ordinary, Julie thought. She felt a slight
oncoming chill that caused her to back away for
a moment.

When the chill had passed, she took two sets
of rope hobbles from her saddlebags with nervous
hands, turned and walked back outside to the animals. She dropped the supplies from the pack mule
and the saddle and bridle from her horse. Using
the mule's lead rope she led them both away from
the hitch rail to a small stand of wild grass surrounding the woodlands.

Julie hobbled both animals and left them to graze beside a thin spring running along the edge of the woods. Returning to the house, she busied herself intentionally, to take her mind off things until she got used to being there. But instead of her apprehension settling, it only grew worse throughout the afternoon.

She knew she could let the horses graze all night without fear of them wandering off; yet, before darkness set in, Julie walked back to the animals, her rifle in hand and pistol in its holster, and led them back to the hitch rail to spend the night. Back inside the house, she hastily went from window to window closing the wooden shutters and bolting them. Then, in spite of the rear door being bolted, she took a chair and tipped it beneath the door latch.

She hadn't noticed her fearful behavior until she'd loaded an armful of kindling and small logs into the fireplace, and found herself hesitating to start the fire and prepare herself a warm meal.

This is nonsense, she heard a voice sounding very much like Baines Meredith's say inside her head. You're right; it is nonsense, she said to herself as if answering to that voice. She walked back to the fireplace, started the fire and cooked a meal of beans and jerked venison that she'd taken from her supplies. After she'd eaten her dinner, she poured her second tin cup of hot dark tea from a pot she'd boiled.

At length, she relaxed, with her boots off in front of the glowing fireplace, but she did so with both rifle and gun belt close at hand. "Go on about your business. Don't let them rattle you," Baines Meredith said somewhere between her consciousness and her dream state.

"I won't . . . ," she heard herself whisper in reply, drifting onto a guarded sleep, fully dressed. The last sound she heard was that of the empty tin cup falling from her hand and clattering lightly on the stone hearth.

The next thing she heard, upon awakening after sunrise, was the sound of birds circling and calling out to one another in the soft morning sunlight. Standing up, she stretched, ran her fingers back through her hair and looked all around her quiet, peaceful home. There had been nothing to fear in the night, only dark shadows, and darker memories.

But that did not mean that her fears from the night before had been unfounded, she reminded herself. Her fears were real; they would remain real as long as Plantz and his men were alive. "So, back to work," she told herself with resolve.

She swung the gun belt around her waist, buckled it, adjusted it and tied it down around her thigh. She slipped the big Colt up and down in the holster, keeping it loose and ready. She looked wistfully at the empty coffeepot hanging in the hearth. *First things first,* she could hear Baines say.

Glancing at the ray of sunlight through the shooting ports, she picked up the rifle and walked to the door with purpose, clearing her mind. She knew that this morning, like every morning for the past four weeks, there would be a dozen targets awaiting her out there. A dozen bottles, limbs or rocks—whatever could be found on hand—

would be waiting out there, waiting to kill her, she told herself somberly . . . if she didn't kill them first.

Nez Peerly and Delbert Reese had been back in Umberton only two days before restlessness began to get the best of them. The townsfolk in Umberton seemed to disappear from the town's only saloon when the two militiamen came in for a few drinks. Card games broke up quickly and the players drifted away, reminding themselves of other things they had to do.

"I say we take a couple bottles with us," Delbert said drunkenly, leaning on one elbow at the bar. "We ride out and meet the others along the trail, tell them everything is just like it always is here— dead and *stinking!*" As he spoke he turned a harsh glare toward a thin young bartender who shrugged, as if to say, *Don't blame me!*

"You want to send Plantz into a killing fit, that would be the best way I can think of to do it, Delbert," Peerly warned him. "Showing up drunk alongside the trail will get you killed quicker than a snakebite."

"We've scouted this place like he told us to," said Reese. "There's nothing going on here, same as always."

"Yeah," Peerly agreed. "The only thing different is that a sheriff is back in town . . . for now anyway." He raised a shot glass and tossed back a mouthful of fiery rye whiskey. "His name's Colbert Daltry. Rumor has it he was run out of Santa Fe without his trousers, in broad daylight, by a piano player who caught him fornicating with his wife."

"I have never seen a piano player try to kill anybody in my life," said Reese.

Peerly just stared at him blankly for a moment, then said, "We've got to ride out and check on the colonel's place. Make sure nobody's squatting there."

"Today?" Reese asked. "Damn, I hate doing anything but drink today. What's Plantz care about that place anyways?"

"I think he likes that place," said Peerly. "Now that the colonel's daughter is gone, don't be surprised if Plantz moves in there."

"What if she comes back?" Reese asked.

"She ain't never coming back," Peerly said with confidence. He poured himself another drink, grinned and raised his glass as if toasting himself. "I scared that woman so bad, she's still running!" He laughed. "Hell, she's somewhere in Canada by now, still ain't about to slow down."

"Yeah, I heard about it," said Reese, raising his glass in unison with Peerly's. "Here's to shy ladies everywhere."

The two drank their rye and set their glasses on the bar. "So," Peerly said, expectantly, staring at him.

"So *what?*" said Reese.

"*So,* are you ready to go?"

"Hell, I guess so," said Reese, taking the bottle off the bar to carry along with them. "It's a long ride. We leave here now or we'll never get there before dark."

"I know it," said Peerly, stepping away from the deserted bar. "We'll ride as far as we can, camp overnight and get there come morning."

They left the saloon, mounted and rode out of town, under the curious gaze of Sheriff Colbert Daltry, who stood watching them through his dusty office window. "That's right, look all around, you sneaking son of a bitch," the old sheriff whispered, seeing Peerly glance back along the empty street before the two rode out of sight. "Now that this war is over, I can't wait to see you step over the line."

He took his eyes away from the window and looked down at a pocket watch he'd reached down and pulled from his vest pocket. A half hour would be about a safe following distance, he decided, mentally marking the time of day and dropping the watch back into his vest.

Across the street, through the window of her boardinghouse, Constance Whirly had also watched the two militiamen leave town. Before turning away, she saw door to the sheriff's office open and Colbert Daltry step outside and close it behind him. "Please don't be coming here, you aggravating old bastard," she murmured under her breath.

But before she'd hardly gotten the words out of her mouth, the sheriff stepped into the street and started walking straight toward the boardinghouse. Well, she knew how to handle the situation, she told herself. She hurried to a hall closet, took out an apron and put it on quickly. Then she mussed her hair just a little, picked up a rug beater and stepped out onto the porch as the sheriff grew nearer.

"Evening, Constance," Colbert said, stopping a few feet away.

"Evening, Sheriff," Constance replied. She

looked toward the west and said, "Evening *already?* And I still haven't gotten all my work done."

Daltry gave her a look, as if he knew that she might be posturing. "Don't worry, Constance, I didn't come for coffee or to take up your time. I wanted you to know that I'm keeping an eye on those militiamen, like I promised you I would."

"Promised me, humph," said Constance. "If we had any real kind of law, I wouldn't need to get your promise. You'd have already had those vermin in your gun sights."

Daltry stared at her. "I've only been back three days, Constance. What do you expect me—"

"I don't expect nothing from you, Sheriff," said Constance, with a sting in her voice. "I never have."

The aging sheriff started to turn and walk away, the same way he had the last time she'd displayed such a nasty attitude toward him. But before leaving, he stopped and said, "I don't know what happened to you since I left to make my rounds to Spotsworth. If we were both still young and foolish, I'd swear there's been another man marking himself a spot here."

"Get out of here, Colbert," said Constance, "before I jerk in the welcome mat altogether."

"All right then, I'm going," the sheriff said. "But I don't deserve this kind of treatment."

Constance's anger relented. "Oh, Colbert. I know you don't. I just haven't been myself lately. I've had things on my mind." She managed to offer him a tired sliver of a smile. "I'll get over it. . . . Pay me no mind."

"I'm a pillar of patience, ma'am," the old sheriff said, touching his wide hat brim, "so long as I know you're not pining for another." He returned her slight smile, with a questioning gleam in his eyes.

"Go on with you," said Constance, waving him away with her rug beater and giving him an embarrassed look. "Who would have either of us old relics?"

"You forget your rug," said Daltry, smiling, nodding toward the rug beater. With his fingertips still to his hat brim, he turned and walked away.

Chapter 20

——◆——

Had Peerly and Reese only ridden another three miles the night before, they would have arrived at the Wilder farm shortly after dark. But being too drunk to ride any farther, Reese pitched sidelong from his saddle and laid along the edge of the dusty trail until Peerly managed to circle back unsteadily and plop down beside him. It was there the two made their camp.

Peerly awakened from his drunken stupor the next morning before daylight, his fingers spider-walking around in the dirt and finally wrapping around the whiskey bottle that had rolled away from him in the night. He took a drink, gagged and coughed and held his hand to his chest until his insides settled. "God Almighty, I'll never drink like that again," he vowed to unseen forces.

A few feet away, Reese snored.

Peerly stared back along the trail for a moment, something having caught his attention. He wasn't sure what it was, a sound, a glimpse of something in the grainy dark light. Whatever it had been, it caused him to reach over and shake Reese by his boot. "Wake up, idiot," he said in a harsh lowered voice.

Reese stirred, then sat up cursing.

"Shut up, gawddamn it," Peerly scolded him. "I believe we're being followed."

"Hell," Reese growled, "who'd be following us?"

"I don't know," Peerly said crossly, working his way up onto a knee and drawing his pistol from his holster. "But get your drunken ass up and let's get out of here. I get the willies, waking up with somebody on my trail."

"Damn, Nez," Reese complained, "it could be anybody on the trail this time of morning. It doesn't mean we're being followed."

"It doesn't mean we're *not* either!" Peerly insisted. "Now let's ride!" As an enticement he held the bottle out to Reese and swished it around.

"Oh God, obliged!" said Reese, snatching it and turning up a drink.

The two stood up, Peerly staring back with his gun in hand. They found the horses less than three yards away, grazing alongside the trail. Mounting quickly, they rode off along the trail and did not stop until they put over two miles behind themselves. When they did stop midtrail and look back, Reese asked, "Think it might be the army? They ain't happy about us not disbanding as quick as they wanted us to."

"Naw, it's not the army," said Peerly, still keeping his voice lowered. "They're too busy disarming every sonsabitch along the Mississippi to care about us ole boys right now."

"I'm starting to wonder if you seen or heard anything at all," Reese said. "Whiskey makes things happen that don't ordinarily happen."

Before Peerly could respond on the matter, a series of six pistol shots resounded steadily in the silent morning air. "There, *Delbert!*" Peerly said sarcastically. "Was that *real,* or was that *whiskey* shooting a gun?"

"Jesus!" Reese exclaimed, having jerked around in his saddle. "That's some serious shooting, is what that is."

"Yeah, that sounds like gun practice to me," said Peerly, "and it's coming from the colonel's place, just over the rise." He looked toward the sliver of sunlight on the eastern horizon, then turned his horse and gigged it forward. . . .

In her front yard, before walking forward and setting up six more targets, Julie opened the chamber of the big revolver—the devil's gun—that Baines Meredith had given her, and let six smoking shell casings drop to the dirt. She replaced them with fresh loads, then closed the chamber, slipped the revolver into her tied-down holster and stooped and picked up the warm casings.

Her first six targets had stood to the west, the same direction they had been standing the past three days at this time of morning, a silvery background of darkness partially concealing them. She made the rough one-foot-square tin targets from the blackened remains of the barn roof. She'd nailed each of them to a stick and poked the stick into the ground, placing them at a different angle from the house each day, to make sure she always fired from varied positions.

Shooting was not something she ever wanted to take for granted, Baines had told her. She thought about his words as she walked forward, gathered the tin targets and carried them to the other side of the yard. Every shot had to be fired as if it were meant to save her life. Someday it would be, she told herself. She stuck the target sticks into the ground in a staggered row, with the glare of rising sunlight standing behind them. Then she turned and walked away twenty-five paces and stood with her back to the tin targets.

She knew when she turned there would be only a split second before that glare of sunlight began affecting her vision. In that narrow instant she had to clearly see all the targets as one as her gun came up and began selecting each target individually. To keep her reflexes sharp, this morning she would do something different. She would take out three of the targets, but fire another shot into the second and third one before they hit the ground.

She calmed herself, let her arms hang limp for a moment longer, before making a sudden move. She turned, and her gun came up cocked and aiming. From left to right she quickly hit the first target with one shot. The second target she hit twice, firing quickly, the second shot hitting only an inch from the first while the target flew backward and fell to the dirt. With the third target she did the same, firing two shots almost as one, seeing each bullet spin the target in a different direction, showing her beyond a doubt that she'd hit it with both shots.

In the stand of woods, Nez Peerly and Delbert Reese had just walked their horses up into a place where they could see Julie standing, facing the two remaining targets. They hadn't seen the first three targets fly backward to the dirt. All they saw was Julie standing with the gun in hand, hanging at her side.

"I'll be damned, she's back," Peerly said quietly. "Can you believe this?"

"She's not only back," said Reese. "She's practicing her shooting."

"Yeah." Peerly grinned. "Practice is what she *better* be doing." He nodded at the two targets still standing and chuckled. "Looks like out of all five shots the only thing she hit was the air and the dirt."

"How's her being back here going to sit with Plantz if he's wanting this place?" Reese asked.

"Not very damn good," said Peerly. "Not very damn good at all. He's going to jump all over me for not getting rid of her like I said I would." He stared at Julie, watching in contemplation while she replaced the spent shell casings from her revolver. "Unless I can get rid of her once and for all before he gets back here."

After her shooting practice, Julie spent the next hour fixing breakfast and a fresh pot of coffee for herself. When she'd finished eating, she cleaned and put the dishes away, poured another cup of coffee and sat back down at the table. She drew the big revolver from her holster, dismantled it onto a soft cotton cloth and began cleaning it, one part at a time. She did not hear the soft boot steps creeping along the front porch until a creaking board caused her to snap her eyes up from the dismantled pistol and freeze, listening intently, realizing that for the first time since she'd arrived, she had failed to lock the front door.

Outside, a thumb reached across a gun hammer and cocked it slowly, quietly. From the table Julie heard another soft, creaking footstep on the porch. Her eyes went to the rifle she'd leaned near the fireplace. She began to make her move just as the door opened a crack, letting in a slanted ray of early-morning sunlight. She hurried. Could she do it? Could she make it in time? Her thoughts raced; so did her actions.

The door swung slowly, all the way open. *"Whoa!"* said Sheriff Daltry, both hands going up, gun and all, at the sight of the rifle swinging up in the woman's hands, pointed at his chest from across the room.

"Your next move will be your *last* one," Julie said with harsh clarity.

"Yes, ma'am! I realize that!" said the sheriff, speaking quickly. "Please don't shoot! I'm a lawman, doing my job! I followed two militiamen here. I saw animals in the corral! I knew the place was supposed to be abandoned!"

Julie did not breathe any easier. She kept the rifle to her shoulder and said, "Lower the pistol at arm's length and let it fall to the floor."

Daltry frowned but did as he was told, settling down with a deep breath. He raised his hands chest high again after the pistol made a thud on the floor planks. "There now, ma'am, see? I ain't trying to cause you any trouble. Allow me to open my duster; I'll show you my badge."

Julie nodded calmly and kept her position, seeing

the sheriff's tin badge come into view on his chest as he slowly opened his faded riding duster. "If you be Miss Julie Wilder, Mrs. Constance Whirly at the boardinghouse told me everything that happened to you whilst I was gone on my rounds."

"You're Colbert Daltry," said Julie. It was not a question; Constance had mentioned the sheriff by name while Julie stayed with her.

"I want you to know how sorry I was to hear about the colonel," said Daltry, "and about having something like that happen in a town under my jurisdiction." Even as he realized that this young woman had heard of him, he saw no gesture from her to allow him to lower his hands.

"Step inside, Sheriff," said Julie. "Close and latch the door behind you."

"Yes, ma'am," said the sheriff.

While he turned and ran the big bolt forward, Julie asked, "You said you're trailing two militiamen?" As she spoke she nodded at the gun lying on the floor.

"Yes, ma'am," said the sheriff. He stooped, picked up his pistol, then turned, closed and latched the door. "I followed their morning tracks to the tree line, after I heard shots coming from here." He nodded in the direction of the sparse woodlands. "Don't get spooked, ma'am, but those two murdering cowards were watching you this morning."

Julie only nodded slowly. She lowered the rifle halfway. "Did you recognize them?" she asked.

"Oh, yes. It was Nez Peerly and Delbert Reese. Both rode under Ruddell Plantz." He lowered his voice as if to keep their conversation between the two of them. "Miss Constance told me these are the ones who killed the colonel and did what they did to you. She described your horse . . . the same buckskin Peerly's riding. I figure I'll never make a charge stick on them for what they done to you and your pa, or the Shawlers. But maybe I can catch them for something else they do."

Julie lowered the rifle the rest of the way. "Obliged for you trailing them, Sheriff. I know there's nothing the law can do for me and my situation. I'm not expecting anything from you."

"I know you've got no reason to think you'll see justice done for the colonel or yourself. But if you write out a complaint against these men, I'll stay on their tails from now on, until I get something on them, or die trying."

"I'm not making a complaint, Sheriff," Julie said in a calm tone. "I know you mean well . . . but after that complaint gets made, you'll be riding off on your rounds again, and I'll be here facing Plantz and his men all alone." She offered a tired and tolerant smile. "Obliged, but I think I'd better leave things as they are. I'll never know for sure who did what things were done here. I expect that's just the Lord's will."

The sheriff gave her a questioning look, noting the pistol dismantled on the table. "Miss Julie, you ain't out to take justice into your own hands, are you?"

"No, Sheriff, of course not," Julie said quietly.

"Because I heard all the shooting going on out there," he probed.

"Yes, I am practicing," said Julie. "But I can't shoot anybody. Ask Constance what happened between me and Peerly in the livery barn."

"She told me." Daltry looked embarrassed for Julie. "I suppose you ain't going to be out for vengeance at that."

"Not me," said Julie, wearing a poker face. "Plantz and his men have no worries about me coming after them. I just want to come back here and live in peace."

"That's an unusual attitude, Miss Julie," said the sheriff. "But I expect that's the best way to look at it, all things considered."

"This is how I want to leave things," said Julie. She leaned the rifle against the table. "I still have some hot coffee here; may I tempt you with a cup?"

The sheriff grinned and swept off his battered, sweat-stained hat. "Yes indeed, ma'am. Consider me tempted."

Chapter 21

Beneath a hot, noonday sun, Nez Peerly jacked a round into his rifle chamber and laid the gun alongside his arm in the tall grass on a rise overlooking the trail toward Umberton. He sipped tepid water from a canteen and sweated profusely beneath his hat brim. "I've quit drinking for the rest of my *natural* life," he said hoarsely to Reese, who lay flat on his back in the grass, his hat sitting over his face.

"Why don't we just go on back to Umberton and get enough whiskey to make us well?" Reese responded.

"Did you just hear me?" Peerly said in a scorching tone of voice. "I *quit,* gawddamn it!"

"All right, you *quit, gawddamn it,*" said Reese, half mocking Peerly. "That don't mean *I* have. I'm whiskey sick, and I need to get well, quick as I can."

"We won't be long," said Peerly. "He has to come this way back to town, unless he wants to ride far the hell out of his way." He capped the canteen and laid it aside. "I ain't letting this chance slip past me. He was out there talking to that woman. There's no telling what they've cooked up for us."

"Are you sure this ain't all about being able to tell Plantz that the Wilder woman is back, without you looking bad?" He spoke without raising his hat from over his face.

Peerly gave him an evil look. He raised his rifle and aimed it at the side of his head under the hat. Slipping his finger into the trigger guard, Peerly eased his thumb over the rifle hammer. But then he got his rage under control and lowered the rifle.

"Hmmm? Is it?" Reese asked, raising his hat from his face and looking over Peerly just as the rifle barrel turned away from him.

Peerly only grinned, gave a little chuckle and said in a friendly voice, "You're a lucky sonsabitch, Delbert. Has anybody ever told you that?"

"A time or two, I reckon," said Reese. He lowered the hat back over his face. "Let me know when you see him coming . . . I'll back your play."

"If you're going to back my play, you best get ready to do it," said Peerly. "I see his hat bobbing up over the rise right now."

Reese jerked the hat from over his face and turned onto his side, facing Peerly. "All right, what do you want from me?"

"Crawl around through the grass and get on the other side of the trail from me," said Peerly. "Make sure you keep out of my gun sights."

"You bet," said Reese, scurrying away on his belly through the tall grass.

Peerly watched the old sheriff ride up into sight,

coming at him along the trail. Picking up his rifle
again, he wiped sweat from his forehead and waited
until Daltry was less than fifty yards away and still
closing. "Time to die, Daltry, you wife-mongering
old turd," he whispered, as if he took personal offence at the rumor he'd heard about the old sheriff
being chased out of Sante Fe.

Daltry had only seen the two sets of hoofprints
the first mile coming back from the Wilder farm.
Once the prints ran off south, he decided he'd done
all the trailing he could for the time being and
stayed on the trail toward Umberton. He could not
have known that the two militiamen had swung
wide intentionally, to make him think they were
gone from the trail. But then they had ridden back
and set up their ambush.

Without concern Daltry had been riding along at
an easy gait, deciding how to tell Constance something about the day's events that might soften her
bristly attitude toward him and get him back on her
good side. He knew Baines Meredith had stayed at
the boardinghouse while he'd been off making his
rounds. Knowing Baines, and well, to be honest,
he thought, knowing Constance too, he had a pretty
good idea there had been some—

His thoughts stopped abruptly when the impact
of Peerly's rifle shot snatched him up from his saddle and hurled him backward onto the hard ground.

Both Peerly and Reese lay silent for a moment
listening to the sheriff's horse's hooves pound away
from them along the trail.

"Is he dead?" Reese called over in a hushed
tone. He remained hunkered down in the grass.

Peerly called out to the sheriff, "Hear that, Sheriff Daltry? My pard wants to know if you're dead or not. What say you?"

"Oh, God . . . Oh, God . . ." the wounded sheriff began to repeat in a weak rasping voice, as if reciting a death chant.

"Sounds like he's mighty damn near it to me," Peerly called out to Reese, in an almost playful tone. Standing from amid the plains grass, he walked carefully toward the downed sheriff, rifle in hand. "There's something I always wanted to ask you, Daltry," he called out, feeling bolder once he saw the sheriff's arms spread out, his hands empty and a spewing gout of blood rising and falling from the large hole in his chest. "Is it true, that story about you and the piano player's wife?" He jacked a fresh round into his rifle chamber.

"I have . . . never been to Sante Fe," the dying sheriff gasped. "Is that . . . why you . . . done this?"

Peerly shrugged. "Not *just* that. What did you and that Wilder woman have to say about me and my pards? I expect she's hell-bent to have us all hanged, after all we done to her?" Peerly liked the idea of admitting what he'd done to the dying lawman, knowing there was nothing he could do about it.

Daltry shook his head. "She . . . don't want trouble. Said she wants . . . to live . . . in peace."

"Aw, now, that's real touching." Peerly grinned. "Hear that, Reese? The poor woman wants to live in peace. Let bygones be bygones. Turn the other cheek, I bet. Love her tormentors, the way the good book says."

"Leave her . . . alone," Daltry pleaded. "She can't . . . hurt you."

I know she can't *hurt* us. I saw her shoot," said Peerly. Laughing, he stepped in closer, stooped down and riffled through the sheriff's trouser pockets. All the dying sheriff could do was watch his money, an old pocket knife and some rolled-up fishing string go into Peerly's greedy hand, then into his pocket. "I'm thinking if she's so obliging, not wanting to put the law on us, maybe she half liked what we did to her."

"Peerly . . . leave the poor woman alone . . . you cowardly little snake," the sheriff wheezed.

"Now you've hurt my feelings, Daltry, calling me all kinds of names," Peerly said, his smile going away. "When me and Reese go visit that woman, we'll be sure and tell her it was you who invited us there."

The dying sheriff's hand tried to crawl to the gun on his hip. But Peerly clamped a boot down on his wrist, pointed the rifle down only inches from his forehead and pulled the trigger.

"Why didn't you let me do that?" Reese asked, walking up beside him. "I wanted to help."

"Why wasn't you right up here where it was all going on?" Peerly responded.

Reese only shook his head, having no answer worth giving. "Think it's true about that woman? I mean about her not wanting any trouble?"

"Yeah, it's probably true," said Peerly. "She scares awfully easy."

"So, are we going to leave her alone?" Reese asked.

"Hell no," said Peerly. "If she's this easy, I plan on going to visit her any damn time I feel like it." He jacked a fresh round into his rifle chamber, turned and walked back toward his horse. "Drag him off the trail if you want to do something to help," he called back over his shoulder. "And hurry the hell up; we've got drinking money to spend."

Shortly after the sheriff had left her house, Julie finished cleaning and reloading her revolver. She checked the rifle and walked to the horse and the mule standing in the half-fallen corral she had patched up with some scraps of timber and fence wire. She saddled the horse and turned the mule loose to graze unhobbled while she was gone. Filling her canteen at the spring, she closed the house without locking it and rode the black to the spot in the woods where Daltry said he'd seen Peerly and Reese.

After only a moment of deliberation, she nudged the horse forward and followed the two sets of hoofprints off in a wide half circle that she began to suspect would lead her back to the trail toward Umberton. Once she saw that she'd been right, she got a sinking feeling in her stomach. Then, at the point where the tracks rejoined the trail she saw Daltry's horse wandering amid the tall grass and knew that her bad feelings had been well-founded.

She collected the horse by its reins and saw the spray of blood on its rump. "Easy, boy," she said, settling the animal when it reacted to having a strange hand on its reins. She roamed back and forth alongside the trail until she saw a wide smear of blood where the sheriff's body had been dragged off the trail and out of sight. She stepped down and followed the blood, leading both horses behind her.

When Julie finally stopped short to keep from stepping on the dead sheriff, she stooped down, looked at his pale, lifeless face and murmured, "God bless you, Sheriff, you did the best you could."

She stood up, took down her canteen and then sat in the tall grass, sipping from the canteen until the afternoon sun had dropped low in the west. If she made a camp overnight. she could ride into Umberton before noon the next day. Or, if she pushed hard, leading the dead sheriff across his saddle, she could ride in tonight after dark.

After considering her choices, she stood up, capped the canteen, and went about the task of raising the limp body upward and over the saddle. After a struggle, she felt the body slide over the saddle and hang there limply until she took a rope from the sheriff's saddle horn and tied the sheriff securely in place. With her mind made up in favor of the darkness, she stepped up into her saddle. Holding the reins to the sheriff's horse, she rode on. . . .

Two hours ahead of her on the trail, Peerly and Reese rode into town just as the sun began to sink in the western horizon. By the time they'd taken their horses to the livery barn and handed them over to Merlin Potts, darkness had taken over the evening sky.

"Are we going to be having any trouble out of you tonight, old man?" Nez Peerly asked the livery tender, grabbing him roughly by his shirt front. He remembered the day he and Kid Kiley had tried overpowering Julie Wilder in the big livery barn.

"I—I only do my job, boys!" said Potts, looking frightened. "I try not to go meddling in any-body's business!"

"See to it you mean that," said Reese, pointing a finger in the old man's face. "You don't know me. I'll gut hook you if you do *meddle* in my business."

Peerly turned the old man loose with a shove and said as the two turned to leave, "See to these horses like they're your own. We'll pay you when we come back for them."

"Yeah, or sometime *real soon.*" Reese grinned.

"Cheap bastards," Potts swore under his breath as they walked away.

Stepping through the saloon doors, Peerly saw three townsmen look at him and Reese and cut their drinking short. "Don't nobody walk out that door on us, gawddamn it!" Peerly warned. "I'm damned tired of seeing every sonsabitches' back-side the minute we come in here to get ourselves a little toot." He spread his arms and herded every-body to the bar. "Besides, the drinks are all on *you* unless me and Reese here say otherwise. Anybody unhappy with that?" He glared from one drinker to the next.

At the end of the bar, Councilman Oscar Bales said under his breath to the barkeeper, Jim Addi-son, "Their attitudes worry me. These two have been up to no good; mark my words."

"Yeah, they act like they know there's no one around to rein them in," said Addison. He wiped his hands on a towel and headed away along the bar to serve the two militiamen.

"Set up a bottle of that *Philadelphia* whiskey that

you keep for the town councilmen, and two glasses without fly specks on them."

The bartender gave Bales a *what-can-I-do* look, reached under the bar, brought up a bottle of whiskey and pulled the cork. He set the bottle on the bar in front of the two and produced two shot glasses as if out of thin air.

"Now, get out of here and give us some room." Peerly sneered, snatching out the wad of money he'd taken from Sheriff Daltry's pockets and slapping it atop the bar.

"Yeah, we've got some serious drinking to do," said Reese.

Chapter 22

Constance Whirly had stayed up way past her usual bedtime. She stood looking cautiously out a front window toward the sound of sporadic gunfire and wild laughter coming from the direction of the saloon. *Where in the hell are you, Colbert?* she asked herself, getting more and more concerned that she hadn't heard anything from the sheriff since he'd left town the day before. One thing was for certain, he wasn't within hearing distance, she told herself. Sheriff Colbert Daltry would never stand for this sort of drunken behavior.

When she heard a sudden knocking at the back door, she turned with a slight gasp. Startled at first, she quickly collected herself, picked up the oil lamp from a table beside the window and hurried through the house, saying aloud, "It's about damn time, Colbert . . . you worry a person to death."

At the sight of Julie on the back porch, Constance was surprised, yet now even more concerned. "Julie Wilder! Get in here!" she said. "There's fools roaming the streets with guns!"

"I know," said Julie, stepping inside with a grim look on her face.

"What on earth brings you back here? I thought you might never leave Colorado." She gave Julie a look full of curious speculation. "Did you find Baines Meredith where he said he lived?"

"I did," said Julie. "I've been living there with him these past few weeks."

"Oh, I *see*," said Constance, with a trace of a wicked grin.

"It's not like you think, Constance," Julie said. "He taught me some things he thought might come in handy, if I ever came back to Umberton."

Constance took on a serious look. "And now, here you are." She studied Julie's eyes closer, saw her clouded brow and asked, "What's wrong, Julie? I see that something bad has happened. Is Baines all right? Because if something has happened to—"

Julie saw the fear in Constance's eyes and cut her off quickly. "Baines is fine, Constance," she said, taking both the woman's hands and holding them firmly. It's Sheriff Daltry . . . I know how close you said the two of you were."

"*Were?*" Constance's eyes widened; she picked right up on Julie's choice of words.

"He's dead, Constance," said Julie. "I—I found his body along the trail on the way here. He's been shot dead."

"Oh no, Colbert!" Constance sobbed into her hands. "I knew it, I just knew it." She shook her head and spoke to him into her trembling cupped hands. "You old fool, I just know you did something stupid and got yourself killed."

"I brought his body here," said Julie. "Forgive me. I didn't know where else to take him."

Calming her grief, Constance breathed deep and said in a crushed voice, "No, dear, you did right. This is where the poor man belongs. I'm the only person he's ever been close to here. I'll see to his arrangements." She sniffled, drew a kerchief from her robe pocket and touched it to her nose. "Can I see him?"

"Are you sure you want to?" Julie asked gently.

"Yes, I'm sure," said Constance.

Julie picked up the lamp Constance had set on the long kitchen table. She reached out, opened the rear door and ushered Constance out and down to where she'd left the two horses tied to the back fence.

After only a few seconds of staring at the dead sheriff, Constance turned to Julie and said, "He left here yesterday tracking two of Plantz's men. They're the ones who did this. Those murdering bastards!" She clenched her fists in rage. "I hope you came back here to kill these sonsabitches! I hope whatever Baines has taught you is enough for you to—"

"Shhh," said Julie, hearing Constance get louder with each word. "We don't want anybody to know what we're saying here." She took Constance by her slim shoulders. "One thing Baines taught me is to keep my intentions to myself. These men masked their faces. I'm masking my intentions."

"I'm afraid I don't understand," said Constance,

sniffling again. "Is Baines coming to help you kill these men?"

"No, I'm on my own," said Julie. "That's why I can't afford to make my intentions known."

Constance looked disappointed. "Are you going to face these men alone?"

"No," said Julie, "all I want to do is live in peace. I don't want any trouble. Can you understand what I'm telling you?" She held Constance firmly by her shoulders, staring into her eyes.

Constance looked confused and shaken. "No, I suppose I don't, Julie. You're making no sense at all."

"Then, you'll just have to watch what happens and keep quiet," Julie said. "Just remember, if anyone asks, I didn't come back here looking for any trouble with anyone, all right?"

"All right," said Constance, nodding, yet with a look of uncertainty.

"Good," said Julie. "I'll leave the sheriff with you. You can contact the barber and make his funeral arrangements come morning."

"Who should I say brought Colbert's body here?" Constance asked. "Is it going to be all right to use your name?"

"Yes, I want you to tell him I found the sheriff along the trail. Make no secret of it. I want the militiamen to know I'm back, that I found the sheriff."

"I hope you know what you're doing, Julie," Constance said in a warning tone.

"So do I, Constance," Julie replied.

All of the townsmen had left the saloon when Julie walked in and crossed the floor to the bar.

She took off her leather riding gloves, shoved them down behind her belt and looked back and forth along the empty bar. At the far end of the bar Delbert Reese stood alone, staring back at her with a drunken smirk.

"Say, I know you," Reese said with a strange whiskey-fueled gleam in his red eyes. "You're the colonel's daughter. Come over here; I want to buy you a drink," he snickered knowingly. "I figure I owe you one."

"Why would you *owe* me one, Mister?" Julie asked in a clipped tone. "I've never seen you before in my life, have I?" She gave him a cold stare and refused to take her eyes off him.

Finally Reese had to shrug and say in a relenting voice, "Hey, I'm just being neighborly."

Only then did Julie look away from him and at the bartender who had stood up from a stool and faced her across the bar. "Pay him no mind, Miss Wilder, ma'am," the bartender said quietly, knowing her name even though she had never stepped foot into the saloon until tonight.

"I'll have a mug of beer," Julie said, shoving her hat brim up on her forehead.

Looking all around the empty saloon, the bartender said with a sigh, "Ordinarily we don't serve womenfolk at the bar, Miss Wilder. But this one and his friend have run everybody off for the night. If you can stand being around them, I'll buy you a beer myself."

"Obliged," said Julie. She jerked her head toward Reese, and asked, "Is that who was doing all the shooting in the street a while ago?"

"Yes, ma'am, him and his friend Nez Peerly," the bartender said. As he spoke he picked up a clean beer mug, stuck it under a tall tap handle and filled it until foam spilled over its edge. "I kept hoping the sheriff would step in any minute and crack both their heads," he said. He stood the foaming mug of beer in front of her. "But I get a sneaking suspicion they know he ain't coming around to stop them." He gave Julie a grim, knowing look.

She didn't respond, not knowing this man any better than she knew the rest of the townsmen. For all she knew she could be talking to one of her worst enemies. "Where's his friend?" she asked, hooking her fingers into the wet beer mug handle. She turned up a long sip of cool beer.

"He went out back to the jake," said the bartender. "I expect he got back there in the stench, heaved his guts up and passed out."

Julie only nodded. She took another long deep drink of beer, then another, this one almost draining the mug.

"Well now, that's some thirst you brought with you, ma'am," the bartender mused. He picked up the mug and started to reach it over under the tap.

"One was all I wanted, thank you," Julie said. She saw Reese watching, listening from the end of the bar. "Now I need to get my horse over to the livery barn and get him stalled for the night."

"You'll be tending your own animal tonight, ma'am," said the bartender. "Ole Merlin rode out of here the minute all the shooting started. I expect he'll spend the night under the stars somewhere."

"Then I best get started," said Julie, her voice raised enough for Reese to hear her. "Obliged again for the beer."

"You're most welcome, Miss Wilder," said the bartender, watching her turn and walk out the door.

Listening to Julie's boot heels resound across the boardwalk until she stepped down to the hitch rail, Delbert Reese grinned slyly to himself, raised his shot glass and tossed back a mouthful of whiskey. He waited a few contemplative minutes, then said as he picked up a cork and stuck it into a whiskey bottle, "When my pard gets back, tell him I'm taking myself a for little walk . . . Need to do some thinking."

"Sure thing, I'll tell him," said the bartender, but under his breath he growled, "I hope he fell down the jake and drowned."

At the livery barn, Julie opened the door wide without looking back to see if anyone had followed her. She led the black into the barn and inside the first empty stall she came to. Using the grainy light of a half-moon through the open door, she turned and closed the stall without taking the saddle off her horse.

From halfway up the street, Reese saw a lantern come to life and glow outward through the open barn door. He stared at Julie from within the darkness as she appeared at the door for a moment and seemed to stare straight at him. Was that an invitation? Reese asked himself. "Damn right it was," he answered himself under his breath, "whether she knew it or not."

Drawing closer, he watched her close the door

and step back. But he noted to his satisfaction that she had not closed it all the way. "Woman, you are toying with me, aren't you?" he murmured. Taking a deep breath to help clear his head a bit, he walked forward, his whiskey bottle hanging loosely in his hand.

At the partially open door, Reese looked inside and saw Julie step over and pitch a fork full of fresh hay into the horse's stall. He grinned to himself again, seeing her gun belt hanging on a wall peg, eight feet away.

"Now, that is plumb dangerous," he said to himself, feeling bold all of a sudden. He shoved the door open, stepped inside and slung it closed behind him.

Julie turned, looking startled. Yet she remained silent, giving a glance toward her gun belt, hanging just out of arm's reach.

"Evening again, ma'am," Reese said, an evil shine to his red-rimmed eyes. "It looks like we just can't *escape* one another." Noting her glance toward her gun belt, he said confidently, "Put the thought out of your mind. I heard all about you and guns." With his free hand on his pistol butt, he gestured loosely with his whiskey bottle toward the pitchfork in her hands.

"Mister, I don't want any trouble," Julie said.

"So I heard," said Reese, remembering the dying sheriff's words. He knew the young woman was harmless, with or without a gun. It didn't matter. "You can just drop the fork where you're standing; get over here and make yourself to home. I'm taking me another taste of you right here and now."

A calmness seemed to have suddenly come over the woman, he noted. "*Another* taste?" Julie asked, letting the pitchfork drop to the straw-covered floor. "You admit that you are one of the ones who killed my father . . . who raped me?" she asked bluntly.

"Did I say that?" Reese replied, looking surprised at himself. He took a quick blurry-eyed look around as if to see if anyone could hear him. "Ooops!" he laughed, satisfied that they were alone. "Just between the two of us," he said, keeping his voice lowered and taking a step forward, "you didn't mind it . . . except when the going got a little rough, did you?"

Julie didn't reply. Instead she reached back and shoved her hands down into her hip pockets. She recalled Baines Meredith's dark eyes. *There's more ways to kill a man than with a gun, you know . . .*

"I thought not." Reese grinned, taking her silence as some sort of admission. Stepping a foot closer, he stopped beside a center post where the lantern hung on a high peg. He sloshed the bottle of whiskey.

"I don't want any trouble," Julie repeated. Yet her words carried no sign of fear, or of uncertainty. Her hands were calm behind her, as if resting and ready.

"Neither do I," said Reese, "if it makes you feel any better. See, I wasn't the one who started all that rough stuff on you. That was Plantz, Peerly and a couple of others. All's I did was what any red-blooded normal man would do. I took what was laid before me." He held the whiskey bottle out toward her, a peace offering. "I figure we ought to keep this as friendly as we can, don't you?" He looked her up and down. "I know you don't want to get hurt. So get those clothes off; don't make me have to slap you around."

"Plantz, Peerly and a *couple of others?*" Julie asked coolly. "Who were the others? All of them," she asked pointedly.

"Hey, I'm the one in charge here," said Reese, his right hand drawing his pistol from its holster and shaking it at her. "Now, start doing like I told you! Step out of your trousers!"

"Their names," Julie demanded. Seeing him start to take another step, she said, "Stop where you are. Tell me everybody's name."

"Well, let me see," said Reese, feigning serious thought on the matter and taking another step toward her in spite of her warning. "There was the parson, Plantz, myself, Peerly, Kiley, Macky . . . That's enough for now. If you're real sweet to me, I'll tell you some more when I'm finished." He started forward, this time as if he would not stop until he'd accomplished what he'd come there to do.

"You're finished now," said Julie. Her hands came from behind her back. Her right hand immediately twirled a bolo quickly into motion, making the apparatus hard to see clearly.

"What the—?" Reese squinted, trying to get a better look at the whirring balls spinning in a dull blur of lantern light. "Are you craz—" His words stopped as the sound of the rawhide bolo strips whistled through the air and wrapped like angry snakes, tightly around his throat.

"I *will* have those names," Julie said coldly,

stepping to the side and watching Reese fall to his knees, his fingers dropping both the whiskey bottle and revolver to the straw-piled floor.

"Arrhhhg!" Reese choked and gasped, his face turning red-purple in only seconds. His hands pulled and tugged at the rawhide strips, but they were too tight to be loosened from the front of his throat. His widened eyes looked up at Julie, pleading.

"Ready to tell me those names?" Julie asked calmly, as if it mattered little to her if he lived or died.

Reese could barely nod his head, but he tried hard to do so, his fingers still grasping in vain at the rawhide strips.

"Are you sure?" Julie asked, taking her time, seeing his face lose its redness and turn more and more purple right before her eyes.

Reese gagged, trying desperately to nod his head.

Julie stepped behind him and hastily untwirled the bolo lines from where they had spun themselves around one another at the center of his neck. "There," she said, staying behind him, "start talking." She reached down, picked up his revolver, cocked it and stuck it against the side of his head.

"I—I— Jesus, woman!" Reese rasped, his voice all but gone. He gagged and coughed and rubbed his red-striped throat. "Don't go doing something you'll be sorr—"

Julie reached down and jerked on the bolo, tightening it around his throat. "The rest of the names," she said in a controlled rage.

"All right, please," Reese said hoarsely. "The

others were Carl Muller, Buell Evans and Clarence Conlon."

"Describe them to me," she demanded.

"All right. Conlon is a big hefty fellow, looks like a bull, wears a full beard . . ."

Julie listened intently as he described each man. She carefully placed the faces and descriptions to the names, committing each man to memory. In her mind it was the same as reaching out and pulling off their masks one at a time until she saw each man clearly. There was relief in knowing the names of the men who'd assaulted her; yet hearing those names also caused her stomach to crawl.

She jerked the bolo again when he'd finished talking. "And that's all? You're sure?" As she spoke she stepped away behind him and swung out a long rope she'd tied around a thick rafter beam on her way to the saloon.

"I swear to God," Reese pleaded. "If there was more, I'd say so! But that was all of us!"

She stepped forward, dropped a noose over his neck; then stepped back, pulling on the rope, drawing it tighter over the beam. "Hey, what the hell!" Reese protested in his hoarse voice.

Backing away two more steps, Julie said, "All right, on your feet. I'm through with you."

"Then let me go!" said Reese, his hands going to the noose around his neck. "What's this, a noose? You're going to hang me? I don't believe I'll allow it!"

Julie said in an almost soothing tone, "I'm not going to hang you, for what you did to me." She rolled out a two-foot nail keg and upended it beneath the rope. "Stand up on this barrel for safekeeping until I ride out of Umberton. I told you I wanted no trouble, and I meant it."

"Woman," said Reese, "if you *really* don't want trouble you best think long and hard about leaving me stranded here, in *shame,* in front of my pard when he comes looking for me."

"Do it now!" Julie demanded.

"All right, damn it, take it easy!" he said, seeing and hearing Julie cock his revolver at his head. "I'm doing it, see?" He stepped up shakily onto the keg.

Julie pulled the slack out of the rope and dogged the end tight around a center post.

Stepping around in front of him, she said, "I told you I wasn't going to hang you for what you did to me." She reached out with her right foot and kicked the barrel from beneath his boots, leaving him thrashing, swinging and gagging in thin air.

"This is for killing my pa." She gave his struggling body a hard shove, making him swing as his hands clawed at the rope around his throat. "And for Shep Watson," she said, shoving him again, seeing dark urine spread down his legs as he choked and gagged and struggled to breathe. "And for poor Jeb Shawler . . . for all the Shawlers. For everybody else you've killed, you murdering son of a bitch."

She stepped back and stared into his red bulging eyes until his last frantic kick turned to a short dying twitch. She let out a deep breath, watching his big hands dangle lifelessly at his sides. "This is a start, Pa," she whispered. "Now I know who I'm looking for." She stepped forward, shoved Reese's revolver down into his holster, turned out the lantern and walked to the dark stall. In the cover of night she walked the horse out through the back door, stepped into her saddle and rode away.

Chapter 23

O n her way across the flatlands, a mile out of
Umberton, Julie eased her horse toward a
campfire glowing high among the tall grass, just
off the trail. When she got within range she saw
Merlin Potts' face in the firelight. He squatted
close to the fire, piling more wood onto the licking flames. A few yards away from him stood a
small one-horse wagon loaded heavily with
firewood.

Julie started to turn her horse away and ride
on, but as she did so, her horse made the slightest
nicker toward the crackling fire. As quick as a
whip, Potts sprang to his feet with a long stick in
his hand. "Who's out there?" he shouted.

"It's Julie Wilder, Mr. Potts," Julie called out,
seeing him give the stick a threatening swing back
and forth.

"Julie Wilder?" Potts said, easing the stick
down to his side at the sound of her voice. "When
did you get back here?"

"A little while back," Julie said, coming into view through the grass above her horse's knees.

"What are you doing out here in the middle of the night? Get on in here, out of that night air."

Stepping her horse in closer to the glowing dome of firelight, Julie said, "I didn't want to disturb you, Mr. Potts. I'm on my way home tonight."

"Tonight?" said Potts, tossing his stick to the ground and rubbing his palms on his trousers. "You can't ride all the way through to the colonel's place tonight. What if your horse founders, breaks a leg in a gopher hole?"

"I'm being careful," Julie said, turning her horse sidelong to him, looking down at his weathered face in the flicker of firelight. "Besides, I like riding on a night with a good moon overhead." She gestured up at a bright half-moon embedded in a sky full of starlight.

"Yeah, well, I'm here because I couldn't stand all the shooting, hollering and carrying on. I had to get out because of them two lousy gawddamned militiamen—pardon my language. The sheriff ain't around and they're going plumb loco."

"The sheriff has been killed, Mr. Potts," Julie said, deciding to tell him. She knew that soon enough everybody would know what happened to Colbert Daltry. "I found his body along the trail and brought him to town."

"Ole Colbert, killed?" Potts pondered it, peeling a worn-out flop hat from his head. "Well, I'll be whipped. Killed how?" he asked.

"Shot dead," said Julie. "It looks like somebody caught him in an ambush." She leaned her crossed wrists on her saddle horn and gave a slight nod toward town. "I left him with Constance Whirly; then I got out as quick as I could, seeing one of Plantz's men at the saloon."

"Them sonsabitches are the ones who killed him!" said Potts, getting angry. "You can bet both boots and your belt on that!"

"I believe you," Julie said, humbly, "but I don't like jumping to conclusions."

"Well, I've already jumped," said Potts. "That explains all the shooting and whooping it up. They knew nobody would be there to stop them. The gawddamned rotten lousy *sonsabitches!*" As he spoke his voice grew louder, until he appeared to be shouting at the militiamen in town.

"Take it easy, Mr. Potts," Julie said. "They can't hear you in town, but you never know who might be in listening distance. Your fire is awfully bright out here in the open."

"I've been tending fires all my natural life," Potts said coolly. "And you are far too tolerant of those night-riding bastards—pardon my language."

"I shouldn't have said anything, Mr. Potts," Julie replied.

But the old man continued. "After what they did to you and your pa, nobody would blame you if you shot them dead in the street like wild dogs!"

"I can't say for sure they did it," Julie offered.

"Ha!" said Potts. "They did it." He seemed to settle a bit and said, "Of course, nobody blames you for not retaliating. You being a woman and all, what could you really do against the likes of them?"

Julie offered him a tired, patient smile. "That's what I've been telling myself all along. 'What can I do?'"

Potts softened. "Well, let's not even talk about the bastards—pardon my language. Step down here and I'll fix us a hot pot of coffee. I ain't sleepy, no way."

"Obliged, Mr. Potts," said Julie, "but I best push on home. I'm avoiding Plantz's men any way I can."

"They've about scared you to death, haven't they?" Potts said in a soft, sympathetic tone.

"I just don't want any trouble," she said, the words rolling effortlessly off her tongue. She backed her horse and turned it, touching her fingertips to her hat brim.

In Umberton, two hours passed before Nez Peerly stood in the open rear door of the saloon, steadying himself against the doorjamb. "Jesus," he murmured, finally pushing off the jamb and staggering a bit on his way to the bar. At the bar, he looked back and forth blurry-eyed for Reese. Shaking his head he turned to the bartender and said, "Pour me a beer, to wash the spiders off my brain."

"Is that all it takes, a glass of beer?" the bartender asked, wearing a smug little grin.

Peerly gave him a wild harsh stare. "Get fresh with me, see how long it takes for me to kill you!"

"Sorry," said the bartender, snatching up a mug and sticking it under the tap. "Just offering friendly conversation."

Peerly grabbed the beer mug, sucked down a

long swig of cool beer and let a deep belch in the bartender's face. The bartender winced at the blast of hot breath. "Damn, that's better," Peerly said, sounding relieved. He took a shorter drink as the bartender stepped away fanning himself with a bar towel.

"I'm selling this place," the bartender murmured in disgust.

Looking back and forth again, Peerly asked, "Where's my pard?" as if he'd left Reese in the bartender's safekeeping.

"Your friend left here quite a while ago," the bartender replied. "Said he needed to do some thinking."

"It's about damn time he did some thinking," Peerly said in wry voice. "Which way did he go?"

The bartender stopped cold in his tracks, turned and said, "You know, somehow I missed that. I meant to follow him so I could report back—"

"Wise son of a bitch," Peerly growled, cutting him off. He snatched his beer mug from the bar and walked out into the empty street. "Reese!" he called out into the quiet night. He heard no response other than a dog who began an endless barking. "Reee*eeese!*" he bellowed louder in order to be heard above the barking.

"Shut up, gawddamn it!" a voice called out along a row of small cottages.

"Go to hell!" shouted Peerly. In a violent response, he drew his pistol and fired it in the direction of the cottages. A cat screamed loudly and sailed up over a fence. The barking continued.

"Where's the sheriff when we need him?" a woman called out angrily.

Addison, the barkeeper, stepped out and down onto the street a few feet behind Peerly, taking an interest.

"Reeeeeese! Answer me!" Peerly fired two more shots, these straight up into the night. Lanterns came alive in the dark windows. "I find you, I ought to shoot your big stinking toes off!" Peerly said to Reese as if he were standing beside him. He staggered forward, looking all around in the darkness; the bartender followed a few feet behind.

In moments, townsmen appeared in nightshirts and trousers, some holding lanterns, some holding lanterns and shotguns. A few followed Peerly along the street and alleyways. On their way toward the livery barn, Councilman Oscar Bales asked Councilman Bill Wilmens, "Who's lost, anyway?"

"One of our *esteemed* militiamen seems to have vanished tonight," Wilmens answered in a sarcastic voice. "As if we should give a damn," he added in a whisper.

Bales stopped short and tossed a hand. "Hell, if I'd known that, I wouldn't have pulled up my suspenders! I'm going home."

"Weren't you drinking with them earlier over at the saloon?" Wilmens asked.

"*Please, Bill,*" said Bales. "I have too much to lose associating myself with these scoundrels. I just happened to be in the saloon when they arrived. I left shortly after." Ahead of them Peerly walked into the livery barn, leaving the door open behind him.

"Sorry, I didn't mean to imply anything," he

said, coaxing Bales to continue walking with him. "Let's stick around long enough to see what's going on . . . Call it our duty as councilmen."

"Yes, well, there's *some* things we are not called upon to do," said Bales, walking along grudgingly.

From the livery barn door, Peerly staggered out with his gun drawn and pointed at the following townsmen. He wore a frightened, surprised look on his face. "Everybody freeze right there!" he shouted. "Any of yas tries to make a move on me, you're *dead!*"

"Good heavens, Nez," said Wilmens. "What's wrong? You look as if you've seen a ghost!"

"Real gawddamn funny, Wilmens!" said Peerly, fanning his gun back and forth from man to man. "I see what you sneaking bastards done to him! You ain't about to get the jump on me!"

"What's going on in there?" Bales asked, venturing forward a half step. "Is Reese in there?"

"Keep it up, Councilman!" shouted Peerly. "I'll blow somebody's head off! You know damn well he's in there. He's hanging deader than a skin full of sausage!"

"He's dead?" Bales asked.

"What did I say, gawddamn it!" Peerly shouted, barely in control of himself.

Bales, Wilmens and the bartender gave one another a puzzled look. Wilmens asked Peerly, "And you think *we* lynched him?"

Peerly kept the gun aimed and pointed, sweat pouring down his sobering face. His hands trembled. "The thought is damn sure crossing my mind," he said. "Somebody's sure put the hemp to him. Who the hell else would do it? You're the only ones around!"

"Wait a minute," said Wilmens. "Who's to say he didn't hang himself?" With his hands chest high, he ventured a step forward. "Has he been *despondent* of late?"

"He did say he was going for a walk and to do some thinking," said the bartender.

"There we have it," Bales offered. "He did some thinking . . . Decided to kill himself. I can see that happening."

"Thinking? Ha! Nothing ever bothered this stupid son of a bitch," said Peerly. "I'm getting out of here. Don't get near me; don't try to stop me. When I come back it'll be with Plantz and the rest of the militia!"

"There was a woman who came in," said the bartender, as if he'd been thinking too hard to have heard Peerly's threat. "The Wilder woman, Julie! She came in, drank a beer and left. I don't know if this means anything."

"What are you saying, barkeep?" Peerly asked. "That a woman did this to my pard?" He almost chuckled at the prospect of Julie Wilder having done it.

"I'm not saying she did anything," said the bartender, spreading his hands. "But she did come in while you were out back in the jake. I think I should mention it."

"She didn't have a damn thing to do with it!" said Constance Whirly, stepping forward in her house robe, a lantern raised in her hand. She glared hard at the bartender. "You ought to be ashamed of yourself, James Addison, casting suspicion on that poor woman after all she's been through. Your brother, the *doctor,* ought to hear how you're speaking. He's a *fine, decent* man . . . but listen to you."

"Constance, I'm sorry," said the barkeeper. "All I'm doing is bringing up the fact that she was here!"

"Then bring up this fact too," Constance continued. "That poor child is so scared of Plantz and his men she can hardly speak when they're around." Her eyes turned to Peerly with accusation. "And for a damn good reason, I have to say."

"Watch you mouth, old woman," Peerly warned. His gun hand had lowered some, and he seemed interested only in getting to his horse and getting out of town. "Me and Plantz and the others are still around. This town don't want to get on our bad side," he threatened, looking from one face to the next.

"See here, Nez Peerly, this is a terrible thing that's happened," Bales said, taking on his council-man tone of authority. "But let's not—"

"Shut up, you ball of spit!" said Peerly. He aimed his gun at Constance Whirly. "You! Old hag! Go get my horse from the hitch rail and bring it over here!"

Old hag . . . ? Constance stared at him with a bemused expression. "Go stick something sharp up your ass," she said.

"Please," said Bales, cutting in, "I'll go get your horse for you! Everybody hold on. Let's keep our-selves civilized!" He turned to a young boy standing among them and nodded toward the buckskin bay at the hitch rail out front of the saloon. The boy turned and ran to get the horse.

"If you had any decency, Nez Peerly," Constance said as she turned to walk away, "you'd go hang yourself beside that idiot, Reese."

"You might want to think about whose side you take, woman!" Peerly shouted at her back. "We've still got power across this blood lands!"

"*Power!* Listen to yourself, Nez Peerly," said Constance without turning to face him. "Yet, you're telling us we need to *side* with you, against a poor single woman whose only purpose is to *avoid* you rotten bastards."

"Why you!" Peerly raged. His hand clenched instinctively around his pistol butt. But the sight of shotgun barrels rising and the sound of hammers cocking caused him to keep himself in check.

"That's it, Peerly, you little worm," Constance called back to him. "Shoot me in the back. Show the world what a craven little coward you are."

Peerly looked back and forth, his face reddened with humiliation. "I shouldn't let her get to me like, huh? I mean, she's just a crazy old woman."

"That woman has friends in this town," Bales warned.

"Yeah, all of them are men," said Peerly, looking from face to face, "and I *know* how she got them."

"You're saying too much, Nez," Bales said just above a whisper.

Peerly turned to the boy who ran up leading the buckskin. Snatching the reins from the boy's hand, he swung up quickly into the saddle. "Plantz ain't going to like the way you've treated me. He's going to want to know more about what happened to Reese," he warned.

"All we can do is tell him what little we know," said Bales. "We had nothing to do with hanging Delbert Reese."

Chapter 24

Leaving Umberton, Peerly raced the buckskin bay along the flat trail, riding much too fast and recklessly in the darkness. At the sight of the glowing campfire, he slowed the horse and reined it off the trail. Thinking it might be Julie Wilder making a camp for the night, he eased down from his saddle and led the buckskin quietly through the grass until he saw the blanket-wrapped figure lying near the fire.

"Now I've got you all to myself," he whispered, stepping into the fire's glow, cocking the pistol in his hand. When he stooped down over the figure he stuck the gun down against the flop hat and said in a louder tone, "Make a move for your gun, woman, and I'll kill you right here and now."

"Woman?" said Potts, smelling the whiskey on Peerly even with a foot of distance and the flop hat between. "You're not just *blind drunk,* you're *blind,* period! Who the hell are you?"

"You old son of a bitch," Peerly said, realizing his mistake. He stood up and stepped back. "What are you doing out here?"

"I came out here to get away from all the racket you and your pard was making. "Now, gawd-damned if you ain't followed me!" He rolled up into a sit and rubbed his bearded face.

"Now I get it," said Peerly, keeping his gun pointed at Potts. "You killed Reese!"

"Killed Reese?" said the old man. "You mean Delbert Reese is *dead?*" He looked surprised for a moment, then said, "How'd the world ever get that lucky? What happened to him?"

"His body is swinging from a beam in the town livery barn," said Peerly, wondering if he could convince Plantz that this old livery-tender had killed Reese. No, he decided, there was no way Plantz would believe it. "Somebody hanged him."

Potts shook his head. "I'm not surprised some-body hanged him," he said. "But I am surprised they did it in the town barn."

Looking all around at the hoofprints Julie's horse had left on the ground, Peerly said, "That woman has been here, hasn't she?"

"Well, yes, she was. I invited her to stay, but she said she was going to push on all night."

"Yeah," said Peerly, now considering Julie as the person to hold up before Plantz, "I can see her hand in all this, the more I think about it."

"That poor scared woman?" said Potts. "I'd love to see you try to convince Ruddell Plantz she did it. He'd shoot you himself." Potts knew better than to push Peerly too far, but he saw that he still had some room. "When are you boys gonna learn to leave that poor woman alone? She's nobody you have to worry about."

"Who says I'm worried about her?" Peerly said. "And as far as leaving her alone, I ain't bothering her." He shrugged. "But I damn sure will, if she's the one who hanged Reese."

"How do you know he didn't hang himself?" Potts asked, knowing this was unusual, Peerly talking to him in a civil tone. He ventured a hand out, picked up his stick and stirred the embers of the fire. "Nobody ever *hangs* a person unless there's a lynch mob behind it. A person is too hard to handle, when they see a noose tickling the top of their head."

"A woman could talk Delbert Reese into eating his own boot," said Peerly, in reflection.

Potts shook his head. "That poor girl. I can see in her eyes that she's never had a good turn come her way in this life."

"Maybe she's never deserved a good turn," Peerly said, his tone turning harsh. "She's nothing but a whore."

"That woman, a whore?" Potts gave him an astonished look. "Where the hell did you ever hear something like that?"

"Her *mother* was a whore!" said Peerly. "The parson can tell you all about *her.* She was camp follower back when the colonel was soldiering."

"Well, even if her ma *was,* that doesn't mean this woman is," said Potts. "Besides, when it comes to whoring, who's the party at fault, the woman who sells, or the man who buys?"

"I got no time for this," Peerly said haughtily, catching himself engaged in a conversation with a livery-tender. "How long ago did she leave?"

"Who?" Potts said. But seeing Peerly give him a flat, cold stare, he said, "All right. She was here about two or three hours ago."

"Old man, I want you to realize that I could have killed you, out here, like this, nobody around. Who would have ever known about it?" He took a step back, uncocked his pistol and lowered it into his holster. "But since you've kept a civil tongue in your head, I'm going to let you live. How does that sound?"

Potts shrugged. "Obliged, I reckon." He continued stirring the stick in the fire. "I wish you'd leave that woman alone though. She's already sadder than a whipped pup over what happened to her."

"Yeah," said Peerly, thinking of the possibilities once he caught her alone, "but there's something I always liked about a sad woman."

Hearing Peerly step away, up into his saddle and turn his horse to the trail, Potts offered himself a thin smile, staring into the dancing flames, "Adios, Nez Peerly," he murmured.

At dawn, Julie set up her first six targets to the west of the house, the same as she'd grown accustomed to doing. This morning she felt the sting of having had very little sleep, being up most of the night on the trail. Yet, the shooting practice had to continue. On the ground a few feet away lay the bolo she'd used on Delbert Reese. Baines had been right. She could not have risked firing a shot and having the whole town gathering around the livery barn, not if she intended to continue wearing her

mask, she told herself. And so far the mask of
being a frightened helpless woman had served her
well. She wasn't going to give it up, not just yet.

Oddly, she told herself as she stepped away from
the targets to her usual distance, but the more she
wore the mask of being afraid, the less afraid she'd
become. The more she'd denounced trouble, to
Constance, to the sheriff or to anyone else who
would listen, the better she seemed to become at
handling it. *And killing?* Well, she thought, killing
was a terrible thing, wasn't it?

She raised the big revolver, checked it and lowered it loosely into her holster. Scanning the targets
from right to left, she let her eyes go across the
woods line. "Time to go to work," she said quietly
to herself.

At the woods line, in the same spot where he
and Reese had watched her shoot before, Peerly sat
with his rifle across his lap. He had ridden nonstop
throughout the night, continuing to push the buckskin bay dangerously hard and fast along the flatlands trail. But that didn't matter now, he told
himself, staring at the woman, her firm hips, her
breasts. He recalled the taste and the feel of her.

"And I like everything I remember of you, Miss
Julie Wilder," he whispered quietly, feeling his
hands tighten around the rifle stock.

In the yard, Julie drew the big revolver, not
quickly, but adequately. She raised the gun out at
arm's length, not firing from hip level the way she
usually practiced. Her first shot barely struck the
target, hitting it on its edge and causing it to spin
backward to the ground. Her second shot missed

her target altogether. He third shot was no better. Her fourth shot hit its target, but her fifth and six shots fell short and kicked up dirt.

From the woods line, Nez Peerly stepped out quietly and grinned to himself. Seeing Julie reach for reloads from her gun belt, he quickly raised his repeating rifle to his shoulder and fired round after round as he walked toward her from the woods. Julie watched the targets fall to the ground with each shot. Then she turned, startled at the sight of Peerly's rifle pointed at her.

"Why don't you drop that gun, sweet Julie, before you hurt yourself?" he said, full of confidence, having knocked down the targets, having caught her with an unloaded gun. This was to his liking; he had her all to himself, this frightened helpless woman. *You're all mine* . . . Sort of like his own private slave, he told himself.

Julie held on to the revolver. "Wha-what are you doing here?" she said in a fearful tone.

"Do you think I'm joking about the gun?" Peerly demanded, taking closer aim at her. "*Drop* it!"

She did. The gun landed at her feet; Peerly came forward and stopped a few feet from her. "You killed my pard, sweet Julie," he said, a slight grin on his lips. "I can't let you get away with that."

"Who?" Julie looked confused.

"Delbert Reese, gawddamn it!" Peerly snapped. "Don't even try denying it." He gestured a nod toward the bolo lying on the ground a few feet away. "Now I can see how you did it. You choked him to death with that Mexican doodad, then hoisted him up on a rope and made it look like he done it himself. Am I right?"

"No, you're wrong!" said Julie. "I haven't done anything, to anybody!" She gestured toward the bolo, taking a step. "This is just something I carry to—"

"Hunh-uh," said Peerly. "Keep your hand back away from it. I like you a lot better *unarmed*. The way you was when we first met."

Julie stopped with a worried look on her face. "Why did you really come here, Mister? This has nothing to do with your friend being dead, does it?"

"Well, it does, sort of." Peerly grinned. "The fact is, you've caused me a bit of a problem." He walked forward, motioned her back away from the revolver lying on the ground. "I've got to not only explain to Ruddell Plantz what happened to Reese; I've also got to explain what you're doing back here after me and Kid Kiley sent you running."

Julie felt anger stir inside her. "Is that what you two were doing in the barn that day, just scaring me away from here?"

Peerly chuckled. "You should have seen your face that day in the barn—talk about scared! You were trembling like a little cold lamb!" His contempt for her showed on his face.

Julie felt angry not only at him for what he and Kiley did; she felt angry at herself for having fallen for it. But that was all right, she told herself, calming her anger. Look where she had run to; look what she had brought back with her.

"All that, just to get me out of Umberton? You two wouldn't have raped me again, had I not run and gotten away?"

"Rape ain't what I call it," Peerly said, enjoying

the fear in her eyes. He liked hearing her talk about it. "I just call it a man doing what a man's got to do."

"Why were you men worried about me being here?" she asked. "I know it wasn't about your conscience bothering you when you saw me."

"Naw, nothing like that." He shrugged. "Picking at you was like picking at a wounded fawn. It was fun because we could do it. We knew there was nothing you could do about it. You'd already rolled over and showed us your belly, so to speak. The only reason we wanted you out of here, I reckon, is because Ruddell wants this place for himself." He grinned and waved a hand, taking in the burnt barn, and the house. "Why do you think we didn't burn the house down too?"

Hearing him talk so freely about everything that had happened here sent a chill through her. He had nothing to hide; he didn't intend for her to be alive long enough to tell anybody. "Now you're worried about Plantz thinking you didn't do a good enough job scaring me away?"

"That's going to change once he hears what you did to Reese."

"But I didn't do it," said Julie.

"It won't matter. I'll convince him you did. He'll be grateful for me catching you and putting an end to things for once and for all."

"You're going to kill me?" she asked flatly.

Peerly gave her a strange look. "I believe that's all up to you, Sweet Julie."

"Oh, I see," said Julie, her eyes looking deep into his, a determined look coming to her expression. She pulled her shirttails from her trousers and began unbuttoning her shirt, starting at the top and working her way down, her eyes fixed on his.

"Yeah . . ." Peerly sighed, watching her. "You're catching on."

"Like you said, it's up to me," Julie replied. With the shirt opened in front, her firm pale breasts exposed, she pulled the shirt down off her shoulder and slipped her left arm from the sleeve. Peerly's rifle barrel tipped toward the ground, his attention no longer on keeping her covered.

"Take everything off," he said in a heated voice, almost panting.

Without answering, Julie pulled her right sleeve down off her arm, slowly, taking her time, her hand drifting back out of sight for only a second. But when her hand came back into sight there was nothing slow about it. Suddenly her arm shot forward with the quickness of a striking rattlesnake. Peerly saw a dull shining object leave her hand in a spinning blur, but he had no time to get out of its way.

He gasped as the flat blade of a throwing knife stuck deep into his chest where his rib cage joined. His rifle exploded; then it fell from his hand. He clutched the knife handle, a shocked look on his face. "I was . . . starting to trust you," he whined.

Julie stepped forward, bare-chested, her shirt in her left hand. She kicked Peerly's rifle away from him, and stood close, almost against him, as if taunting him, letting him see what he would never have. "All you had to do was leave me alone," she said in a soft, almost soothing voice. "You just couldn't do it."

She stooped down with him as he sank to his

knees. She stared into his eyes as his chest bucked violently. His face lost all expression. His hands fell limply; he weaved back and forth until Julie gave him a slight nudge. When he landed lifeless on his side, she grasped the knife, put a boot on his chest and pulled it out of his heart. In doing so she saw the silver necklace her father had given her lying around his neck. She reached down, unclasped it and gathered it into her hand.

"You wore this to remind you of what you did to me," she said to his dead blank eyes. "You sorry bastard."

Standing, the silver necklace firmly in hand, she waited a moment before putting her shirt back on. In the silence, a gentle warm breeze swept over her like a lover's caress. There were no longer masks to hide the faces of these cowardly men, she told herself. Remembering clearly the names Reese had given her, she whispered them to herself as if reciting a death chant.

Chapter 25

——

Riding beside the parson in front of the five riders, Ruddell Plantz raised his hand and stopped the men less than a thousand yards outside of Umberton. Beside him the parson looked back and forth pensively and asked, "Where do you suppose they are?"

"I don't know," said Plantz, "but they both better hope to God we don't ride in and find them drunk out of their minds."

"Peerly has been toeing the mark pretty good ever since we started riding on our own," said the parson.

"Yeah, but he's still a fool," said Plantz, looking forward, from one side of Umberton to the other. "And Reese would have been better off had his mother dropped him down a well."

"There's a rider," the parson cut in, nodding toward a horseman bounding forward through the tall grass on their left. The rider joggled loosely in his saddle, one hand planted down atop his derby hat.

"It's Wright," said Plantz, watching the rider.

"There are men who should not be allowed to ride a horse," he mused quietly.

"I don't like the looks of this," said the parson.

"Neither do I," said Plantz.

"No, I mean *him* showing up, and two of our men not riding out to meet us, like always."

"Wright's a worrier," said Plantz. He gave the parson a sidelong glance and asked, "How's your premonition coming along? Anything new on the woman?"

The parson gazed at him for a second, unsure if he was serious or making a mockery of him. Unable to decide, he finally said, "No, nothing new . . . but I feel just as strongly about it today as I did when I first started getting it."

"You still don't see the outcome?" Plantz asked.

"No, I still do not," the parson said somberly. "But it's not good."

"Still think some *mysterious* woman is going to cause you to die?"

"I don't know," said the parson, clearly uncomfortable talking about it. "All I'm saying is we best all watch our step. These things are not to be taken lightly."

Plantz turned his eyes back toward the men behind them and said, "All of you watch your steps, you hear?"

The men just looked at one another curiously, not having heard what the two were discussing. The parson looked puzzled. It was not like Plantz to treat his visions and insights so casually. He wanted to comment on it, but seeing Councilman Wright drawing closer, he decided to wait for a better time.

A moment later Wright rode in close. Slowing his horse to a jog the last fifty feet, he turned it crosswise to Plantz and the parson and said in a worried tone, "Thank God I found you!"

"All right." Plantz shrugged. "Thank you God," he said sarcastically toward the sky. Then he turned back to Wright. "Now what the hell is going on? You look like you've been caught with your hand in the till."

Wright saw no humor in Plantz's words. "Your man Reese has hanged himself in the livery barn!"

"Reese *hanged* himself?" Plantz gave the parson a disbelieving look. "Reese ain't smart enough to tie a knot for himself."

"Well, either he hanged himself, or somebody else hanged him!" said Wright. "I've been watching you ride in for the longest time. I figured when I saw nobody else ride out to you, that maybe I better . . . to let you know what's going on."

"Obliged, Councilman," said Plantz, "although I know your main concern is whether or not anybody finds out that you made a little something for yourself off the money we charged to protect Umberton."

"Okay! I admit that's something that troubles me all the time. But the best way for me to make sure it doesn't happen is to make sure you don't ride into town and get caught unawares of anything."

"Good thinking." Plantz smiled. "Where the hell is Nez Peerly? I should have heard it from him about Reese being dead."

"Everybody said he rode out of town last night," said Wright. "Word has it he's going out to the colonel's place. He blamed the colonel's daughter, Julie, for hanging Reese. He left town drunk and angry; hasn't been seen since," he concluded.

"Julie Wilder is back?" Plantz asked. As soon as he asked, his eyes went to the parson, who only gave a solemn nod.

"Then I can tell you why Peerly's disappeared," said Planz, getting a dark expression. "That little weasel son of a bitch knows I'll kill him. He told me she'd never come back here after the scare him and Kid Kiley put into her." Glancing back over his shoulder, he shouted, "Kiley, *get up here!*"

Kiley bolted forward on his horse and slid to a halt beside Wright. "Yeah, what's going on?" he asked Plantz, giving Wright a look.

"The councilman here says the Wilder woman is back at the colonel's place! Want to tell me again how bad you and Peerly scared her?" Plantz asked wryly.

Kiley tried to play it down with a shrug. "She left town at a run is what I heard. If she's come back, maybe she forgot something."

"Are you being *funny* with me?" Plantz asked, his voice becoming enraged.

"Sorry, Captain," Kiley said quickly. "Want me to go put a bullet in her head? Get this over with?"

Wright winced and looked away. "Jesus!" he said, "I didn't hear any of that!"

Plantz gave a half grin. "Yeah, watch what you say, Kid." He gave Kiley a knowing look and said, "But maybe you ought to ride out to the colonel's place, take a look around . . . make sure that young woman is safe out there all alone." He winked. "Whatever you do, try not to scare her again."

"Sure thing," said Kiley, getting the message. "Then join the rest of yas in town tomorrow?"

"That's right," said Plantz. "I don't want you fooling around either. Get out there this evening. Get back here by morning, no excuses. Ride all night if you have to, but get here before sunup."

Kiley gave a sour expression at the thought of being in the saddle all night. But seeing the ugly mood Plantz had begun to fall into, he wanted to get out of his sight as quickly as he could. "I'm gone, Captain," he said, turning his horse and nailing his spurs to its sides.

Turning to Harold Wright as Kiley rode away, Plantz said, "Councilman, unless you want to be seen riding into Umberton with us, you better cut some dust on out of here yourself."

"I just wanted to get what information I could to you," said Wright.

"Yeah, yeah," said Peerly, a bit impatiently. "Now ride. I'm tired of sitting out here in the sun."

Wright turned his horse and rode off, making it a point not to go in the same direction as Kid Kiley. Plantz said to the parson in a quiet tone, calming down, "She *is* the woman you've been seeing, ain't she?"

"I don't want to say just yet," said the parson.

But judging from his tone of voice and his expression, Plantz nodded and said, "Yep, I thought so."

"Then what're we going to do?" the parson asked, not sounding sure of himself the way he did most times.

"Well," Plantz sighed. "We're going to ride in, get a meal, some whiskey to clear the dust out of our gullets, and we're going to see who rides in come morning, either Peerly and the Kid . . . or Miss Julie *by God* Wilder."

"You think she's got something to do with all this, with Reese hanging, with Peerly not showing up?" asked the parson.

Plantz gave him a look. "Hell no. She wants no part of us. I'm just trying to humor *you.* Keep your mysterious vision woman from troubling you too much."

"This is not something to joke about," said the parson, a serious look in his eyes.

"Who said I'm joking," Plantz replied, nudging his horse forward.

Julie saw the rider in the evening sunlight, following the trail though the tall grass toward her house. She stood on her front porch sipping coffee from a tin cup until she was certain the rider saw her. She pitched the remains of her coffee, turned and quickly went inside.

Kiley had watched her as he drew nearer. Once she disappeared inside he kicked his horse up into a quicker pace until he arrived in the front yard. Knowing the woman had run inside at just the sight of him, he trotted his horse back and forth, feeling confident. "Listen in there! If I wanted in, I'd get in!"

Seeing the shutters closed on every window, he stopped his horse and called out, "Do you think these shutters can stop me? There's *nothing* you can do to stop me. Do you hear me? There's no use in you trying to hide from me. You may just as well come out and face me!"

When no response came from the house, Kiley

stepped down from his saddle and looked all around the yard. In the corral, he saw the big buckskin bay staring at him from the other side of the fence. "Ah ha! Nez Peerly's buckskin!" he said. Turning back to the house with a bemused look he called out, "Nez, you sly sonsabitch, are you in there?"

Again there was only silence as he stood staring at the house. After a moment his expression darkened. "All right, gawddamn it! I didn't come here to play around all evening. Whoever is in there better come on out before I lose my temper!"

He sprang up onto the porch and gave the heavy door a solid kick. But all he got for his effort was a stir of dust. "All right, that's it!" he shouted. Losing control he began kicking and beating the door like a madman, cursing at the top of his lungs.

It wasn't until he'd spent himself and stood panting and rubbing his knuckles that he heard Julie's calm voice call out from the middle of the yard behind him. "Are you through roughing up my door?"

In his surprise, Kid Kiley spun around and saw her staring at him from ten yards away. For some reason he felt embarrassed, knowing she'd been watching him attack the big thick wooden door to no avail. "Damn it, woman!" he said, trying to compose himself. "You shouldn't be sneaking up behind a man like that. You could get yourself shot!"

"What do you want here, *Kid* Kiley?" she said, calling him by name. He noted the way she said his name, a bit sarcastically, he thought.

"What I want, first of all, is for you to tell me

where the hell Nez Peerly is!" He stepped down off the porch and stood facing her with his hand poised near his pistol butt in his tied-down holster.

"I have no idea," Julie said.

"You're lying," Kiley said flatly, jerking his head toward the corral. "There's his horse. What the hell is it doing here?"

"That's my horse," said Julie. "It belonged to me before it belonged to Peerly. Now it belongs to me again."

"How the hell did that come about?" Kiley said. "I know Peerly wouldn't give that horse to you, no matter how he got it in the first place."

"When you see Peerly, have him explain it to you," said Julie. "We both know how *he* got it."

"Hey, don't get sassy with me, woman," Kiley threatened.

"I'm not getting sassy," said Julie. "I'm telling you that's my horse. There's nothing more I have to say on the matter." She stared at him with a look that somehow made him uncomfortable. "Unless you want to talk about how Peerly acquired the horse in the first place."

He decided to drop the subject, since they both knew it had been her horse. He wasn't about to say anything about how Peerly happened to come by the animal. Yet, as she spoke, Kiley caught a glimpse of the rose medallion hanging on the necklace around her throat, and said before he gave it any thought, "That's *his* necklace you're wearing too."

"Oh?" Julie said. "Nez Peerly wears a silver rose on a necklace with *my mother's* name engraved on it?"

"I don't know what's gone on here," Kiley said,

not liking the way their conversation kept leaving him short on answers. His eyes went to the gun on her hip. "I think you best drop that gun, before I get riled."

"This gun?" Julie said, the gun coming up into her hand too slick and sudden for him to even react. She cocked it on the upswing and said calmly, "I've got a better idea, Kid Kiley. Drop *yours*."

It took Kiley a few seconds to collect himself. But when he did, he managed a smug grin. "You must be out of your mind! I was in the barn that day, remember? The day you let your gun get taken away from you?" He stood with his feet spread shoulder width. He looked as if he might take a step forward. "Now drop that—"

Her revolver bucked in her hand, kicking up dirt between his boots. "My next shot will be three feet higher. It'll cut your nuts off at your belly."

The look on her face told him she would do it. This was not the same woman he and Peerly had frightened in the livery barn. "Easy now," he said, raising his hands chest high; then slowly he eased his right hand down, lifted his Colt with two fingers and let it fall to the ground.

"Now your trousers," Julie said quietly.

"Huh?" Kiley gave her a peculiar look.

"You heard me, Kiley," she said. "Skin out of them. Then get on that horse and ride. Tell Plantz you didn't scare me nearly as much as you thought you would. And tell him I said if he wants to drop this here and now, I'll oblige him. Nobody is wearing a mask any longer. I know everybody's name . . . I've seen everybody's face."

Kiley looked humiliated; yet, he loosened his gun

belt, let it fall, then dropped his trousers and stepped out of them. Crossing his hands modestly over the blaring fly in his knee-length underwear, he gave Julie a look and said, "You don't really mean that, do you, about wanting to drop all this?"

"Get out of here, Kiley," Julie said. "Go tell him what I said. . . . tell him while you're standing before him in your drawers."

Chapter 26

In the middle of the night Herbert Wright awakened to the explosive yapping of a spotted bitch hound who maintained a litter of pups beneath the back porch. Pushing himself to his feet, Wright cursed and padded barefoot to where a shotgun leaned inside a closet door. Beside it a big Colt hung on a peg. He grabbed both guns and checked them quickly. "There better be a good reason for all this racket, or I'll turn these guns on her flea-bitten hide!"

"She never carries on this way without cause," said his wife, Margolin, with a concerned strain in her voice. She sat up on her side of the bed and pulled a house robe around herself. "I'm going with you," she whispered.

"Yes, come on," said Herbert. "Here, take this horse pistol and follow me. Lock the door behind me. Stay inside with the girls. There might be Indians prowling around out there."

"Indians? Oh my!" said Margolin. Snatching the heavy pistol from her husband's hand, she hurried along behind him.

Venturing out onto the porch, Wright stepped down onto the soft ground in the moonlight and squinted all around, giving a barefoot kick toward the yapping hound. But his kick only brought a renewed round of even louder barking. Walking along furtively, he stopped and raised the shotgun when he heard a horse nicker softly and saw movement at the side of a woodshed. "Who's there?" he shouted. "Make your presence known or I'll shoot!"

He heard a voice call out, but the constant barking of the dog kept him from understanding the words. "What? Who's there?" he said, keeping the shotgun leveled and cocked.

"I said, *it's me,* Kid Kiley, gawddamn it!" Kiley called out, at the same time trying to keep his voice level, under control. "Will you shut that damn dog up?"

Wright kicked again, only a glancing blow, but one that sent the hound racing under the porch to her pups with a growl of warning rattling in her throat. "Kiley, what are you doing out here?" Wright asked. "I don't keep anything valuable out here. Nor do I keep any money or valuables in the house," he added quickly.

"I'm not here to rob you, Wright!" said Kiley, stepping out into view in his underwear. "I need some trousers!"

"Trousers indeed," said Wright. He lowered the shotgun without uncocking it. "You were wearing trousers when last I saw you. What happened?"

"It's a long story, Wright," said Kiley, stepping forward. "I hoped maybe you'd have overalls in the wood shed."

"No, I don't," said Wright. "But I have a pair of older pinstripes in the house—if you don't mind a hole in the knee."

Stopping two feet away and letting out a sigh, Kiley said, "I don't mind the hole. Just get them on me. I've got to get to Umberton and tell Plantz what the Wilder woman did to me."

Looking him up and down curiously, Wright said, "What *exactly* did she do?"

Sounding ashamed, Kiley told him the story he'd been practicing all the way from the Wilder farm. "She got the drop on me," he said. "Snuck up behind me while I was on the front porch and cracked me on the back of my head. I woke up, my trousers were gone and my gun was stuck in my face." He paused to get an idea of what Wright might think of his story.

"My!" Wright said. "How is your head? Is it bleeding?"

"Bleeding?" Kiley hadn't thought of that. "No, it's better now," he said, touching his fingers to the back of his head. "The swelling's even gone down. Now, go get those trousers."

"Certainly," said Wright.

But before he could turn and go inside, Kiley reached out and put a hand around the shotgun stock. "I need a gun too."

"Not this gun," said Wright, not wanting Kid Kiley armed under these circumstances. He wasn't about to mention the horse pistol in the house. "This is all I have to protect my family!"

"Give me the gawddamn gun," Kiley demanded, jerking the gun hard, tearing it from Wright's grasp.

"Watch it! It's got a"—Wright's next words were

lost in the sound of the shotgun blast—"hair trigger," he concluded, amid the orange-blue explosion that fired straight up only an inch beneath Kiley's chin.

Inside the latched door, Margolin Wright heard her husband scream for the first time in all the years she'd known the man. "I'm coming, Herbert!" she screamed in reply, throwing the latch up on the door and swinging it wide open.

In the yard, Herbert stood bowed at the waist, walking in a short aimless circle with his arms spread wide. His scream had stopped as the hound's barking started again. Margolin's eyes widened when they came upon the faceless body lying spread-eagle on its back in the moonlight. "Oh my God! Herbert, what happened? Are you all right?" She looked at her husband, covered with blood and bits of bone and human matter. "You've killed him!"

"No, I— I— He—!" Wright pointed at Kiley as he used his free hand to swab blood from his eyes. "The gun went off! Oh God! Margolin, this is one of Plantz's men! Do you understand me? This is the one they call Kid Kiley."

"What did he expect, Herbert?" Margolin asked. "Prowling around at night in his underwear? What did he want anyway?"

"He wanted *clothes,* Margolin," Wright said, a snap of impatience in his voice.

"Where's his?" she snapped back at him.

Wright just shook his head. "Please shut her up," he said, referring to the hound.

Margolin gave a silencing kick toward the hound. The animal turned, tucked its tail and shot under the porch. A chorus of pups whined softly. "Then what do you suppose Ruddell Plantz is going to say about this?" she asked, the two of them looking down at the smoking gourdlike hull that had been Kiley's face.

They stood in silence, staring at Kiley's body, the pups whining and stirring gently beneath the porch. "What *will* you tell him?" Margolin said finally.

"I don't know yet," said Wright.

"The truth, maybe?" Morgolin suggested softly, just to see what he thought of the idea.

"Maybe . . . I just don't know," said Wright, shaking his bloody head. "After what happened to Delbert Reese, the hanging and all. There's no telling what Plantz will do if I lead this man into town, his head blown off."

"He'll just have to understand that accidents happen, Herbert," said Margolin, reaching out, wanting to put a hand on his shoulder, but thinking better of it and stopping at the sight of all the blood.

"No, Margolin," said Wright, "accidents don't happen. Not in the mind of men like Plantz and the parson. If I take this man to them, they will think right away that I had something to do with this." Thinking aloud, he said quietly, "I can tell them I found him on his horse wandering around out here . . . act as if the Wilder woman might have had a hand in it."

"Not if you ever expect to spend another night under this roof, you won't," she said, propping a hand on her hip. "That poor girl has had enough misfortune to last her a lifetime."

"All right, *dear!* I was only considering the consequences," said Wright.

"I just *told* you the consequences," Margolin said firmly. "The best thing you can do is pitch him over his saddle and get him away from here before daylight. We'll clean up this mess right now and act like nothing ever happened here."

"Yes, that's what we better do," said Wright. "I'll take him a long way from here and give him a shove. Nobody ever has to know." Behind them inside the house, a lantern glowed as their daughters' bare feet padded hastily across the wooden floor. "Dear God, Margolin," Herbert Wright whispered, "please go keep them inside!"

"All right, little ladies, back inside," Margolin said, hurrying in between her daughters and the body lying on the ground.

"We heard a shot, Ma," Herbert Wright heard one of his daughters say behind, her words moving away from him as his wife shooed the children back inside and latched the door.

"Jesus," Wright whispered, staring down at the mangled corpse. What had he been thinking, ever getting involved with men like Plantz.

In moments, Wright had dragged Kiley to his horse and pushed him up over the saddle. Remaining blood rushed down from the open cavity and splattered heavily onto the dirt. *Oh God . . .* Wright hurriedly washed himself in a bucket of water he'd drawn from the well. Then he dressed, saddled a horse for himself and, anxious to get the body away from his home and family, led the dead man's horse away by a lead rope.

For the next hour he rode straight out across the rolling plains. Even on the vast empty grasslands he looked all around, making sure no one saw him

when he topped a wide knoll, stopped and un-
hooked the lead rope from Kiley's horse. *Never
again, so help me God* . . . He vowed to himself as
he gave Kiley's body a shove, knowing that once it
fell into the tall grass, the odds of it ever being
seen again before being picked clean by buzzards
were slim.

Buzzards circling were commonplace out here,
he told himself, watching the body fall, hearing the
solid thud. Nobody would investigate. If they did,
so what? This was a long ways from his home. He
reached out and slapped the horse soundly on its
rump. There was no reason for anybody to think
he had anything to do with—*Oh no!*

The horse shot out through the tall grass. Wright
sat stunned, staring in wide-eyed disbelief. When
he'd shoved Kiley's body off the saddle, somehow
as it slid down the horse's side, an arm slipped
though a stirrup, twisted at a sharp angle and stuck
there. *Jesus, no . . . !* Wright could only sit and
watch transfixed as Kid Kiley's faceless corpse went
bouncing and skipping out across the dark plains.

Standing on the boardwalk out front of the saloon, Plantz threw back a shot of whiskey and
pitched the glass out into the street. He eyed the
glass in the grainy morning light as he took a sip
of cool foamy beer. Beside him the parson said, "I
don't like the way things feel around here
anymore."

"Oh? Have a drink then. You always feel better
after breakfast." Plantz smiled, raising his big Colt
from its holster. "I thought you did a hell of a job
telling these pumpkin heads what I told you to last

night." He fired a shot and the glass disappeared in an upward spray of dirt. "If I hadn't known better, I'd have thought you and me gave a damn about Delbert here pulling hemp."

In a wooden chair leaned back against the front of the building sat Delbert Reese's body. His eyes stared blankly straight ahead, his lids and cheeks having turned the color of rotting fruit. Someone had shoved a lit cigar into Reese's mouth and propped a mug of beer in his gray hand. A fly walked around on the bridge of his nose.

"It's all in the delivery," the parson said, proud of himself for a job well done. "Leaving the blame for Reese's death on their shoulders was a good idea. It sets the stage for us squeezing these folks a little bit harder if we choose to."

"Yes, and we choose to, Parson," said Plantz, tipping his beer mug toward his comrade. "I'm glad to hear you starting to talk like your old self. Go on, have yourself a good eye-opener. Maybe it'll help settle the rest of your willies."

The parson nodded and jiggled the bottle of whiskey hanging from his fingertips. "I don't have the willies. I'm just practicing caution. I can't deny my premonition. That would be foolhardy."

Plantz shook his head, chuckled under his breath and dismissed the matter. "I told Kid Kiley to be back here at daybreak." He sipped his beer and stared out along the street leading out of town. "The son of a bitch is late already," he said.

"What if he doesn't show?" the parson asked.

"You already know the answer," said Plantz. "I'm not going to fool with this woman. If I have to ride out there and put a bullet in her head . . .

well, I suspect that's how life will have to end for her."

No sooner than he'd spoken, the sound of horse's hooves resounded along the empty street. "Who's this?" said the parson, squinting into the silver gray of morning.

"Kiley, is that you?" Plantz asked, catching only a glimpse of Kid Kiley's horse in the silvery mist. It took a second longer for him to see that the saddle was not only empty, but hanging loosely down the horse's side.

The parson saw the body dragging alongside the horse, on its side, its arm tangled and flopping up and down with each step. "My God," said the parson. "She's blown his damn head off."

The two stepped down from the boardwalk and walked to the horse, stopping it on its homeward journey to the livery barn a block away. "Shotgun," Plantz said flatly, staring down at Kiley's faceless body.

"You think that frightened woman did this?" the parson asked.

"I don't know what to think," said Plantz. "Get the men ready to ride. We're heading out to the colonel's and getting rid of her for once and for all. It's time I move in anyway, take that place for my own."

The parson turned and started back onto the boardwalk to the saloon. But seeing Buell Evans and Carl Muller standing in the door, he said, "Get Conlon and Macky. We're riding out."

"Get them, hell, they're gone," said Evans.

"Gone where?" the parson demanded.

"Gone to hell, far as I know," said Evans.

Gesturing a nod toward the body in the street, he said, "They walked over here, took a look at that mess; the next thing I knew they was shoving one another to see who got out the back door first!"

"I'll kill the sonsabitches," said the parson.

"Let them go," said Plantz. "There's still four of us. I'd hate to think us four can't handle one scared woman. Especially one who's got no fight in her."

"No *fight* in her?" said the parson. He looked down at Kiley's body. "This *is* the woman in my premonition, make no mistake about it."

Chapter 27

At the end of a good night's sleep, Julie had gotten up, fixed herself breakfast and eaten it on the front porch, watching the first light of day grow into morning on the far horizon. After coffee and target practice, she returned to the porch and cleaned her guns while she had a second cup of coffee. Then she emptied the morning grounds from the coffeepot, washed it and put it away.

She kept track of the time and estimated how long it should take for Plantz and his men to arrive after Kiley met them in town. She thought about it as she cleaned house, brought in kindling for the cookstove, made the bed and brought in fresh drinking water from the spring.

When noon arrived, Julie walked to the corral, saddled the black and rode off toward the woods line, her rifle, revolver, bolo and throwing knife close at hand. She rode all the way through the woods and stopped at the far edge where she had a good view of the trail from Umberton. She stepped down from her saddle, canteen in hand, and waited.

Nearly an hour had passed when she first spotted the four riders come up into sight over a grassy rise. She watched a full ten minutes until the riders swung off the main trail and onto a thinner path running through the tall grass toward her house. "Here we go," she said to herself, standing and dusting the seat of her trousers. She mounted the black, hung her canteen from the saddle horn and rode quietly back through the woods, catching glimpses of Plantz and his men through the trees, keeping the four ahead of her.

At the front yard, Plantz raised his hand, stopping the other three cavalry style, as if leading an entire battalion. "Take a look at this," he said as the parson and the other two gathered around him.

"Yeah, that's Peerly's horse," said Muller, his hand going instinctively to the pistol on his hip and resting there. "What do you suppose *this* means?"

Evans looked all around, as if searching for Peerly. "I think it means he's turned traitor on us, over this woman."

"You stupid bastard," Plantz growled at him. "Don't say anything else, if that's the best you can do."

"This woman wouldn't have anything to do with Peerly," said the parson. "Any woman he ever had, he had to take her by force."

"It looks like there's nobody here," said Plantz, his eyes moving across the yard, going to the front door, then across the shuttered windows.

"Or, if she is here, she doesn't want to come out and be sociable, like before," Muller said with a hint of a smile on his broad bearded face.

"Good then. I'm not here to be sociable either," said Plantz.

The parson nudged his horse forward slowly, seeing the tin targets lying in the side yard. "What have we here?" he asked idly. Plantz nudged his horse alongside him; the other two followed.

"Looks like this young woman has been doing some serious target shooting," the parson said, stepping down and holding up a target riddled with bullet holes.

"How much target shooting does it take to blow a man's face off with a shotgun?" Evans asked.

"What did I just tell you, Buell?" Plantz said in a sharp bristly voice.

Evans brooded in silence, his face red with embarrassment. Beside him, Muller looked away, stifled a laugh and shook his head. "Dumb goat-fucker," he said under his breath.

"Take a look at this, Ruddell," said the parson, stepping back from a wide spot on the ground. "Something was dragged away from here."

Plantz swung down from his saddle, still looking all around. Then he looked down on the spot where Peerly had fallen with the throwing knife in his heart. "Yeah, I see," he said in a guarded tone. "Either something or somebody."

"What do you say?" the parson asked.

"I say this situation has Baines Meredith written all over it. This woman ain't the type who'd blow a man's face away, but that's exactly Meredith's cup of tea. He brought her to Umberton when she was down. I can see that sonsabitch sticking his nose into this . . . especially if he figured he could get her to wiggle out of her trousers for him."

"Jesus, Baines Meredith?" said Evans, looking all around again.

"Keep your stool from slipping out on you, Buell," said Plantz. "If he's around here he's only human." He drew his pistol and cocked it, the slightest look of uncertainty in his eyes.

"Everybody *spread out;* see what we can find lying around," said the parson, seeing Plantz grow preoccupied with the thought of a killer like Baines Meredith lurking nearby.

"This is starting to interest me all over." Plantz said. He pulled his horse over to the hitch rail, spun its reins and stepped up onto the porch.

From inside the cover of the woods line, Julie watched Plantz pound his fist on the door, still looking back over his shoulder and all around the yard. Raising the rifle to her shoulder, she took close aim on the center of his back. A good wide full target, she told herself. But then she lowered the rifle and decided against the shot. Plantz was the leader, the one who had put all the killing into motion.

She didn't want to kill Plantz this way. She wanted to look into his eyes, up close, the way she'd done with Peerly and Reese. This went against all Baines Meredith had taught her. He'd taught her to take the best shot while you had the opportunity; yet, that was exactly what she did. *Sorry Baines . . .*

She moved her sights over to the parson, then to Evans, then to Muller. They fit the description Reese had given her before he died. These were the ones; if by some fluke they weren't her attackers, her father's killers, too bad, she thought. If that was the case, they had simply picked the wrong day to come calling.

Her sights homed onto Muller, the one farthest away, the one most likely to get atop his horse and make a run for it. She rested the sights there and waited, breathing slowly, calmly.

Strange, she thought, how not long ago she had looked for the slightest reason not to kill these men, these men who had violated her, who had taken her father's life, and in that sense destroyed hers. But that had changed. Now, if they fit the description, or matched the names, or came close to doing either, she wanted them dead.

The killing had begun. The quicker they were dead, the sooner she could live in a home of her own—something she'd never had. And more than that, she could hold her head up and live there in peace, like regular everyday folks—something she'd never known. A tear glistened in her eye, but there was no time to wipe it away. She wouldn't let it affect her aim.

In the yard Muller stooped down and touched his fingertip to a dark spot on the dirt. Looking a few feet in front of him, he saw another dark spot on the ground, then another. "Captain Plantz!" he called out toward the porch where Plantz stood. "There's spots all over the ground here; looks like blood." He stood up and held up his middle finger up toward Plantz. "See this?"

"Is he *trying* to get me to kill him?" Plantz asked the parson, who came stepping up onto the porch.

The parson looked back over his shoulder at

Muller, then said to Plantz, "Hell, don't waste your bullets. It's hard to tell which one of them is the most stupid—"

Suddenly Muller went flying backward before their eyes, a hole opening up in his chest and a spray of blood exploding from his back as the rifle shot resounded from the woods line. "Up there!" shouted Evans, pointing toward the smoke along the edge of the woods.

"Get down, you damn fool!" warned the parson, both himself and Plantz leaping from the porch and taking cover around the corner of the house.

But his warning came too late. A rifle shot hit Evans in the center of his back as he turned to run, causing him to stiffen and freeze in his tracks. He didn't move until the next shot hit him an inch higher. Then he stumbled forward, blood gushing from his wounds, and fell dead on the ground.

"We're going to be stuck here if he decides to go for our horses!" said Plantz, hugging his back against the house.

"*He?*" The parson gave him a strange look.

"Meredith, damn it!" Plantz shouted at him. "Who do you think? This is no scared woman shooting at us. This is a killer! It's Baines Meredith!"

"You couldn't be more wrong, Ruddell," said the parson, shaking his head. "This is the woman . . . my *premonition*. Her day is at hand! She's going to kill us all before she's through! I see the end now! I see it clearly! She will be victorious! She will kill us both!"

"You're dead wrong there, Parson, you crazy son of a bitch!" Plantz raged. He turned his pistol toward the parson and shot him. "There now, satisfied? She didn't kill you; I did!"

"Damn you!" The parson staggered backward, seeing his wound and knowing it was mortal. He raised his pistol toward Plantz, but as he fired, he staggered back another step, out of the cover of the house. Just as his shot went off, a rifle shot from the tree line hit him in the left side of his neck, sliced down and came out the side of his chest in a blast of blood.

Spinning, he hit the ground and gagged and choked until he caught his breath and struggled to form his words. Plantz stood in the same spot, protected by the corner of the house. He held his gun aimed at the parson. His other hand squeezed the bullet hole down low in his belly where the parson's shot had hit him.

"I told you . . . didn't I?" said the parson. "She killed me . . ." He turned loose of his wounded neck and let the blood fly until his eyes glazed over in death.

"Yeah, you told me," said Plantz in a strained voice, speaking to the dead face staring blankly at him. "A woman killed you, but you didn't see it coming!" He backed up against the side of the house and slid down into a squat, still holding his wounded side.

Knowing the others were all dead, Julie stood up from her crouched firing position against the side of a tree. She gazed long and closely at the side of the house before backing away from the edge of the woods. Plantz was still there, she was certain of it. Yet, as if to assure her, as she reached her horse and shoved the rifle down into her saddle boot, she heard him call out, "All right, Meredith, it's just me and you! Is this the way you wanted it?"

Julie stood for a moment just listening. She wasn't about to say anything. Not yet. Instead, she stepped up into the saddle, turned the horse and rode through the woods to the main trail. From the trail she could see Plantz hunkered down against the house, and the parson's body lying a few feet from him.

Plantz's rifle butt stood up from the saddle boot on his horse, at the hitch rail twenty yards away. But even though she knew she was out of pistol range, she stepped down from the horse, led it to the front yard and let its reins fall to the ground. Even though it had now been several minutes since Plantz had called out Baines Meredith's name toward the tree line, Julie replied, "It's not Meredith. It's me, Julie Wilder. I'm the one who killed all your men, Plantz."

"The hell you are," said Plantz, pushing himself up from against the side of the house. He gave a look toward the tree line, appearing concerned about not stepping out of his cover. "He's still up there, backing your play. You had no guts for doing this."

Julie stared at him for a moment, realizing there was nothing she could say to convince him that the same woman he and his men had raped and beaten had returned and done such damage. "Where're Macky and Conlon?" she asked.

"They lit out when you and Meredith sent Kiley in wearing his drawers, with his face blown off," said Plantz. "If that was meant to scare them, it worked. But I don't scare." He straightened up, facing her, having slipped his pistol back into his holster when he saw her ride down to the trail. The woman wanted a showdown, one-on-one. Well, he would give her that, he thought, so long as he didn't have Baines Meredith firing on him from the woods, ambushing him the way he'd done these other three.

His face blown off? Julie kept her surprise from showing. She had no idea what he was talking about, nor did she care. If Kiley was dead, that was good enough for her. Julie took a breath, her hand poised near the big revolver holstered on her hip. "I knew someday I would be standing here, looking you in the eyes," she said. "I must've thought a thousand different things that I would say to you."

"Then you best get them said," Plantz replied. "I'm not one to stand around when there's fighting to be done. Let's get at it."

"There's nothing I've got to say." Julie shook her head slowly. "Let's get at it," she repeated his words.

"One thing though," said Plantz, cutting a glance toward the woods line, then back to her. "Once I kill you in a fair fight, is he going to let me make it out to my horse and get away from here?"

Julie thought it over for a second, then answered with a poker face, "That's up to him."

"Yeah, gawddamn it, see?" said Plantz. "You're a big tough gunslinger so long as you've got somebody backing your play. I'm not getting a fair shake out of this, either way it goes."

"You're getting far better than you ever gave, you son of a bitch," said Julie. She didn't have to wait for him to draw. She knew it was coming; if

it wasn't it should have been. The big revolver
streaked up from her holster and fired, one shot,
dead center. Plantz flew backward, dead on the
ground.

Holstering the big revolver, Julie stood with her
hand resting on its bone handle. She looked off in
the direction of Umberton, making a note of those
two names, Conlon and Macky. But she didn't have to
hurry. She would catch them. Now that she knew
their faces and names, they would keep until she
decided to go after them. They were cowards, and
they knew someone was coming for them, sooner
or later. That's all it took. She could let them sweat
for a while.

She took off her hat, shook out her hair and
touched her fingertips to the silver rose at her
throat. She had her work cut out for her here, she
reminded herself, looking all around, seeing the
bodies on the ground, the burnt barn. There would
be cleaning up to do, hauling away, a lot of rebuild-
ing . . . *other things,* she concluded. But she
didn't mind.

"It looks like I've finally made it home, Pa," she
heard herself say quietly. She felt a tear spill from
her eye and run slowly down her cheek. *Let it
run . . . ,* she thought, feeling a breeze blow in
warm and sweet from across the grasslands.

GUNSMOKE
by Joseph A. West

The all-new Western adventure series—based on the CBS television series.

Marshal Matt Dillon is keeping Dodge City safe from rustlers, gamblers, and desperados—and rejoining Doc Adams, Kitty Russell, and all the characters from the classic TV series.

Gunsmoke #1:
Bullets, Blood, and Buckskin
0-451-21348-3

Gunsmoke #2:
The Last Dog Soldier
0-451-21491-9

Gunsmoke #3:
Blizzard of Lead
0-451-21633-4

Available wherever books are sold or at
penguin.com

S310